LOVED ONE

LOVED ONE

Aisha Muharrar

VIKING

VIKING
An imprint of Penguin Random House LLC
1745 Broadway, New York, NY 10019
penguinrandomhouse.com

Designed by Cassandra Garruzzo Mueller

LIBRARY OF CONGRESS CATALOGING-IN-PUBLICATION DATA
Names: Muharrar, Aisha, author.
Title: Loved one : a novel / Aisha Muharrar.
Description: New York : Viking, 2025
Identifiers: LCCN 2024041426 (print) |
LCCN 2024041427 (ebook) | ISBN 9780593655849 (hardcover) |
ISBN 9798217060542 (international edition) | ISBN 9780593655856 (ebook)
Subjects: LCGFT: Novels.
Classification: LCC PS3613.U3835 L68 2025 (print) |
LCC PS3613.U3835 (ebook) | DDC 813/.6—dc23/eng/20241025
LC record available at https://lccn.loc.gov/2024041426
LC ebook record available at https://lccn.loc.gov/2024041427

Printed in the United States of America

The authorized representative in the EU for product safety
and compliance is Penguin Random House Ireland, Morrison Chambers,
32 Nassau Street, Dublin D02 YH68, Ireland,
https://eu-contact.penguin.ie.

For Ben

LOVED ONE

ONE

There was no bride. There was no groom. No seating chart with my name in calligraphy—a blue dot next to *Julia* indicating a preference for fish. No DJ coaxing guests to the dance floor with a multigenerational crowd-pleaser, no maid of honor fiddling with a sheet of white printer paper, unfolding it from eighths to fourths, then taking a theatrical deep breath before she says, *Okay! So.*

Which made sense because it was not a wedding.

But there were approximately a hundred of us gathered at Berkeley City Club, a grand Italian Renaissance Revival building often rented out for private events (like weddings), and there were two sections of dark wood folding chairs separated by a wide stripe of hardwood floor (an aisle if you will), and more important, it just *felt* like it should have been a wedding. It's what we did that year. We went to weddings. Not together—though Gabe did ask, the year before, when the invitations went out and before he'd started dating Elizabeth, if I'd be his plus-one to the Tokyo wedding of his percussionist and backup vocalist. They'd met on tour with him. I would have loved to go to Japan, but I already had another wedding on the same day. By September, I'd been to six and RSVP'd to three more. I was thirty—Gabe, born the same year but in December, was twenty-nine—and apparently we'd entered that stage of life where if you haven't nailed down your version of semiformal cocktail attire, you'd better do it quick because that's what your weekends were going to be for the next decade. This perpetual wedding season was such a well-known truth about people our age that I could feel an awareness of it in the room as I stood up, clutching my own folded sheet of printer paper, and began to speak about my dear friend Gabe. It was one of the things I had to avoid saying in Gabe's eulogy—the obvious thing—that he was only twenty-nine, and his death was so sudden, by anyone's estimation, it would have been more likely I was speaking at the happiest day of his life.

My dear friend Gabe. This was the one line I'd prepared and now I'd said it. I'd hoped to come up with more by the time I arrived at the funeral. In my studio as I packaged orders. On the flight from LA, the car ride from the airport. But no, nothing. I lowered the microphone, stalling for time, and tried to remember how I was supposed to feel about Gabe. Outside, UC Berkeley students chatted on the street below us, cars and trucks drove along the city's concrete hills. It was a beautiful cloudless day.

"Gabe was the kind of friend who was more like family," I said. This was true. Having briefly dated as teenagers, when we met again in our twenties, we became friends so quickly it was clear we worked better that way. And we'd remained close for years.

"I could always count on him," I continued, launching into one quickly delivered anecdote after another to prove this point. As I scanned the faces in front of me—mostly Gabe's music associates and peers, plus both sides of his family: his father, his cousins, the aunts who'd flown in from Colombia, and his mother and her relatives and friends—I was sure none of them could tell, but I knew there was a disconnect between the words I was saying and what I was feeling. Not because I was in shock or numb. Though I probably *was* both in shock *and* numb. And not because the stories weren't real. I had plenty of examples of Gabe being sweet and constant.

Of course it would never have been painless, giving that eulogy. But it should have been easier.

The problem was even though Gabe was one of my closest friends, the month before, we'd made a dumb mistake and slept together.

AN IMMEDIATE AND IMPORTANT CAVEAT: GABE AND I WERE ACTUAL friends. I won't mention this again, because then the lady doth protest too much, but the point has to be made. We weren't the kind of friends who were never really friends. The kind of friends you see in a romantic comedy where there are two incredibly attractive people who are deeply emotionally invested in each other, and we're supposed to believe they have never once considered the idea of sexual intercourse. The kind of friends who are secretly in love with each other and only realize minutes before one of them is about to get married or leave town, and the next thing you know they're jumping in a car, or on a horse, or running down the street, *whatever*, and they tumble into bed, or out of frame, depending on the rating of the movie. Having several male friends, this depiction of male-female friendship was always a pet peeve of mine, but somehow

Gabe and I had tumbled (onto a couch, not a bed, but then, yes, eventually a bed too), and we'd ended up in this exact ridiculous situation, except we'd done worse than that because we hadn't even gotten a stolen honeymoon or new zip code; we'd just made a real, and awful, mess of everything.

But—you may be thinking—there's always a chance to make things better. Even if it gets really bad, if you're truly good friends, then you can work it out. And absolutely, totally you can. Unless, three weeks later, one of you dies.

"Oh, Julia, he *loved* you." The first person I spoke to after my eulogy was Gabe's manager, Kathy Liu. We were in the restroom. It was small, with two narrow stalls and two side-by-side sinks. Kathy was middle-aged, probably closer to my mom's age than mine. She was wearing a Tina Turner concert tee over a long-sleeved black dress. Gabe's mother, Leora, had asked that instead of the usual funeral garb, in honor of Gabe's career as a musician, we wear our favorite concert tees. I'd chosen a Billy Joel's *The Stranger* shirt (an inside joke for no one but the deceased) under a black tuxedo jacket. It was clear Leora wanted Gabe's funeral to be a departure from traditional mourning and as much of a celebration of his life as possible. His producer and frequent collaborator Jabari Bernier was currently leading a twenty-minute musical tribute with a jazz quartet. *A time of reflection* is what it said in the program. A time for a bathroom break is how several people interpreted it. I'd avoided the long line for the women's room and found an empty restroom downstairs. Well, empty until Kathy walked in. She hugged me, then took a step back, concentrating with concern as if she were appraising car wreckage.

"He just adored you," Kathy said, clutching my hands in hers. "I remember we were headed to a show in Houston, and he kept saying, 'Julia's going to be near here. You have to leave some time so I can see Julia.' And I said, 'Okay, where's Julia staying? Which hotel in Houston?'"

I knew this story. Kathy had told it to me before. She was one of those people who connected with acquaintances by continually reminding them of the single experience they shared, imbuing an anecdote with dramatic reverence, as if it were Kerri Strug's Olympic vault or some other monumental event worthy of its own ten-part docuseries. Now finally we'd reached the episode about the dismount.

"And *then* he said, 'Oh no, Julia's staying in *Austin.*' Austin! I said, 'That may as well be a different state, honey.' But I got him there. So sweet."

I had once found this story sweet too; now it was, at best, proof that Gabe was terrible at state geography.

Kathy rested her funeral program on the edge of the sink. *Gabriel Wolfe-Martel, 1986–2016.* "I'm sorry we couldn't reach you directly, our priority was Leora."

"Of course," I said. I'd found out the same way everyone else had. Through the internet. I was at a workbench in my studio, tightening the prong setting of a bespoke ruby ring, the chain nose pliers gripped between my thumb and index finger. Mandy, the new production manager for my jewelry line, was at her desk.

Mandy had only worked for me for a few weeks, but we'd hit it off instantly after realizing we'd both grown up the only Black girl in a mostly white suburban school. There was often an immediate bond with other onlies, a shared interest in things that would probably go on some ill-conceived this-is-for-white-people list that we'd come by honestly and early before realizing those things weren't made with us in mind. Somewhere Mandy had a photo of herself with her all-white soccer team and somewhere I had a similar picture; we got each other. But we hadn't known each other that long, and it can take some time for me to open up to people, which is why it wasn't her fault when she looked up from her laptop and gasped. "Wait, don't you know one of the guys from Separate Bedrooms?"

"It's just Gabe," I said. This was a common mistake. Separate Bedrooms wasn't a band of four or five guys, it was a stage name for one person.

"Oh," she said, her voice tentative. "People are saying he, like, died?"

Kathy pulled a handkerchief from her purse. A handkerchief. You didn't see those too often. I pointed to it. "Am I going to need one of those?" I was sort of trying to make a joke, sort of genuinely afraid. I'd never been to a funeral. Which I knew at thirty was lucky. Though it's hard to feel lucky at a funeral.

"Oh yes, dear," Kathy said. Her face softened into a maternal tenderness. "You may not feel it yet, but at some point, it will hit you. And then you'll be back to normal, talking to someone, just like we are now, and it will hit you all over again. Grief comes in waves." She patted my shoulder. You let me know if there's anything I can do."

There was something Kathy could do. What I'd realized I needed as soon as I entered the bathroom, ironic because I'd purposely avoided the long line of women waiting for the upstairs restroom and was now on my own. "Do you have a tampon?" I asked.

She didn't. ("Oh, darling, I'm menopausal!") I checked the bathroom tampon dispenser, but of course it was empty. Or broken. Either way, nonfunctional. (Had anyone ever seen a functional public restroom tampon dispenser?) I searched my bag again, then ducked into a stall. I was in there, preparing to make a toilet-paper-constructed menstruation nest, when someone walked in and entered the other stall.

"Sorry, excuse me? Do you have a tampon?" I asked.

"I do actually," a voice said in an English accent. The stalls were the type where you could see the feet of the person next to you. In this space, a woman's hand, long fingers with short, unpolished nails, appeared. A tampon in the palm. It was the European kind, no applicator. I took it from her, and as I did, I noticed a large statement ring on her index finger, a garnet in a silver setting.

It wasn't unusual for me to notice the pieces people wore. But it wasn't the first time I'd seen this ring. I knew that burgundy oval, the chunky cigar band. But from where? Then with a mental click, a memory popped it into place like a bone reset.

It was from Gabe's texts. A selfie, and in the corner was a woman's hand—with this ring—on his shoulder. I was pretty sure it was his most recent ex-girlfriend. I'd seen other pictures of her too. She was white, a brunette. What was her name? They'd dated off and on for a year. She lived in London and Gabe had moved in with her at the end of his European tour.

I took the tampon. "Thanks," I said.

"Of course," she replied. "Just make sure I get it back."

Funny, I thought. Given the day's events, it was the equivalent of me guffawing.

When I exited my stall, she was at one of the sinks. Kathy had left her funeral program balanced on the edge. Between us, Gabe looked up. Sitting on some steps, leaning forward, his forearms on his knees. His black hair spiked up away from his face. A slight squint, like the sun was in his eyes.

I turned on the faucet of the other sink, glancing over to confirm her identity. Reddish-brown hair, wavy and just past her shoulders. A strong jawline and the kind of skin I'd heard pale friends complain resisted a tan. Taller than me. A statuesque womanly figure that I, still waiting for a growth spurt, had never possessed. She was wearing a black wrap dress. Great boobs, I thought. Nice pull, Gabe.

She turned toward me. Elizabeth! That was her name. And it was definitely her. Her eyes narrowed, I assumed because she was trying to place me.

I extended my hand. "Elizabeth, hi. We've never met. I'm—"

"You're Julia." There was an abrupt downshift in her tone, her words a shove. As she pulled a paper towel from the dispenser, she said, "I know who you are. I know exactly who you were to Gabe." Then she walked out, tossing the crumpled paper into the trash as she went.

I stood for a moment, dazed. I didn't go after her. In the same way you wouldn't pursue a bear after it mauled you or pick up a sizzling-hot pan that had just scalded you. It was how she'd said it, like an accusation, but also with total confidence, like she already knew everything.

When I left the restroom, there was no sign of Elizabeth. I walked into the assembly room where I'd given my eulogy. The jazz quartet was playing a fizzy party anthem from the third Separate Bedrooms album. People mingled, talking softly. I scanned the room for a tall Korean man in a Fiona Apple shirt. Finally I spotted my friend Casey. Long face, warm eyes, the perfect posture of a man who'd put a lot of time into core training. He was standing in front of a diamond-paned window. When I caught his glance, he and his fiancé, Will, a thin, wiry Black man who was never without his round-frame glasses, headed over to me. The three of us met in the middle of the room, facing the quartet. We were silent, our usual conversation topics paused. What would we have been talking about if we weren't at Gabe's funeral? The headlines of that summer: the election, Zika, more takes on Beyoncé's *Lemonade*, the swimmer who'd been accused of lying about being held up at gunpoint at the Rio Olympics. Our own lives: Will was training to become a therapist, he'd recently completed an intensive graduate study program and was now a supervised intern. Casey was a lawyer at the LA office of a big global firm. He could never tell us the specific details of the cases he was working on, but he *would* share how stressed he was working seventy hours a week on them. Then I'd talk about a professional nuisance of my own, like the frustration of invoicing (why could not *one* outlet I worked with remember to pay on time?). There were so many things that had been on my mind before I heard about Gabe, but now I didn't have the energy to discuss even one.

Instead I listened to Jabari conclude his tribute. I smoothed over a crease in my shirt. Casey put his arm around me. He'd never really had his own friendship with Gabe, but they'd hung out a ton when we were younger, usually in groups with me; Will had met Gabe

9

once. If it weren't for me, they probably wouldn't have been at his funeral. I'd told them they didn't have to come, but now I was glad they were here.

After the tribute, one of Gabe's uncles announced that those of us who'd been asked ahead of time should head to the cemetery. Only I'd been invited, so Casey said he was going to take a quick work call and then he and Will would meet up with me later. He went to find a quiet spot for his phone conversation, which left me and Will alone.

"How are you?" Will asked.

"Okay," I said.

We walked out of the building onto the front steps. Most people were either still inside or heading to the cemetery. Kathy had said she'd give me a ride there and I was waiting for her. Will was watching me—I think hoping I'd say more, maybe give an honest response to his question. He wasn't like me and Casey, content to keep communication light, packed with nineties pop culture references or a tally of what we were currently watching. We liked to tease Will about his failure at small talk, his instinct to search for the hidden hurt in everyone. Always hopeful for a transformative breakthrough, he spoke in eighth-grade Earth Science terms: *metamorphosis, energy, capacity, a shift.* When he asked *how are you*, he genuinely wanted to know. And maybe it would help, I thought. If I told him.

I said, "So Will, say you *were* hypothetically a therapist."

A proud look slid across his face. "Almost there."

"Right. So what would you say if I were your patient and I told you Gabe and I slept together?"

Will looked puzzled. "You did? Oh, from when you dated a long time ago?"

"No. We actually didn't have sex then. I meant more recently."

"How recently?"

". . . Like a month ago?" I chuckled, awkwardly. "It's actually pretty funny." It was not at all funny. "Because then after that, I didn't hear from him."

"What do you mean?"

I spoke quickly. "We said we'd be in touch and then I texted him and called him, but he didn't respond. And then he kept not responding."

Will clasped his hands together and slid them down his forehead, across his head, his hair was buzzed to the scalp, just the impression of a curl. "That's a lot."

There was more. By the end I wasn't too proud of my own behavior, though I blamed that also on Gabe.

"Does Casey know?" Will asked.

"No," I said. "And please don't tell him." I'd considered this. Aside from Gabe and Casey, my other closest friends were my college friends Nneka and Rose. When someone said "best friend," I thought of these four people as a group, even though they were not close to each other. I imagined telling my three remaining closest friends what had happened with my fourth. Nneka would listen, then give me a pragmatic summary. Rose would cry, somehow even more hurt than me. Casey would want to tie a big romantic bow around the whole thing. It was enough trying to figure things out on my own, I didn't want to hear anyone else's interpretation of events.

Which was why it was strange that I was *still* thinking about Elizabeth. Even after I left Will on the steps and drove with Kathy to the cemetery, I was replaying our conversation in the bathroom. Elizabeth had seemed so sure in her assessment. *I know exactly who you were to Gabe.* And I envied her certainty. For years I'd known exactly who I was to Gabe. It was a long story but I could tell it confidently, like a bartender sharing the recipe for her signature cocktail. Now things were so jumbled up in my head, I had no idea where to begin.

The actual beginning would have to do.

TWELVE YEARS BEFORE, DURING A DIFFERENT SUMMER, BETWEEN MY senior year of high school and my freshman year of college, I attended an arts and architecture program in Barcelona called the Hayes Emily Yarborough Summer of Art. It was founded by a painter named, you guessed it, Hayes Emily Yarborough. Hayes Emily had gone to Barcelona in his midforties and the art there had radically transformed his approach to his own work. But, he lamented, it was too little, too late. Lucky for him—and I guess lucky for me too because I received one of the program's scholarships—he had family money and a generosity of spirit, and thus the Hayes Emily Yarborough Summer of Art was born. HEYSA was technically an arts education program for young adults, but both "young adults" and "arts" were broadly defined. There were twenty-five students total, ranging from high school to college and continuing adult education. As far as courses, there was art history and the architecture of Barcelona—expected standards that I, hoping to get college credit, signed up for—but there was also welding, feminist poetry, a class called Dance Memoir, and another that was dedicated solely to Picasso's pieces created during the Spanish Civil War—if you so much as mentioned the Blue Period, you were asked to leave the classroom.

Years later, I saw Hayes Emily at a CFDA (Council of Fashion Designers of America) party in a sculpture garden. Three Calders and a Truitt away from me was a man in his seventies wearing a black tuxedo and black turtleneck. Hayes Emily often wore all black; he had tall, stiff white hair. There was a certain Andy Warhol thing going on (which he'd been criticized for, *New York* magazine quipping, "even his wardrobe is derivative"). I knew it might be my only chance to ever speak to him in person. I was wearing this electric-blue minidress with a train twice the length of the dress, so I was running in heels, holding this cascade of silk in one hand and a champagne flute in the other, weaving through an obstacle course of passed canapés, runway models, and priceless artwork, nearly crashing into Hayes Emily in the process, all so I could say, "Excuse me? I went to HEYSA in Barcelona. You changed my life." He replied, not at all shocked, "Thank you. I get that all the time."

The weekend after the first week of classes, I was invited to a party at my art history teacher's apartment. Professor Roberta Donnelly was one of the few teachers who wasn't visiting for the summer, she was American but she lived in Barcelona full time. "She's amazing," I told my mom when I called home. I'd only ever had two Black teachers, so I knew my mom would find Roberta interesting for this reason alone. But then I went into specifics of how fascinating she was. Everyone agreed she was the best professor. It was rumored she'd partied with Basquiat, she and her ex-husband shared custody of a four-year-old, but more interesting to us art students, they also shared custody of an original Norman Lewis painting. Now, instead of an architect like Gaudí, I was thinking I'd become a professor like Roberta. I saw myself walking through the campus of some foreign university, wearing a chic tweed blazer with velvet elbow patches, carrying a brown leather satchel.

My mother stopped me. "Julia, you're describing an outfit, not a career."

ROBERTA'S APARTMENT WAS IN GRÀCIA. ON THE WAY FROM MY STU-dent apartment near Plaça de Catalunya, I passed crowds of people drinking under the outdoor umbrellas of restaurants, smoking, laughing, but then gradually the streets quieted, it felt more residential.

I heard the party as soon as I stepped into the building—the rumble of a sound system, multiple conversations crushed together into sprinkles of indistinct chatter. By the time I reached Roberta's fourth-floor apartment, it had quieted down. There were a few people clustered by the doorway. I waited for them to move forward, but instead they lingered, focused on what I now realize had grabbed their attention and everyone else's at the party: "Through the Fire," a slow melodic tune from the early eighties, by genius diva Chaka Khan. But it wasn't genius diva Chaka Khan singing. Someone at the party was performing a cover. I knew the voice, I'd heard it before. Or at least I thought I had.

In a program focused on the arts within a city known for its architectural risk-taking, the uninspiring office building where we had our classes was a surprising visual dud. But the outdoor court-yard was lovely, with a few trees, some plants and flowers in coral-pink pots, a round concrete table where people gathered: students met between classes, the office workers took their smoke breaks, and sometimes people would perform. Fifteen minutes into the first lecture of my Architecture of Gaudí course, we heard someone sing-ing outside. Our classroom didn't face the courtyard, but with the windows open (there was no AC and it was June in Barcelona, so the windows were always open) we could still hear the outside world.

"Annie Lennox," one of the older students shouted (he looked nearly thirty). He leaned back in his chair, proud of himself, as if we'd all been participating in this guessing game and he'd beat us to it.

At the time I didn't remember the song was called "Why," I just knew it wasn't the famous one she did as part of the Eurythmics. "Why" starts out quiet, so we were probably too far away to hear the first part, and that's why the song seemed to burst mid-chorus out of nowhere. Everyone paused, including our teacher. He lis-tened, rubbing his mustache. "Beautiful, beautiful," he said, mo-mentarily enchanted. Then he clapped his hands as if that summed it up and returned to his lecture on Casa Milà.

But he'd lost my attention, I was still listening to the music. It was a pure, powerful voice, like a gospel choir soloist or an opera virtuoso. Beautiful, yes. But there was something else there. It was hard to explain, but it was like the singer *needed* to sing this song. Like if they didn't sing these words right now, they'd be dragged away. All together it created a disquieting comfort, like someone sliding their hand under my skin and resting it over my heart.

Next class it happened again. Same time, same singer. Different songs. I was pretty sure it was a male voice, but the artists covered were almost all women. Carly Simon, Nina Simone, Joni Mitchell, Joan Armatrading. The songs started at 4:05, right after class began, and then ended promptly at 4:25, with the singer shouting, in a strangely cheesy voice, "Thank you for your ears! Keep your coins!" It was a grating discordance in an otherwise flawless set.

Each time, when I walked through the courtyard after class, the singer was packed up and gone, without a trace. Well, without a physical trace. I swear I noticed a difference between when I walked by before class and after—a subtle undulation in energy, the last pulses of an echo, the lingering gratitude on the faces of the people who had just had the good fortune to witness the little concert.

Now in Roberta's hallway, I thought there was a good chance the singer at her party might be the courtyard voice. I squeezed by the people in the doorway, ducking under a man's elbow, the cocktail in his hand tipped and spilled into my sandal. I made it into the apartment and saw Roberta dancing with a thin, small-boned white woman with long black hair, so dark and glossy it was like a raven's wing. Roberta's long braids were braided into one larger braid and thrown over her shoulder. Both women wore flowy linen shirts. They shimmied, snapping their fingers and pointing at each other. They held pretend mics, silently lip-synching along, pointing to the front of the room. Here was the singer. A boy around my age wearing a white T-shirt and blue-and-yellow basketball shorts, very high school jock, though his physique was more wrestler than basketball player: compact, sturdy. He looked up and I watched him notice Roberta's friend's dancing. His eyes widened in horror, then he vigorously shook his head as if trying to erase the image. He was so completely mortified I knew the woman had to be his mother.

I'd noticed from my classroom perch that he had what sounded like a wide range, employing an impressive falsetto, then dipping back down to a deeper reservoir of sound. He ended the song reaching an impossible high note. The party went wild.

I wanted to talk to him, to confirm he was the voice in the HEYSA courtyard, but some of my classmates arrived and I got pulled into conversation, losing track of him. I figured Roberta might know who he was, but I hadn't been able to talk to her yet. She was the host, everyone wanted to talk to her. When I finally found her, she was standing in the very back of the living room by the windows. She had a wineglass in one hand and the woman next to her, the one she'd been dancing with, was pouring from a bottle of red wine. Roberta saw me and lifted her glass as if to toast my arrival. "Julia! I'm so glad you made it! This is my friend Professor Wolfe, she's a poet and she's teaching a writing class in the program this summer."

"You can call me Leora," she said. I could tell when she spoke she was American too. "Are you going to college in the fall, Julia?"

I said yes, I was attending Brown and looking forward to it.

She said, "Of course you are," as if that settled some matter, and declared, "You have to meet my son." She pointed behind me, waving someone over. It was the singer from the beginning of the party. "Gabe, this is Julia," she said. "Julia was just telling me how excited she is to be off to college."

He rolled his eyes. "Come *on*."

"What?" Leora said, throwing up her hands. "I thought it would be good for you to talk to someone your own age who clearly appreciates art *and* also wants to get a full education." Leora turned to Roberta. "He's threatening to not show up at NYU in the fall."

"Casually mentioned it at dinner," Gabe corrected.

"Playing for tips at HEYSA isn't a long-term plan."

So it was definitely him.

Roberta waved to someone entering the party, she told me she'd be right back and headed in that direction. I was left in Leora and Gabe's conversation. "I'm not against it," Leora was saying, feigning indifference. "Try it out, give it a shot. That's what a gap year is for."

"You know those dreams," Gabe responded. "Always accomplished in three hundred sixty-five days or less."

"Just be grateful it's not a leap year," I interrupted. Their heads swung toward me at the same time. Gabe had the same shiny black hair as his mother's, though his, aided by some kind of product, traveled upward and out.

It was at this moment, when I jumped into their conversation, that Leora would later say she saw a spark of interest in her son and decided to make herself scarce. She left, saying she had to find Roberta. But I didn't see any moment, all I saw was Gabe scowling. I wasn't sure if I should take it personally—if his lack of enthusiasm to meet me was anger with his mother pushing college or just a lack of enthusiasm to meet me. I knew I didn't want to be somewhere I wasn't wanted. When Leora walked away, I did too.

I drifted over to the corner of the room where party snacks were laid out on a folding table. Gabe followed. "You're not eating?" he asked.

It hadn't been my intention but I guess I wasn't. I looked at the various snacks available, most were wrapped in ham, the others topped with sausage. I said, "I don't eat meat. I'm a vegetarian. I eat fish."

Gabe nodded, not questioning this contradiction. "There were some potato things earlier, and some bacalao . . ." His gaze traveled the table. "Oh, I think those are gone." He gestured for me to follow him.

We headed into Roberta's kitchen. It was teeny. The floor tiles had a marigold-and-orange geometric print. Gabe stood on one side of the kitchen, against the sink. I stood on the other, a wall of wood cabinets behind me. Between us there was a narrow butcher table with the remnants of party prep: two empty wine bottles, a bucket of melting ice, a large cutting board with the jellied remnants of a tomato, the last few slices of a loaf of bread.

"I know where Roberta keeps the good stuff," Gabe said. He opened a cabinet above the sink, then turned back to me, revealing a jar of peanut butter. He grabbed a jar of jam from the fridge, then opened the silverware drawer and took out a knife. He dropped his haul onto the counter and began to assemble the ingredients, spooning out dollops of jam onto a slice of bread, spreading peanut butter on another. When it was complete, he glanced up at me. "Which way?" He mimed cutting it straight down the middle or diagonal, rapidly switching back and forth between the two possibilities.

"That way," I answered.

He cut it diagonally, put the sandwich on a plate, and slid it across the table to me.

"Thanks," I said. I took a bite.

"So you're in Roberta's class?" he asked.

I nodded. My mouth was full, peanut butter stuck to the roof. It took me two tries to swallow. By the time I did, it felt too late to answer. Gabe hoisted himself onto the counter, in front of the window. It overlooked the neighborhood's rust-colored rooftops.

"What else are you studying?" Gabe asked.

"The Architecture of Gaudí."

He glanced at the city below. "I haven't seen any Gaudí yet."

I swallowed a bite. "I mean, you probably have seen some. You just didn't know you were seeing it."

There was a pause, I feared that might be the end of the conversation. I had to say it now, what I'd been thinking since I realized he was the one singing in the courtyard.

"You're really good," I said. "I mean, I've heard you singing at HEYSA and you're really good."

"Why do you think I'm good?"

Oh great. I'd known plenty of boys in high school like this. Flatter me, make yourself tiny so I can feel important.

Gabe must have seen the repulsion cross my face. He rushed to explain himself. "No, no, no, I'm not looking for compliments. I mean, I'll take them, but not only. I'm looking for specifics. So I can improve, you know."

"Oh." I swallowed the last bite of my sandwich. "You want my crit."

"Crit?"

"My criticism," I explained. "It's something we do in art classes."

"Okay."

"Well. I guess I thought your voice reminded me of home."

"Like an Americana feel?" He wrinkled his nose.

"No, not our actual home. Like, I mean, it was familiar."

The truth was I hadn't clicked with any of the other HEYSA students. Not having friends the first week of a summer abroad was no emergency. It wasn't indicative of how college would go, or even how the program would go. But I didn't know that then. At the end of high school, I'd had the realization the people I'd been hanging out with weren't actually *my* people. I'd made friends with them through sports, and most of them were pretty popular, so there were social benefits to hanging out with them. But did I really *like* them? No. It was one of the reasons I'd applied to HEYSA, to get away as soon as possible. But then to not click with anyone in the program? I worried I was the problem. And I was lonely. When I heard the singing in the courtyard, for those twenty minutes, I felt less alone. Now in Roberta's kitchen, I found I felt that way talking to Gabe too. It was easy, like I'd made my first friend in Barcelona.

I couldn't say all of this to Gabe. I tried again to describe how he sounded to me. I closed my eyes, placing myself back in the classroom above the courtyard. "Well, it's like, your voice has a solid base." I was unsure at first but gained more confidence as I spoke. "It felt rich, like if it were a color, it wouldn't just be red or orange, it would be ochre." I'd learned that word recently in Roberta's class. I opened my eyes to see if Gabe understood. He looked confused. I said, "It's just like a deep earthy pigment. Think of clay." I stuck my tongue into the corner of my mouth, unsure if I had any more to say. "Is that helpful?"

He smiled. "Yeah. It is."

I remembered the end of his sets. "Thank you for your ears, keep your coins," I parroted. "Where did that come from?"

"You don't like it?"

"It's not my favorite part of the show."

He looked at me. A fraction of a second, then we both laughed.

"Laughed" is not enough. I went bwahaha. He made a sound from the middle of his throat. Hay hay hay. Our laughs overlapped together were greater than their parts and engendered more of this sound, increasing in volume and strength.

Bwahayhay.

BWAHAYHAY.

A man and woman walked into the kitchen, both somewhere in that nebulous age range between students and parents. "This is *silk*, Peter," the woman said. She was examining a large red wine stain on her oversize white-and-purple-patterned shirt. Silk, apparently. It looked like someone had spilled an entire glass on her. Peter, apparently. They headed straight for the refrigerator, leaving less space on Gabe's side of the kitchen. He crossed over to mine. The two of them found a bottle of seltzer and headed back into the party. Gabe remained on my side of the kitchen. We turned to face each other, shoulders leaning against the cabinets.

Something about him being next to me, as I now faced the empty space where he'd been, made me aware of how I'd looked when he was across from me. I was wearing a thin-strapped red ballerina dress with white sneakers. My hair was relaxed at the time. It was straight, shiny, and smelled of chemicals and heat damage. We both had dark brown eyes. His slightly lighter with a hint of amber shimmer, like tortoiseshell.

"Do you write your own songs too?" I asked.

"No, can't do that yet."

"Oh, you don't know how to write?" I joked.

"Not anything good," he said. And he looked so sad I felt bad about my joke.

I apologized, overcompensating by rambling on about my song-writing ignorance. "I don't know why I thought it would just be saying whatever came to mind in some random melody. I mean, I make up little songs all the time about making breakfast or running late, whatever I'm doing. But of course, obviously it's more than that."

"Running late? How does that go?"

"I'm running late," I lightly sang. "I'm running late. This is the running-late song."

"Instant hit," Gabe said, smiling. He had one of those faces that when he smiled, his entire face changed. It pulled his features up. In repose, he looked brooding, now he was a gleeful little kid. It was like a party trick. I wanted to see it again.

I said, "I could show you some Gaudí now, if you wanted?"

I TOOK HIM TO PARC GÜELL, THE PRIVATE ESTATE GAUDÍ HAD designed that became a public outdoor space and landmark. I directed him to the crowd favorite: *El Drac*, a dragon made of a collage of broken tiles. People gathered around, taking photos with it. It was my third time at the park. I found it interesting to see what approach people took for their photos with *El Drac*, some hugging it like a family dog, others attempting to ride it, others mugging faces of terror as if they were about to be devoured.

I asked Gabe what he was doing in Barcelona for the summer and he said he was tagging along with his mom while she taught and worked on her next collection of poetry. His parents were divorced, he lived with Leora. For the past five summers, he'd gone to a performing arts program in Michigan. He was classically trained in voice and piano, he always got the lead in school theater productions, and for a long time he thought he'd do something in the theater space, maybe even become a teacher. But his focus had shifted senior year.

"My voice teacher always said that my voice was enough, I didn't need a band or pop production. But then I was like, what if I want to do that? I could create my own full-on theatrical spectacle myself. Sing, perform, write." He held up his hand, ticking each of these off.

"Totally you can," I said, as if I knew anything about performing or the music business.

We left the park and headed back to my student apartment. On the way, we walked down Carrer de Sardenya and I pointed out La Sagrada Família, Gaudí's unfinished masterpiece. We joined a long line of tourists. Inside we stared at the kaleidoscope ceiling. Gabe took a picture of me with the disposable camera I'd been carrying around. Neither of my parents had ever been outside the country, I was also documenting my trip for them.

There was something I'd wanted to ask Gabe. "Why do you only sing songs by women?"

"I like them."

So did I, but I thought that was because I was a girl. I didn't know any guys who liked anything done by a woman as much as they liked something done by a man. I was always arguing for them to even consider a woman.

It might seem hard to imagine because it wasn't 1952 or anything, but back in the early aughts, it was rare to come across a boy who talked like this. And we weren't at the point we'd eventually get to when men started using equality catchphrases as pickup lines. Gabe and I talked about how women had been treated in the music industry, I told him about the female painters and architects he should know. We were in the middle of an architectural marvel and a boy feminist was the most striking part of the experience; it thrilled me.

Back on the street it was after sunset, and we passed restaurants, debating where to go for dinner, attempting to find the student-abroad holy grail: (1) really good and (2) really cheap. Twenty minutes into our search I spotted a place with a line out the door and a chalkboard menu in front with prices we could afford. It was a balmy evening. The air had weight, the day was clinging to us. The waiter brought over a pitcher of sangria. We ate pan con tomaté, patatas bravas, stuffed piquillos. We talked. And we talked. And we talked and talked and talked. As we left the restaurant, after splitting the bill, a car drove by, blasting a reggaeton song. It had been popular that summer and we sang along.

By the time we reached my apartment it was dark. The moon seemed to appear out of nowhere, like someone had flicked a dime into the sky. We stood outside the building, still talking. Then from some part of the night, there was a loud noise. We jumped. A car backfiring? Someone unloading a truck? Who knew? It was enough to pause our conversation, the first real silence we'd had in hours. We looked at each other, wondering what would happen next;

maybe we were unsure even then what it was we were feeling for each other—romance, friendship, some other unnamed kinship—but what we settled on was a kiss.

AT FIRST NO ONE COULD BELIEVE IT. THERE WERE ONLINE THEORIES, media speculation. People assumed there had to be more to the story. A young, successful musician couldn't just die. And if they did, it had to be the result of their own reckless behavior, the cumulative pressures of fame, or some sordid combination of the two.

In the end, that all quieted down and was replaced with the facts.

Gabriel Wolfe-Martel, aka Separate Bedrooms, twenty-nine, popular indie musician, preternaturally talented, at the height of his career, deceased after performing a secret show at Hotel Frank in Downtown Los Angeles. After the concert, back in his room, while stepping out of the shower, Wolfe-Martel slipped and hit his head on the marble sink. He was dead instantly. Found by housekeeping in the morning. Here was an accident in a hotel room that involved a musician in his twenties but did not involve cocaine, a firearm, or heroin. A beer bottle, but he wasn't over the limit, and room service drinks aren't illegal. His death, in its banality, was miraculous. The only thing more miraculous would have been if he'd survived.

AT THE CEMETERY, JABARI AND THREE GUYS FROM GABE'S TOURING band lifted the coffin from the hearse. The rest of us followed behind them into a wide, green space with tall oaks. And many grave-stones. Once the coffin was placed, Jabari stood near me, under one of the oak trees. He wore large, dark sunglasses and I wondered if he was crying behind them. We were all crying. Tears slid down my face. I had been crying every day since I heard. They didn't have any aim or origin, those early tears. It was a physical response, a leak in my face, similar to sweat in that I had completely exhausted myself and it had to come out somehow.

The rabbi was making the rounds, pausing to speak to each person. When she got to me, she gripped my hand in hers. "May his memory be a blessing." She said the same thing to Jabari. I heard her say it to the next group of people. Then when she spoke to another group in Hebrew in the same brief, somber way, I knew this had to be some kind of traditional funeral parting, a wish people had been making for each other for millennia. And had it been granted? How did people get through this? If I was going to get through this, I would need an addendum. May *some* of your memories be a bless-ing. The rest of them? Recently? I thought of the story Kathy had told me about Gabe making time to see me. I'd never thought that story was as cute as Kathy thought it was, but I'd *liked* it. Now it was another sliver of our history that would eventually, like all my memories of Gabe, have to be carefully reexamined. Others around me bowed their heads in silence, wishing Gabe peace and love. That's what I should have been doing. Instead, as the rabbi spoke, the spark of rage I'd been smothering burst into an inferno. I looked down at the coffin and thought about what I had really wanted to say in my eulogy. What I had wanted to say all day. Now in my head, the words writhed around, tangled in an anger I'd hoped could be pushed down.

You fucking jerk. You're lucky I even came to your funeral.

Then the burial. It was wretched. They actually put him in the ground.

TWO

“A nger is very common in grief,” Will said on the ride to the airport. We were in a rental car, an unremarkable sedan that smelled of cleaning solution and fast food. I’d told them about Elizabeth’s comment. I wanted their opinion, but also if we talked about that, we wouldn’t have to talk about what I’d told Will. He’d said he wouldn’t tell Casey and I was hoping I could count on him to honor the confidentiality of his pending profession. He was already eager to behave like a therapist in other ways, he’d recently gotten into casually diagnosing people. “Or she could have emotional regulation issues,” he offered.

“Yeah,” I said, reclining in my seat. I was in the back and had craned forward to talk to them. “It probably had nothing to do with me.” This explanation would have to be enough. It’s not like I thought I’d get a better one. I didn’t think I’d ever see Elizabeth again.

I LIVED ALONE IN A RENTED BUNGALOW WAY UP A HILL IN BEACH-wood Canyon. The driveway was in the front, but the real entrance was a white gate off to the side of the house, obscured by jasmine vines. Past the gate there was a grassless, drought-tolerant yard and a small brick area where the owner had left a grill I never used.

I dropped my keys and bucket bag by the door. I hadn't needed to pack a suitcase. The flight back to LA was only an hour, so we'd been able to fit the entire funeral trip into one day. It was hard to believe I'd left home no more than sixteen hours ago. I felt like I'd lived through a week. Obviously impossible, it hadn't even been a week since Gabe died. Jewish custom was to bury the body as soon as possible; Gabe had never been observant, but Leora sometimes was, so everything had to come together as fast as possible.

I took off my clothes, not bothering to put them away or hang them up, then drew myself a bath. A framed Alma Thomas print hung on the wall behind the tub. *Cherry Blossom Symphony*. My favorite painting, an abstract blur of pink and cobalt blue. I lit a candle, then stepped into the bath. I stayed until I pruned. When I got out, the candle, which had already been low, was almost finished. I could see straight down to the base, the wax translucent.

I didn't sleep well that night. The next morning, I went back to work. I had two assistants, one administrative and one to help out in the studio. Between the two of them they'd stayed on top of things. I was only recently the boss of a team. For years, aside from crucial social media help from my friend Rose, I'd done all the jobs myself, making the jewelry, photographing the pieces, packaging the orders. And at first, it was just a lot of thinking. When I'd worked at a boutique I could never find the kind of jewelry I wanted to wear, but also I didn't know how to put into words what I was looking for exactly. Some reflection of myself I guess, a reminder of the woman I wanted to become: free, sure of herself, daring. What started out as postcards on a mood board—Diana Ross in a sequined top and jeans, shimmying with her shoulder so low it looked like she was doing the limbo, Elsa Peretti with her arms bent, leaning back into the New York skyline, cigarette hanging from her lip, Anjelica Huston in a Calder necklace—became manipulating hot metal, failing several times, smoothing the coarseness of my first attempts, until I held in my hands a ring I was proud of, then a necklace, then earrings, followed by requests for gifts and loans to famous women, well-circulated, well-lit photographs of these famous women, the pieces out of my hands and onto their bodies where they became symbols of cool. Somehow wondering who I was became *this is who you should be*. The brand, My Grandmother's Collection, was a cheeky nod to a rich girl who'd gone to my college that Rose, Nneka, and I would quote—whenever anyone gave her a compliment on her jewelry, she'd say, "Oh, this? Just something from my grandmother's collection."

After catching up on work emails, I tackled my personal inbox, which I'd avoided since the initial round of condolences came in. There were a few more of those and a message from Leora about tracking down Gabe's things. He'd sold his house in LA in 2013. Ever since, he'd been staying in rentals, hotels, friends' places, living out of a duffel bag, moving from location to location, leaving bits of his life behind, promising to collect them when he was back again. When he played in LA, he usually stayed in my home studio (which, given all my jewelry tools—saw, torch, pliers, hammer, tweezers— he called my serial killer lair), and he'd left some stuff at my place.

Nothing important. I found a pair of sunglasses and a hoodie and put them in a box to send to Leora.

When I texted Casey to see if he had anything of Gabe's, he said probably not, he couldn't think of a time that Gabe had been to the new apartment he shared with Will, but then later he texted *could this be Gabe's* with a photo of a long wool scarf, black with green stripes. I replied no and texted a photo of two interlocking rings I'd designed for an engagement last year. *Inspiration?* Casey had given me his grandmother's engagement ring and I was going to repurpose the diamonds and emeralds to make wedding bands for Casey and Will. This was my specialty. Taking heirloom pieces and turning them into something new. Casey texted back a thumbs-up. I tried to get back to work, there were other orders I had to fulfill, but it was hard to focus. I took a break and went to Cupcakery, a vegan bakery near my studio.

Cupcakery was set up like a miniature fifties ice cream soda shop, with a cutesy white-and-blue gingham motif. After I paid for my pistachio cupcake and waited for my sencha, I noticed two tip jars by the register. This was something they did sometimes; you could pledge your tip money to one of two categories: Lakers or Dodgers, Madonna or Lady Gaga, Nicolas Cage in *Face/Off* or Nicolas Cage in *Wicker Man*. Turning it into a competition made them more money. That day there was one jar with a picture of Kurt Cobain. The other jar had a picture of Gabe, labeled *Separate Bedrooms*. He was onstage, frozen in a midair jump, hair wild and angled away from his face.

Here's a tip, Cupcakery: Kurt Cobain died decades ago. Gabe? Days ago. Too soon for the tip jar.

Gabe was not a celebrity, not really; he was only semi-famous. It was cool to know his music but that was exactly it: people knew his *music*. He wasn't a pop star with a physical identity as ubiquitous as the songs; unless you were in a specific subgroup of devoted fans, you wouldn't recognize him. He was known for raucous, danceable (or at least enthusiastically swayable) indie music and tenderly written emo anthems, both of which appealed to a smaller demographic of people. But my life was at the center of that demographic. Los Angeles, creative job, hipster bakery. Of course I would hear the news at work, of course my local baker and baristas were engaged in their own mourning rituals.

I checked my phone. I had a missed call from my cousin Ines. I knew she was calling about Gabe. I looked back at the tip cups. The fame thing was weird, but I'd been trying to think of it like this: Separate Bedrooms was the topic of discussion. It wasn't about Gabe. But now in Cupcakery on a tip jar, there he was.

IMMEDIATELY AFTER OUR FIRST DAY TOGETHER GABE AND I WERE inseparable. In 2004, you could enter Parc Güell without paying a fee and we spent a lot of time going back to that park, making loops around the now familiar landscape. Other times we'd walk Las Ramblas or buy fresh smoothies from La Boqueria. Or we'd go to this outdoor café, at its center was a tree with wood planks for seating built around it. I liked to study there, Gabe would come along, bringing the small black notebook he'd started carrying around, along with a ballpoint pen to jot down song ideas. Whenever I asked to see, he'd say, "Not yet." Sometimes we'd head to Barceloneta and spend time at the beach. The sharp smell of the sea stung my nose like the white anchovies in vinegar we brought with us, eating them straight up, out of their tin. They were called *boquerones*, which led us to jokes that we were *brokerones*. Though in different ways. Leora had money, so Gabe was in a financial holding pattern tied to youth. Whereas my brokeness was the inverse. I did not have to pay rent *yet*, I was still eligible for educational scholarships where I could look at buildings and hold hands with a musician.

For dinner, we'd stop at the grocery store and get some frozen tortilla española. It fascinated us that you could buy them in the freezer section. We'd heat them up in my student apartment kitchen, then watch a DVD on Gabe's laptop. More than a few times, we'd watch *The Last Days of Disco*. We loved the quick, heady dialogue and were obsessed with the late seventies and early eighties. Gabe for the music, his number one was Bowie, me for the fashion and films. I refused to pick a number one but: Grace Jones, *The Wiz*, Diane Keaton's vest.

We made out a lot. In high school, there'd been a kiss or two, some sweaty grinding at school dances, but that was it and I didn't see myself going from zero to one hundred.

My cousin Ines had a different summer objective for me. When I called her to give an update on my summer, she said, "You just need to do it." Ines is four years older and has been giving me blunt advice since the day, as I'm told, she stood over my crib and screamed, "Walk, baby, walk!" I ignored her advice then and that summer. I wanted to take it slowly.

I imagined—based on teen TV shows and stories from friends— that going slow would mean an escalating series of physical encounters, one step after the other, eventually leading to intercourse. But Gabe took going slowly as an instruction for how to set the pace. It

was less like a game of rounding bases and more like we were training to compete in the entire Olympics and each event required its
own skill set, its own precise talents, yielding its own gold medal. So
one night we might spend hours seeing what we could do with an
earlobe, then the next afternoon we'd see how many times I would
squeal, then fall back against my twin bed, breathless, after he wove
patterns around my nipples with his tongue. I didn't tell Ines. I thought
she'd laugh at me. It wasn't going all the way, so it didn't count. She
had been having sex for years, and I was still catching up. It's only
recently I've considered that what Gabe and I were doing was more
intimate than sex. But at the time, I didn't see it that way, and once I
have a way of looking at something, it's hard for me to see it differently.

Anyway, I was in no rush. Which matched the pace of summer in
Barcelona. The days went on forever, we were bathed in near constant sunlight; night in the city was also endless, it started at nine
and went past dawn. We had all the time in the world.

THE ONLY PERSON ASIDE FROM WILL WHO KNEW THAT GABE AND I
had hooked up, and that he'd disappeared after, was Ines. When the
news of his accident at Hotel Frank broke, Ines reached out, leaving
voicemails and texts. I'm sure she was wondering what had happened between me and Gabe. While I waited for my tea, I sat on a
stool by the counter. I pulled the wrapper from my cupcake, then
nibbled at it. When I finished, I called Ines. Water ran in the background. There was a loud motorized sound that I'd come to recognize as her portable breast pump. After offering her condolences
she asked, "How did you two leave things?"

I told her we decided we'd be better off as friends. I told myself this was how I was sure we would have resolved it. We'd made a mistake, it got awkward, but with time we would have figured it out eventually.

We weren't exactly on the best terms before Gabe died. But he had died.

If you took the average of who we were together, considering our decade-long friendship, we were golden. What could I do? Spend the rest of my life haunted by one aberration?

I tossed my cupcake wrapper and left my empty teacup on the counter. I noticed the tip jars again. Kurt Cobain had more dollars in his. Annoyed, I left a dollar in Gabe's.

Right before turning thirty, I'd felt acutely aware that I'd reached the end of something. Not just my twenties, but also that feeling that life was completely fresh, newly unfolding. Experience and routine were settling in. Gabe's death had made me a novice again. Now that I'd returned to this state, I saw that I'd romanticized being a beginner. There was a queasy unease to treading new waters, building the compass as you sailed, every choice a guess. Except it was worse now. Because it was expected at eighteen, or even twenty-five, but at thirty, it was embarrassing.

I returned to my studio but was unable to get any work done. Eventually I gave up and went for a drive. The next day followed the same pattern: I went into the studio, tried to work, failed, then went for a long drive, an even longer one this time, nearly making it to Joshua Tree before turning back home. A week went on like this and it felt like it would repeat forever until I received another email from Leora.

THREE

Leora's email, addressed to family and friends, said she was ready to receive visitors. This time, when I went up to Berkeley, I drove. I'd been driving all the time anyway, mostly at night. A six-hour trip to see Leora was no trouble. Gabe and I used to talk about our parents getting older. We were both only children, being solely responsible for their care was an anxiety people with siblings wouldn't understand. No matter how I was feeling about Gabe (I knew how I was *trying* to feel: forgiving, calm, at peace), I had to go see Leora.

The house where Gabe grew up was one of those big Northern California houses with aged redwood shingles. High in the hills, with a forest-green trim around the windows and doors, it blended in with the trees, like a Swiss Family Robinson hideaway. I'd been to the house twice, once for a seder, another time for the sixty-fifth birthday party Gabe threw for his mom. He set up a karaoke room in their house and Leora sang "Ironic" by Alanis Morissette. She was surprisingly good, rocking out, throwing herself into it. After her rendition, in his toast, Gabe said, "Ladies and gentlemen, the true rock star of the family."

A couple in their sixties, an Indian woman and a white man, were leaving as I arrived. Leora's brother Howard, Gabe's uncle, let me in as they walked out. The entryway was lined with flowers and baked goods. I placed the muffins I'd brought on top of a box of chocolate chip cookies.

Howard said Leora was expecting me, so I waited in the living room. I sat on a faded green couch. Across from it was a fireplace and built-in bookshelves. On one of the shelves, there were several copies of Leora's poetry collections. When Leora entered carrying two mugs, I sprang up. "Oh, thank you, you didn't have to," I said. If anyone was offering tea to someone, it should have been me to her.

As she handed me a mug, we leaned into each other, touching shoulders for a quick hug. She motioned for me to sit back down as she took a seat in the armchair by the fireplace. The last time I'd seen her, at the funeral, her hair had been in a braid, but now it was loose, wild, and falling over her shoulders. She was wearing small platinum stud earrings, one of my designs. She'd never been much of a jewelry wearer, but she'd supported me from the beginning, making the earrings part of her uniform of loose jeans and men's shirts. In Barcelona, she'd been like a surrogate mother to me, always checking in on how I was doing in the city, making me home-cooked meals. Over the years, I'd had two or three catch-up lunches with her, sometimes we texted. She'd requested that I give a eulogy, but it was Howard who had contacted me. We hadn't talked much at the funeral. What was there to say?

"How are you?" I asked. Well don't say *that*, I thought. It was what I meant, I did want to know how she was doing, but they weren't the right words, it wasn't enough. How are you, considering everything. How are you in this moment. That's what I meant.

"Ramiro tried to sit shiva with me."

"He did?" I'd seen Gabe's father, Ramiro, at the funeral. Gabe would admit that his father had taught him Spanish and a few things about the technical aspects of music, adding, "All things I could have picked up in a high school elective." Gabe was close to the Colombian side of his family; at the funeral, his aunt had spoken about his vacations in Colombia. But his relationship with his dad was always difficult. The last Gabe mentioned to me, Ramiro was "living in Boulder with some woman barely older than me." I tried to imagine Leora and Ramiro sitting shiva together. As far as I knew, they didn't even speak. Gabe said the only way they'd be in a room together again was if he got married.

"What was that like?" I asked Leora.

"I didn't do it. He can't stand that I don't turn to religion. 'You don't have to go to mass, but at least do your thing,'" she said, imitating him. "*My thing*? It's called Judaism. And it's not my thing." She had a limitless well of disdain for her ex-husband, and plumbing its depths seemed to energize her. "He wants me to be the mourning mother. Like someone out of *General Hospital*. He wants me to slap him and say something like, 'Don't you know I've lost my son?' I think the only way he *can* mourn is if I slap him. Some men need that. They can't access an emotion without their handy female cipher. He'd love it if I just slapped him."

It seemed like she'd also love that.

I said, "I'm so sorry."

How are you. I'm sorry. Useless phrases. I was useless.

She thanked me for sending along Gabe's things and filled me in on her progress with the rest. The spare keys to her house had turned up in Jabari's studio, but the Mingus live recordings Jabari loaned Gabe were in her pantry. The guitar Gabe usually played at performances was recovered at the hotel. Gabe's manager, Kathy, had gathered most of the others, but there were two more still out there. "Everyone's responded, it's been very helpful. There's only one person I haven't heard from." She took a sip of her tea.

I felt a prickle under the skin behind my ears. Why did I know immediately who she was talking about?

"Gabe's recent ex-girlfriend." She rested her cup on the end table next to her chair.

"Elizabeth?" I asked.

"Yes, her."

"How many times have you emailed?" I asked. "Did you follow up?"

"Of course! I emailed five times. That's the limit."

That was beyond any email limit I knew, but I didn't say anything.

"I don't know what to do. The most important things are still out there. And if they're with this woman, she could be going through her house one day and think, *What's this junk?* And toss it."

"No," I said. "Anyone who knew Gabe wouldn't just throw away his stuff."

"If he meant so much to her, why wasn't she at the funeral?"

"She was there," I said.

"She didn't speak to me."

She didn't? Why come all the way from London and not speak to Gabe's mother? "What's the stuff you're still looking for?" I asked.

"A guitar, it used to be mine. It has a brown leather strap. I stamped my initials on it in college. Back when I thought I was going to be Joni Mitchell."

I knew the guitar. It was the one Gabe had played in Barcelona. The one he'd learned on. It wasn't the best guitar, he didn't play it onstage, but it was his first and most familiar. He knew the sound well, so he often took it with him when traveling.

"Then there's the sheet music for 'I Left My Heart in San Francisco.' It was a little joke my father and I had when I moved to Berkeley. When Gabe left home, I gave it to him. And a baseball hat. Ramiro wants that."

"The Mets cap?"

She nodded. I figured it would be that one. I knew baseball was one of the few things they shared, and when Gabe was nine, Ramiro had given him the cap. It was too big for Gabe then, he'd had to grow into it.

"Ramiro wanted to . . . he wanted him to be wearing it when we buried . . ." Leora folded her arms across her chest. "But then we couldn't find it. Which I think was best. Nothing he owned in life went with him."

"What about his bracelet?" I asked.

"His bracelet? Of course, oh my goodness. I don't know where the bracelet is."

When reviewing my memories of Gabe, there were gaps, things I couldn't make sense of, especially in recent weeks. But if there was anything I could still count on, it was that bracelet.

———

THREE WEEKS BEFORE MY SUMMER PROGRAM ENDED, GABE AND I were lying in his bed, reading Paris travel guides together. We wanted to take a trip out of Barcelona. It would have to be somewhere nearby in Europe and it would have to be cheap. Paris was the splurge, it was probably going to end up being Seville, but if the combination of his busking and my babysitting Roberta's four-year-old daughter, Tamara, earned us enough, we wanted to be ready.

"Hey," he said. "What do you hear?" He gestured with his chin down to his chest. I pressed my ear against the left side of his chest, over his heart. I didn't know what I was listening for. His heartbeat was faint. The phrase *heart murmur* crossed my mind. I tensed up. Even though I didn't remember what exactly a heart murmur was, I thought of death.

Gabe leaned back and used his elbows to slide himself up. "That's not where my heart is. It's on the right side." He tapped the other side of his chest. I repositioned myself and rested my head on the spot he'd pointed out. His heartbeat had sounded faint because I wasn't in the correct place. Now I heard it beating strongly. Gabe said he had situs inversus. His organs were reversed. "Your heart is on the left side, mine is on the right. Your spleen is on the right side. Mine's on the left. And so on," Gabe explained.

We'd only been dating three weeks, but we'd spent most of that time together. How could there be something I didn't know about Gabe? Now as an adult, when I'm in a relationship, learning anything new about someone familiar is a thrill—and expected. There's an understanding we've lived lives before each other. But Gabe and

I were teenagers. There wasn't much life to cover, and considering how talkative we were, it felt impossible that there was anything we'd left unmentioned. "How did you find out?" I asked.

"I was having chest pains. Turned out just to be stress, but first they did all these tests. And then the nurse was like, 'I think the machine's broken. No wait! Your *body* is backwards.'"

"What were you stressed about?"

"AP exams."

"Sure," I said. Those were stressful. "And now? Are you . . . ?"

"Yeah, I did okay on the exams." He saw the worry on my face. "I'm fine," he assured me. "It's not a problem. The only thing is if I'm in an accident and they don't know about my condition, they could cut me open on the wrong side when they operate."

"Oh, that's the only thing?"

"But I just wear a medical ID bracelet so they know not to do that."

I checked even though I already knew both wrists would be bare. I may not have known everything going on inside of Gabe's body but I'd happily memorized every inch of it I could see. I knew he'd traveled with a week's worth of clothes and rotated them, and he wore the Mets cap on particularly sunny days. I'd never seen a bracelet. "Where is it? Why aren't you wearing it?" My voice was getting higher.

"I don't have it yet. My mom ordered one, but it hadn't arrived before we left."

"And you're just walking around without it?" Now I was shrieking. I jumped out of bed. Gabe reached for my hand.

He laughed. "It's okay. Seriously. It's fine."

It didn't seem fine. The only reason I let it go was because I knew there was something I could do about it.

GIVEN MY AFFILIATION WITH THE PROGRAM, IT WAS NOT HARD TO find somewhere in Barcelona where I could make a bracelet. I spoke to the program's sculpture professor, who led me to a local sculptor who worked with metal and also made jewelry. She was happy to invite me into her space and gave me access to her equipment in exchange for some light assistant work. I'd taken metalwork in high school and had been making jewelry as a hobby for years, but I was far from a professional. It would have been easier to make a bangle or a cuff, but I knew a linked chain would last longer and be easier to adjust over time. To pay for the silver I needed, I used the money I'd saved from babysitting. This was more important than Paris.

Meanwhile, I continued with my courses. We had two options for our final project in Roberta's class: curate the works of a classmate from the painting course, basically committing four nights to being a docent in the student show, or write a paper on an artist of our choosing. Wanting my nights free to be with Gabe, I chose the paper. Roberta and I met in a café near the HEYSA campus so I could finalize my topic with her. I saw her often out of class now, when I babysat Tamara or when she had Leora, Gabe, and me over for dinner, but today was official business.

"So what are we doing here?" Roberta asked. She picked up her cup of coffee, lightly blowing across the top. "I can't wait to hear what you've chosen, Julia."

"Um, well, it's going to be Georgia O'Keeffe. O'Keeffe's landscapes." I showed her the book on the topic I'd brought with me. Always helpful to have a visual.

Roberta's expression slumped. She tapped a finger against her mouth. "Are you sure? O'Keeffe has been written about. A lot."

I'd thought this might happen. "I'm not going to write about the flowers," I said quickly. "That's why I chose the Abiquiú works—"

"Which have also been covered. I expected you to bring something new to the table?" She squinted, as if reassessing her opinion of me. I was not used to teachers looking at me like this and I didn't like it.

"O'Keeffe is new to me," I continued, talking faster as I explained that my father was a local bank manager, but on weekends he painted, he was always bringing home art books from the library, specifically African American art books. I knew Romare Bearden, Alma Thomas, Betye Saar. These were artists and pieces often excluded from the curriculum, he explained. They hadn't been excluded from Roberta's, but by the time I was in her class, they were old hat to me, they were canon, and O'Keeffe was the undiscovered outlier. Roberta understood and commended my father for his forethought, but I was still embarrassed, bringing up my dad had made me feel like a little kid, and I kept talking even though she'd accepted my explanation.

"It's like love," I said. "I'm in love right now."

"Gabe?"

I nodded quickly. "And you've been in love before, right?" I asked.

"Yes." She smiled, a tiny, private smile, either thinking about that love or amused with the teenager in front of her comparing it with her own limited dating experience.

"But I've never been in love," I continued. "It's never happened to me. So should I just say, oh, this isn't interesting. Everyone does this. Why should I care? Just because it's common doesn't mean it's not remarkable." I hugged the O'Keeffe book to my chest. "Obviously, I want to get a good grade, and if you really don't like it, I guess I can find another artist. But O'Keeffe is the one I discovered this summer."

Roberta reached for the book. I passed it to her. She said, "There are better books. It will be up to you to research and find them. At least you can contextualize your new feelings."

I beamed. "Thank you."

Two weeks left in my summer session, and Leora, Gabe, and I were at Roberta's place for dinner. The bracelet was complete, and my plan was to give it to Gabe that night after he walked me home. As I pulled out my chair, Leora asked me, "How are your classes going, Julia?"

"They're fine," I replied, with a casual indifference and a hint of boredom. We were in a little dining nook off the kitchen. Gabe was in the kitchen, within earshot, and I knew she was aware of that too. She had not given up on the plan for Gabe to go to college, finding any way to bang the drum for higher education, but I wasn't going to defect from Gabe's side (which was currently undecided, but unwilling to give his mom the satisfaction of knowing he was probably, most likely, going to attend college in the fall as planned). I would never dream of withholding information that might cost my parents money, but that was me.

"So are you in Roberta's army of docents?" Leora asked.

"No, she took the hard way," Roberta said, entering from the kitchen. Gabe followed with a pitcher of peach sangria. He sat next to me. Roberta set down a platter of grilled shrimp and said, "She's writing a paper on Georgia O'Keeffe."

Electricity gathered at the back of my neck.

"You won't be the first!" Leora joked.

Roberta laughed. She leaned over the chair next to Leora. "That's what I said. I thought I was encouraging her, but I was limiting, very art snob of me. It's not like I'd tell her never to read Audre Lorde or listen to Mozart." As she sat down she said, "And Julia made an excellent point."

I loved Roberta's spontaneity in class. She said whatever came to her and it was always delightful. Now I saw the drawback to her personality. My eyes darted to Gabe. It felt like we were in love. I'd always wanted to be in love. But we had never said I love you.

Gabe gnawed on a shrimp, unaware of what was about to play out.

Maybe it could be stopped. "I don't eat shrimp," I said.

"Oh, I'm sorry," Roberta said. "I didn't realize you were a vegetarian now."

"I'm not. I'm a pescatarian. But shrimp are basically bugs."

"But aren't bugs less than fish?" Gabe asked.

"No," I said angrily.

"Wait, so what was Julia's great point?" Leora asked.

"It wasn't," I insisted.

"It was!" Roberta slid her hand across the table, patting mine. "She said that yes, to me, to us, O'Keeffe is old news, but she's seeing it for the first time. So should Julia not write about it just because the work is old? Julia's feelings are new." Roberta smiled. Then the death stroke. "Just like falling in love with Gabe."

Leora widened her eyes in surprise. I felt Gabe freeze next to me, but I didn't look at him. I could never look at him again. I was Orpheus. I had made my deal. If *he* had looked up from that shrimp tail seconds ago, we could have had a proper goodbye. Now it was too late. He'd walk home with his mom, and I'd jump into the Mediterranean.

I hadn't even used the phrase *falling in love*! Roberta ad-libbed that. Maybe I could say the whole thing was her improvisation. I'd tell Gabe later, *I guess she just ran out of things to say and started making up stories about me.* I could save myself if I threw Roberta under the bus. *I guess she's just a bit of a liar. Weird!*

"And when you have that first love," Roberta continued, "it is exquisite. Just because others have been in love before, it doesn't make it any less intense or important. If it did, we'd never want to hear another pop song again."

"I don't want to hear another pop song again." Leora chuckled.

Roberta gestured with wide arms toward me and Gabe. "But they do!" She laughed. Leora laughed. I stared at Gabe's shrimp. Gabe stared at Gabe's shrimp. Our gazes burrowed through the shrimp, into his plate, through the table, down to the earth's mantle, its magma and molten core, and still our eyes never met. We shared embarrassment, but no further glances for the rest of the meal.

IT WAS A QUIET WALK BACK TO MY STUDENT APARTMENT. I TOLD MY-self Gabe and I only had two weeks left in Barcelona, so this was why we were silent. We were taking in the city. The motorbikes parked alongside the gray brick buildings, the celebration and chatter from smoke-filled restaurants, another Barcelona night for our memories. Maybe we were. But it didn't change the fact that neither of us knew what to say.

In front of my apartment, Gabe asked about the surprise I'd mentioned earlier. My stomach dropped three floors. I was hoping he'd forget that I'd said that, give me a good-night kiss, go home, we'd start fresh in the morning. The bracelet was a grand gesture. Roberta had already forced my hand on another grand gesture and look how that had gone.

We entered my room. It wasn't the right moment for it, but he was already expecting a present and I didn't have anything else to give him. Maybe I could somehow convince him that the copy of *The Namesake* he'd seen me reading all week was for him? But the small wrapped gift was sitting on my desk, plainly visible. I handed it to Gabe.

"It's like *El Drac*." He smiled. I'd peeled the labels off the packages of tortilla española we'd shared and used them to decoupage the box. He gently opened it.

I'd slipped up a few times, trying to connect the links and melting them in the process. The nameplate came out crooked and wrong. I'd started again. The engraving was the last part. I'd been practicing as I worked on the rest of the bracelet. When it came time to write Gabe's condition, the letters came out perfectly, not in cursive, which would have been a lovely flourish, but in delicate capital letters, evenly spaced, legible for an EMT in an emergency. It was more complicated than anything I'd ever made. I never would have been so ambitious without the life-or-death motivation, but once I realized I could meet the challenge, I became obsessed. Soon I was looking forward to working on the bracelet more than going to classes. I'd canceled on Gabe once when I'd lost track of time while soldering.

He held the bracelet between two fingers. "Oh wow. This is definitely something I needed."

Definitely something he needed? What did that mean? Did he like it? I told him I'd made it.

"You *made* this?"

"Yeah."

Gabe flipped it over. "It's engraved."

"Yeah, I did that too. I borrowed a Dremel."

"What's a Dremel?"

"It's a little gnome creature who helps with metalworking. He's quite strong but has a terrible attitude."

"What?"

"It's just, like, a tool," I quickly explained. Something was going on. We were awkward with each other. Or I was being awkward and the sheer force of it was ricocheting off Gabe back to me. I said, "You can fall off a mountain now and whoever rescues you will know what to do."

"That's probably when I'll need it. All the mountain climbing I'll be doing."

He was joking. I was annoyed. "Yeah, I mean you probably won't wear it. It was just something to try." I tossed my hair back. "It was a great learning experience."

"A great learning experience?" He sat on my bed. "Kind of like this whole summer? You want to see if you can get college credit for this?"

"What's going on? I feel like you're being mean."

"Really? I feel like *you're* being mean. You don't care if I wear it. 'Great learning experience.'"

"I already told you how I feel."

"No, Roberta told me."

I didn't know what he wanted from me. I was the embarrassed one. Why was he making it worse? I noticed he hadn't offered his own declaration of love. "Do you like the bracelet or not?"

He let out a loud exhale and raked his hands through his hair. "Sorry. I love it. I really do. You made me a bracelet that could save my life. And it's way better than one from some random medical catalog. This is—no one would ever think to do something like this for me. It's the kind of thing I would think about doing, and then cop out because I was scared of seeming too intense."

"I *was* scared of that."

He held out his hands, reaching for mine. "Thank you is what I meant." Our fingers interlaced.

"You're welcome," I said. Whatever tension had erupted seemed to be dissipating. I helped him put the bracelet on, holding on to one end of the clasp. "I'm glad you like it."

"Like it?" He shook his wrist. It fit. Loose, but not too loose. "I'll never take it off."

He kissed me. It was a quick peck, a conciliatory end-of-an-argument kiss, like the mandatory handshake after a middle school soccer game. I could feel the effort to make everything right in that kiss. And then to make it even clearer, he said, "It's okay."

"I know," I said. I knew couples fought, my parents rarely did, or at least not in front of me, but I knew in general people did. Lovers' quarrels. Makeup sex. I'd heard the phrases and got the gist.

But it wasn't okay. *That* I understood at the time. It's only recently that I can look back on this memory, one of our last Barcelona nights, the bikes, the cafés, and us, and understand what was going on in that room and exactly what wasn't being said.

Two days later we broke up.

The one place we wanted to go in Barcelona and hadn't visited yet was Tibidabo, the hill that overlooks the city. At the very top is an amusement park. We took the funicular up, passing rooftops, then power lines and trees, mountainsides, until our view stretched to the sea. In the station the ticket taker immediately began speaking Spanish to Gabe, which happened all the time in Barcelona. They never started with Catalan—after weeks in the sun, his skin had a darker, more golden undertone than most locals'—but they never started with English either. After we got our tickets, we headed toward the amusement park. The roller coaster looked ancient, like it might be as old as the mountain itself, but we got in line. While we waited, we took in the real show—the panorama view of Barcelona. Two girls ahead of us, backpacks slung low over their shoulders, twirled with their arms out. It was the kind of view that made you want to twirl.

"I can't go to Paris," Gabe said. It was so abrupt, I wasn't sure if I'd heard right. I asked him to repeat himself. When he did, I said that was fine. I hadn't saved up enough for Paris either.

"No," he said. "I can't go to Paris because I'm leaving Europe."

"Yeah, we're all leaving Europe." Gabe and Leora were staying a week after HEYSA ended, but then they'd return to America too.

"No, I'm leaving, like as soon as possible," Gabe said.

"How soon?"

"The day after tomorrow. I decided last night."

I stepped out of the line, letting the people behind us go ahead.

"You decided last night you're leaving the day after tomorrow?"

He pulled at his hair. "I *decided* last night. After thinking I was pretty sure about it last week."

Last week. Even before Roberta's dinner. We hadn't spoken about the dinner, this was the first time we'd hung out since, I'd had to work on my O'Keeffe project the night before.

We walked away from the line as Gabe explained. "I've been talking to these guys, good musicians, we've been trading stuff. We're thinking about starting a band. But they're back in America. They're sophomores at Oberlin. And they want to get in some practice time before school starts." NYU was definitely not happening, he'd told Leora he might apply to Oberlin, but between us, he didn't think he would. "I *could* say, let's keep dating, but it wouldn't be right. I'd be doing that thing guys do when they leave and say they'll come back for the girl, but they don't."

"Come back for the girl? What are you, a country-western singer now?"

"I just need to focus on this opportunity, Julia."

"So you're breaking up with me because you *might* form a band?"

"When you say it like that it makes me sound like a dick."

53

I didn't know how to talk about what he was doing without making him sound like a dick.

I'd never been in this position before, never had a boyfriend, never broken up. I confused the personally unprecedented with the universally undeniable and argued, "But I don't *want* us to break up." I can't remember for sure, but I may have even put my hand on my heart. God help me if I put my hand on *his* heart.

Gabe nodded, appearing to be in agreement, then said, "I know, I know. But we are."

We thought it best if we took the funicular down separately.

I saw him once before he left Spain. He was playing in the courtyard. I don't remember the song, I was trying not to listen. I was trying not to look at him either, but I gave in. His hair had reached its highest heights of the summer, he needed a cut. He gave me a half smile, I turned away.

That was the first time I thought I'd seen Gabe for the last time. We were over, though I noticed he was still wearing the bracelet. He said he'd never take it off and he never did.

I'D ASSUMED HE'D BEEN BURIED WITH IT.

"No, I haven't seen the bracelet," Leora said. She sighed. "I guess it's missing too."

"But at the hospital?"

"No, he didn't make it to—"

Right. The point of the bracelet was to alert medical professionals, in the event of Gabe's incapacitation, of a rare condition to prevent a surgical error. We had imagined his cause of death and solved for it, as if eliminating this cause would eliminate death altogether. It had nothing to do with why he died, so in that way it didn't matter if he was wearing it or not.

"I'm sorry, Julia. I don't know where it is. I can't believe I forgot about that." Her face sank, then rebounded. "Maybe Elizabeth has it?"

"Maybe, but they weren't still living together," I said. I wasn't going to tell Leora that I knew for sure Elizabeth didn't have it because I'd seen Gabe wearing it a month ago, after they'd broken up. I didn't want to lie to her and there was no way I was going to tell the truth when she asked the inevitable follow-up question: *Oh, what were you doing with Gabe last month?*

"But he went back to England a few weeks ago."

He had? Though, I hadn't heard from Gabe in weeks, which was enough time to travel around the globe. But why would he have even taken off the bracelet? I asked Leora if it could have been left behind at Hotel Frank.

"The police went over everything. Then the insurance company. They returned it all. His clothes. A belt." She placed a hand on each side of her waist and pressed in as if demonstrating the belt. She winced, like she'd actually cinched herself together.

"And are you sure—" I caught myself in time. I was interrogating a grieving mother.

Leora didn't seem to notice I'd stopped talking. I don't think she was even listening anymore. Before I could suggest that I head out, she stood up briskly and walked into the kitchen. She called back to me, "I was able to catalog most of his stuff. Do you want anything? We have so many concert tees. And there are other guitars." She

55

gestured down the hallway, to the room that had been Gabe's bedroom and then became her office and was now, in a way, Gabe's again. A warehouse for Gabe. The door was closed. Which was good. I did not want to go in there. I said no thanks.

She returned with another cup of tea. I glanced at the full one already sitting on the end table. She shrugged, like, now I have two cups of tea, what are you going to do? Was there anything anyone could do for Leora?

"I can help," I offered. "With Elizabeth."

"But I already emailed her. How?"

How to explain it politely? Especially to someone like Leora, who thought of herself as a cool parent. Compared to her, I was Sherlock Holmes. Nancy Drew. Batman. The greatest detective out there. Because I had Facebook. Instagram. All of social media, the entire internet. Email was only the beginning. If Elizabeth didn't respond to my DM or tweet or poke or whatever other digital nudge I gave her, then I'd shake her social tree. *Hey, your friend Elizabeth is holding private property hostage from an older American woman who's lost her only child. Please get in touch!*

I could help Leora. And I did think maybe this would lead me to the bracelet.

I'd been convincing myself that Gabe and I had made some mistakes, we'd ended up in an awkward place, but eventually who we were would have remained the same. But if he had taken off his bracelet, it was more than that. Discarding the bracelet was discarding us, making the last month more serious than one isolated incident. If I could find out where Gabe had left it, I might be able to figure out why he wasn't wearing it and if that reason was connected to what had happened between us. And, either way, if the bracelet was out there, I wanted it back. As a souvenir of our time together, as a personal token of the earnest art student who I used to be, as *proof* that at one point when Gabe gave me his word, he meant it.

I told Leora not to worry about contacting Elizabeth again. I'd take care of this. When I got home, I didn't try to work, I didn't try to sleep. I googled Elizabeth. It was a relief to have something to do, other than crying and driving. I was a set of house keys buried at the bottom of a purse, finally plucked out, jangling with purpose.

FOUR

Elizabeth was seven years older than us.

She started out as a floral designer, then at a wedding where she provided the flowers, she befriended a caterer named Emmanuel Oyi.

Together they hosted a supper club in London, which then became a pop-up in London and Paris. Last year they'd opened a restaurant called Fleur Bleue, focusing on seasonal European cuisine.

Elizabeth's personal profile was private, but I pieced this together from the "About" section of the Fleur Bleue website, some press on her, and Emmanuel Oyi's wife's frequently updated social media. A few constants emerged from my search: Elizabeth worked in a little white building with a neon-blue sign; she hopscotched between Paris and London. She was always photographed with her work. Her signature pose was facing away from the camera, holding one of the lush, garden-style bouquets she made over her shoulder. She arranged elaborate private dinners. Long tables set with taper candles and handmade serpentine floral centerpieces. With every photo, the tables got longer and the candles got taller, until both were stretching out of frame.

I found an interview with her on a culinary podcast.

"And your restaurant is called Fleur Bleue. The blue flower," the podcast host explained. "Which in French has a whole different meaning."

"Yes," Elizabeth said. "It was inspired by my time in Paris."

It was inspired by my time in Paris.

Though to be fair, one time I'd been interviewed and said, "Rose gold is death."

I did consider that the items Leora wanted might be elsewhere. Gabe had played a lot of music festivals that year and I reached out to other musicians on the rosters. The lead singer of a band in Brazil said one of Gabe's guitars was on their bus, and for a few days I thought I had solved it, but then the guitar didn't match the description of the one Leora wanted. They would send it along anyway.

Then nothing. No further leads. Elizabeth was the only person left.

Good, I thought. I wanted it to be with her. She was in my head now, with her candlelit gatherings, her garden-style bouquets, and her *I know exactly who you were to Gabe.*

AFTER TOO MUCH TIME DOWN THE INTERNET RABBIT HOLE, I TOOK a break from my Elizabeth sleuthing and went over to Casey and Will's to look at fabric swatches. I'd used a professional connection with one of Casey's favorite menswear designers to get a discount on their wedding suits. Will thought this was a frivolous waste of money, even with the discount. Casey was ecstatic. We sat at their kitchen table with the swatches spread out in front of us. Lately Will had gotten into cooking on the weekends, and the countertop was crowded with kitchen appliances: a blender, a rice cooker, a stand mixer, a different more powerful blender, and a large cardboard box housing some new arrival to the countertop gang.

"How are you doing?" I asked Casey.

"I'm fine," he said. "How are *you*?"

Will glanced at me, probably waiting to see if I'd tell Casey what I told him about me and Gabe.

Instead I filled them in on my visit with Leora and how I was helping her. Minus the part about my own search for the bracelet.

"His poor mom," Will said. "Tracking down his stuff won't bring back Gabe."

"She knows that," I said. I hoped she knew it. Though I could tell Will and I disagreed on the importance of "stuff." My entire business was based on creating sentimental items. Things were things until the thing *meant* something and then it was invaluable. Did I have to break out *The Velveteen Rabbit*?

Casey held up a tartan swatch.

I dismissed it. "Too Trey MacDougal."

My phone was in my lap. I returned to googling Elizabeth. I scrolled, not seeing anything new. Was that it? Had I exhausted every online source about her? The last page I'd looked at had a photo of Gabe and Elizabeth together. They'd broken up not too long after. Something about schedules not lining up, and she didn't want to move to America.

"Not even New York," Gabe had said.

"New York is America," I reminded him.

"Barely. It's just hanging on the coast. There are so many good restaurants."

"Wow, I can't believe she didn't pack her bags and leave all her friends and family for you."

"Like I did?"

I didn't mention that a few months wasn't the same as a long-term commitment.

Casey leaned over the table, craning his neck down to see my phone. "I googled her too," he said. "You know, you both kind of have this 'I make beautiful things, I own my own business' thing going on. Maybe Gabe had a type."

"I met Gabe before I had a career."

Casey sat back in his chair. "Then maybe you were the *proto*type." He folded his arms. "And I was thinking about what she said to you. She could have been joking. It's very hard to tell tone with the Brits."

Will twirled three swatches around with his fingers in a little concentric circle dance. "Or she was at a funeral."

"'She was at a funeral?' What does that mean?" Casey asked.

"At my grandmother's funeral, my mom and her sisters got in a *physical* fight."

"What?" Casey laughed. "Why?"

"It wasn't hand-to-hand combat or anything. Just a few slaps from my aunt Camille."

"Oh, Aunt Camille," Casey said, as if that was just the kind of thing Aunt Camille would do. He held up a silk swatch and rubbed it against his face.

Will continued, "Something about how there were four of them, but only three seats in front of the coffin. It was this whole thing about who was the favorite and then it became about some vacation they took in 1972."

I wanted to know more about Aunt Camille (who wouldn't?), but I returned to my phone. I'd reached the end of Elizabeth Thompson's presence on the internet, with no leads. Also, despite my original idea, I hadn't reached out to her or her friends. I'd realized I'd only get one shot and I didn't want to blow it. Email was never going to work. Elizabeth could just ignore it. Same with a letter or a call; she could tell her friends to do the same. The only way was to approach her in person. Then she'd have no choice but to engage with me. I searched for a home address but couldn't find one in my texts with Gabe. I mentally reviewed everything I knew about Elizabeth, everything I'd come across about her in the last few days.

The little white building with the neon-blue sign.

I could tell from what I'd learned of Elizabeth that she, like most women I knew, was always at work. She had no social media, no website. But her restaurant did. And there on the home page was the address:

23 Turville Street

Greater London, England E2 7HX, United Kingdom

". . . and one of the therapists in my program shaved her head." Will was still talking. "People do strange things when they're grieving . . ." He checked in to see if I was paying attention. "Julia?"

"Huh," I murmured, only half hearing him. I was searching flights to Heathrow.

FIVE

I left the next night and—with the ten-hour flight and eight-hour time difference—arrived in London the following afternoon. From the back seat of a black cab, I felt a faint tourist delight as we passed red double-decker buses. The cabdriver had asked if I'd ever been to London, and when I said no, he offered to take the scenic route. I accepted, knowing this passive form of sightseeing would be as good as it got. When Gabe talked about touring, he'd said after he played a city, it felt strange to say he'd been there. Yes, technically he had been physically there, but he'd only seen his hotel room, the concert venue, and the mode of transportation between the two. He never expected to know a tour stop city in any real way; it was a work event, not a vacation. I was approaching my first trip to London the same way. This would not be my chance to wander through the Tate or climb the steps of the Tower of London, but letting my driver take an extra few minutes to go through the roundabout in front of Buckingham Palace, I could do. It was Thursday and I was staying four nights, a long weekend. September was usually one of the quieter months for My Grandmother's Collection, right before the holiday gift-buying rush, but even so Mandy and I figured I'd have to be back by Tuesday to avoid falling behind. Whether or not it would be enough time to track down Elizabeth and find Gabe's stuff, I didn't know.

We pulled up to Hotel J, a gray brick building with steel-framed windows and doors, a boutique hotel, part of a global chain. I'd stayed at one in Brooklyn when a New York fragrance brand, wanting to collaborate, put me up for a week. The hotel's trademark aesthetic centered around purposely ironic, overstuffed kitschy decor with large, bright (often neon or light-bulb-studded) knickknacks from the city where each outpost was based. When I checked in, I was greeted by a giant bejeweled painting of Big Ben behind the front desk. Techno-pop music blared at a volume that could only be called undeniable. I'd chosen the hotel because it was in Shoreditch, the same East London neighborhood as Fleur Bleue, only a six-minute walk away.

In my room, I washed my face. The bathroom was small, with the shower, sink, and toilet only a finger away from each other. I leaned over from the sink and turned on the shower. I stripped down, but I didn't get in. The most I could do was tilt my head so one ear was *slightly* in the vicinity of the water. And then, feeling a sense of vertigo as I imagined the various combinations of slips and falls that might lead to head trauma, I immediately pulled that lone ear out again. No one had told me that when mourning someone's death you might also start to fear your own. Since hearing how Gabe died, I'd avoided showers. I'd stuck to long baths, washing my hair over the kitchen sink like my mom used to do when I was a kid.

Maybe this was good. Without a tub, I'd have no choice but to take a shower. It would be mandatory exposure therapy. I stood at the edge, staring at the torrent of water as if we were facing off in a duel, waiting to see who would blink first.

The shower won. I turned it off, then dropped a towel on the floor to soak up any rogue specks of water that might have escaped.

Whatever. I could conquer this newfound fear later. I washed up in the sink and changed into a pair of jeans and a lightweight cream button-down. In the elevator, I mentally rehearsed my approach. The story was I happened to be in London on business. I was walking by when I saw the restaurant, I realized it was Elizabeth's and thought I'd stop by for a quick hello. Oh, by the way, was she aware Leora needed to reach her? Since I was in town, why not avoid shipping costs and allow me to transport everything back to California? On my way through the lobby, I passed a line of people at the front desk. A bellhop lifted a suitcase onto a trolley, placing it on top of an already precarious Tetris-like tower of luggage. Outside, the hotel doors slid closed behind me. I glanced at the map on my phone to make sure I was headed in the right direction, then began walking to Fleur Bleue.

I USED A PAPER MAP WHEN I FIRST MOVED TO LOS ANGELES IN 2008. It was essential. I kept it stuffed in the glove compartment of my used Volvo. And when I say paper map, I don't mean one folded piece of paper. *The Thomas Guide* was a giant book of many pages, with LA street maps. You would search the index for the street address you wanted, then find the grid code for that address, then find the map page corresponding to the grid code.

I can't imagine why this system was replaced.

My first month in town, I was determined to explore as many LA neighborhoods as possible, the map integral to the type of destination-less driving I liked to do. I'd park wherever I could find free parking and then continue on foot. One morning, it was early, probably just past 7:00 A.M., I ended up in Echo Park. I walked down Sunset Boulevard, passing restaurants that wouldn't be open for hours. I'd just noticed a boutique across the street, with handmade leather shoes and bags in the window, when someone whizzed past me. A nose, ears; that's all I had to go on, but I thought it might be—

My eyes darted away from him; at the same time, he called out, "Julia Hendricks?"

I turned around. "Gabe Wolfe-Martel?" I asked, hoping my feigned surprise would resemble the genuine shock I'd felt seconds earlier—before I knew without a doubt it was him. Four years older, slightly lankier. He still dressed like he was on his way to a high school gym class: basketball shorts, T-shirt.

I braced myself for the pain of that summer's rejection, the boomerang of forgotten feelings. Neither arrived. Instead I was distracted by Gabe's haircut. It was awful. A bowl cut. A Caesar situation. Like a nineties boy band member in the early videos before they saw themselves on MTV and adjusted accordingly. How had this happened to him? I didn't know, but I was grateful. I had a hormonal breakout on my chin. I was wearing a loose short-sleeved smock dress that—to borrow a phrase from my grandmother—did nothing for my figure. But any insecurities about my own appearance were supplanted by the mess on Gabe's head.

A prayer for the rejected:

Oh if ye be noble and true, may ye be blessed with running into the boy who dumped you after he's had a terrible haircut.

And then there was his method of transport. I raised an eyebrow. "Is that a scooter?"

"It is." He wheeled himself forward a few feet so we were now directly in front of each other. Keeping one foot on his steerable skateboard, he placed the other on the sidewalk.

And may he be on a scooter.

"Why are you on a scooter?" I asked, in a slightly teasing way, although with genuine curiosity. Eventually there would be scooters all around LA and several other major cities, but at the time, I thought of them as the ridiculous little cousins of the Segway, which had become, in recent pop culture, a well-established sight gag.

"I thought I'd try it. But you know, early. Before anyone would see me, in case I fell over or looked like a tool."

"Someone did, and you do."

He laughed, then motioned to me, mimicking my earlier eyebrow raise. "And why were you running so slowly?" He spoke deliberately, with curiosity, as if I'd just witnessed a natural disaster and he was the first reporter on the scene. I knew I was being set up for something but responded anyway. "I was walking."

"Just walking? Cool. Like the old ladies who do laps around the mall?"

It was my turn after the scooter ribbing. I bopped my head in an *okay I get it* rhythm, then gave him the finger. "Can you even be out in public? Now that you're a rock star?"

"Not a rock star," he said emphatically, brushing away my claim, but also, it seemed, reminding himself of a personally disappointing fact. It was true—at that point, he wasn't quite "a thing" yet. He'd put out *Separate Bedrooms*, a self-titled EP. It had its fans, though it was a small following. Still, he was more of a rock star than anyone I knew.

"So you've been following my music?" he asked.

"Had to," I said. "For a while I was one of your only fans on MySpace."

Gabe ran his hand through his hair, a bit self-consciously, I thought. A silver halo sparkled around his wrist. I couldn't help myself; my mouth sprang into a grin. "You still wear that?"

"Yeah, of course." He shook his arm so the bracelet slid up and down. "I told you I'd never take it off."

"And it could save your life," I joked.

"Yeah, that too." He smiled at me. The smile was the same. I looked away, not wanting to find out if it still had the power to melt me. A tall white woman jogged by, in running shorts and a neoprene tank. Her face was beet red.

"I can go this way," he offered, pointing his chin in the direction I'd been walking.

"Sure," I said, grateful to start moving, looking at the sidewalk instead of directly into each other's faces. Gabe wheeled his scooter along. Ahead of us, a bus pulled up to a stop with that loud sinking sigh buses make when their doors open. An older Asian woman holding a clear plastic umbrella stepped off. The doors closed, whatever mechanism that had produced the sigh now reversed into a groan, and the bus heaved itself like some lumbering extinct beast back into the flow of traffic.

"So what are you doing in LA?" Gabe asked.

I told him I was starting my first year of law school.

"Why are you going to law school?"

"I got in."

"Of course you got in. I just can't believe you're *going* to law school."

"Well I am."

"I mean, we haven't seen each other in a long time, but I can't imagine it."

"Gabe, deal with it. I'm in law school."

"Do you like it?"

"No."

BWAHAYHAY.

The truth was I was in law school because I needed to make money. My parents, in an unsurprising move considering their climb from lower-middle to middle-middle class and the recession-based concern that in a generation our family could slip-slide back, had explained that law would provide a financial safety net for whatever I ultimately chose to do. I'd start at a law firm, working for however long was needed to essentially create my own trust fund, and then I could do what I wanted. Eventually I could pursue something in art or design, and if that didn't work out, I'd still have the law degree to fall back on. Of course I was driving around LA trying to suss out any whiff of adventure before school started in a week and I found myself in lecture halls and study groups 24/7. The only reason I wasn't fighting law school as a backup plan was because I didn't even have a first plan. Maybe Gabe was disappointed that he had yet to meet the heights of his ambition, but at least he had a goal. I had no idea what I really wanted to do.

"Which law school?" Gabe asked.

"UCLA. I thought if I'm going to law school, I can at least be near the beach."

"I would have thought Yale."

After researching law schools for a year, I knew enough to clock the specificity of his question. "How'd you know Yale is the top law school?" Most people assumed Harvard.

"Oh—um, my ex-girlfriend. Her brother got into Yale Law."

"Oh!"

"Yeah!"

Our banter had taken off at such a breakneck speed, we were bound to flip over and crash. Of course he'd dated other people since we last spoke. So had I. Most recently my long-term college boyfriend, a philosophy major named Eric. Eric and I had officially broken up the beginning of senior year. But we'd continued to hook up casually and emotionally torture each other for months. After graduation, he'd moved back home to Durham to take over his dad's lumber business. We were still in touch, we talked on the phone all the time, another step in protracting the slowest-moving breakup in history. Believe me, if there had been any graceful way to bring up Eric, I would have. Right, so, speaking of law school, you know, as a citizen of this country, *Eric* is required to abide by our nation's laws. Oh, who's Eric? College boyfriend. Not to be confused with my first college boyfriend, *Aaron*, the guy I had sex with for the first time. Oh, did you think that was going to be you? You snooze, you lose.

I didn't feel the same magnetic pull I'd felt with Gabe when we were dating. But I did feel the need for him to know I'd been pulled toward others since him, and more important, for him to know they'd been pulled to me.

At the corner, we turned down a side street. "That's my car," I said, pointing to my used Volvo, a few parking meters from where we were. I hadn't meant to lead us to my car, but then once we ended up on the street, there it was, and it felt weird not to acknowledge it. But I knew in doing so, I'd ended our stroll.

"Oh!" said Gabe, also clearly surprised that our wandering had a destination after all.

I said, "So I'll see you around," and he said, "Yeah, see you around."

He hopped on his scooter and turned it back in the direction we'd just walked. But then he turned it around again and asked, "Wait, how? Just run into each other?"

I loved him for that.

"I'll check your MySpace," I joked.

He nodded his head slowly as if what he was about to say needed time to ferment. "Hey, were you going to pretend you didn't see me?"

My eyes hit the ground. The street, recently paved, was bright black.

"Maybe I deserve that," Gabe said. He smiled weakly, waiting for my response.

Come on, I thought. Tell the truth. "Yeah, I saw you. I was surprised. But I don't think I would have just walked away."

"We'll never know because I started yelling your name down the street." He cupped his hands around his mouth. "Hey, Julia! It's me, Gabe! Remember me? We used to date in Barcelona! It's Gabe, remember?"

He hadn't said all that, but he was saying it now; the swiftest acknowledgment of what we used to be to each other. Early morning had receded, bright yellow daylight flooded the street. Hot, insistent, it was not unlike the sunshine of Barcelona. We were standing in a memory. Then it was over. We laid our past on a pyre, and as it burned, I made an offering. Maybe we could be something different.

"Do you still have the same email?"

"No, I got a new one a while ago. And yours isn't the college one anymore?"

"Yeah, I have a new number too." I took out my phone. "Let's just give each other all the letters and numbers we have."

I STEPPED ACROSS SMOOTH PAVEMENT AND TURNED ONTO A COBblestone alley. There it was. A small building, painted Santorini white, with a neon sign: no words, just a blue flower blinking back at me. It was only half past six, but already there was a line at the door. When it opened, I saw the restaurant was packed inside, every table filled. Fleur Bleue was the place to be. My stomach clenched. Already my plan to breezily saunter by was in jeopardy. I mentally scanned for my next move, but found my thinking slow, muddled by jet lag.

Four people approached, work colleagues it seemed. They cradled blazers in the crooks of their arms, they were complaining about someone named Curtis. "Are you waiting?" one of them asked. I said yes and stepped forward, responding to an instinct not to lose my place, then immediately worried I'd made the wrong choice.

A white woman with white-blond curls and a small elfin face moved briskly from the entrance toward the line. She wore white overalls with a blue shirt underneath. She held up a wine bottle, pausing in front of each person as she asked, "Gewürztraminer while you wait?" The restaurant's windows were semi-opaque. From outside, I watched the shadows and outlines of people moving around, but no faces. One of these figures turned toward me. It was a man, I could tell that, but it seemed like he was staring right at me and it made me wonder if Elizabeth was in there somewhere, if she'd seen me join the line. If she had, it wouldn't look like I'd just *happened by*. It would look like what it was—that I desperately needed to get in.

Now that the jet lag was in my limbs, I had to fight to keep my eyes open. If I could have curled up on the sidewalk and fallen asleep, I would have.

"Gewürztraminer while you wait?" the hostess asked two men ahead of me. I was next, close enough to read the label and see the condensation droplets clinging to the curve of the bottle. Under normal circumstances I would have taken the free pour and chatted with her. Instead, before she could once again demonstrate her proficiency with this German tongue twister, I stepped out of line. I headed back down the alley. I was retreating, but at the same time forming a new battle plan. I'd get some sleep, then tomorrow I'd arrive right at five. I'd pass by as the little blond woman came out to offer her first glass of wine, wave her down and say, *Oh, I know the owner. Mind if I say hello?*

On the way back to the hotel, I counted two bookstores, three bars, a bagel shop, and restaurants on top of restaurants. Shoreditch was unlike the London areas I'd passed in the cab. There were no palatial buildings or business district towers. Most of the buildings were fewer than four stories and either tan or red brick. Building walls were covered in colorful street art. Perfect, I thought. I'd unintentionally chosen a fun area. At the next bar, there were a few guys out front, midtwenties, ties loosened, jackets slung over shoulders. Yeah, mate. Here we go, mate. Did people really say *mate* this often? I thought that was something British cinema amped up for American viewers. One of them yelled something I couldn't hear, but in the universal quick staccato of a diss. His mates howled with laughter, pointing to the one guy not laughing, the butt of the burn.

I don't know what I'd been expecting: the gloomy gray of early industrial London I'd read about in nineteenth-century novels? Thinking perhaps I'd bring my mood, and the city would adjust around me? Nope. It was seven in the evening and the sun was still shining, people were *out*. Then another bar with more people outside, a group of four in their early twenties, beers in hand. They were young and wasting time, and I immediately hated them. I couldn't have been more than five years older than them. I'd never felt more ancient.

LOS ANGELES WAS THE PERFECT PLACE TO MEET GABE AGAIN. Everything there was new to me. Why not add a friendship with Gabe to the list? It's also where I met Casey. We were both at UCLA Law. We'd decided over the summer, based on a few emails and one long phone call in which we discussed and analyzed every scene from *The Devil Wears Prada*, that we should live together.

Casey's older sister, Jeanette, was already living in LA. During our first semester, she took us out to a famous diner in Hollywood. I was expecting her list of places to see, things to do, but she had different advice to impart. Within five minutes of meeting me, she asked if I was dating anyone. I told her I was single.

"Okay, so dating in college is completely different," she said, aggressively dunking a French fry into a small plastic ramekin of ketchup. Jeanette was only four years older than us, but I noticed, like my cousin Ines, she wielded her age gap with great authority. Her thick black hair was piled into a loose topknot. It slid slightly to one side as she shook her head. "Girls have the power in college. But after college, men have the power."

"And then after that?" I sipped my milkshake, rapt.

"There is no after that," Jeanette declared. "We have a window of four years. They get the rest of it."

I exchanged a look with Casey to see how he was processing this *Cosmopolitan*-magazine approach to dating. He rolled his eyes but remained silent, robbing me of what I thought might be an opportunity for us to use the word *heteronormative* in casual adult conversation, the secret goal of all liberal arts students who graduated between 2005 and 2010.

"I'll lower my expectations," I said gamely to Jeanette.

"Lower them even further," she said. "Especially in LA. LA's the worst. No one falls in love in LA."

I considered this. In college, I'd dated two guys seriously and hooked up with a few others. All of them seemed grateful for the opportunity. But recently in LA, I'd met someone, a guy named Sean. Sean seemed like the guys I dated in college: smart, thoughtful, a bit nerdy and insecure, but still sweet. A law school classmate brought him to a party. After, Sean walked me to my car, then we made out for ten minutes. It was fun. We hung out again, the third time turned into a week of sleeping over at each other's places pretty much every night. It seemed like everything was going well, when he suddenly broke it off, emailing, *It feels like it's time for us to go down our own paths. I think I'm doing me, and you're doing you.* We'd been doing each other, but per his last email, that was over.

"Right," Jeanette said after I shared this story. "Like I said, no one falls in love in LA."

There were many reasons for this, she opined. For one, it was too bright. The city resisted a romantic vibe. You could disappear into a dimly lit corner of a bar with someone, sinking into a sultry mood. Then you'd walk out the door, and bam!—it was still too bright out. There were cars everywhere all the time, their headlights flashing a spotlight over any flaw. The fear was that everyone in LA was fake, so there was a premium placed on being organic. You had to find out if someone was for real. But that meant getting to know people, which no one had time to do. Traffic was constantly gobbling up our lives, so everyone was late to arrive and in a hurry to leave. Lastly, people were already in love: with their careers or their dogs or themselves. You could not fall in love in LA.

Which meant I could not fall back in love either. Helpful because since running into each other, Gabe and I had exchanged a few emails—mostly with music recommendations or tips about things to do in LA: free events, restaurant openings, stuff like that—and now we were planning to meet up. When I told Jeanette this, she said, "You dated this guy and now you want to be friends with him?"

This question apparently eroded what was left of Casey's patience for his sister. He leaned back against the booth, sighed, and with his arms folded said, "Jeanette, men and women can be friends, you know? Nora Ephron proved that in the eighties."

Now it was Jeanette's turn to fold her arms. "I'm not talking about men and women, I'm talking about exes. And have you seen that movie? They fuck and then they get married."

A MONTH OR SO AFTER OUR ECHO PARK RUN-IN, GABE AND I MET for brunch at The Hungry Hound, a twenty-four-hour diner in Hollywood with cheap drinks. In the short span of time since we'd reconnected, the single from Separate Bedrooms' first full-length album, *Dodger Stadium*, had come out. It was topping college radio charts. The week before, Gabe had been on a late-night show. Casey and I watched the performance together, on a couch we'd found on Craigslist and, with some law school classmates, carried two blocks to our apartment. Gabe, wearing a bespangled jacket, was joined onstage by a drummer, a bassist, and Jabari on keyboard. According to Gabe, Jabari—who'd also produced *Dodger Stadium*—was a genius, he was Jamaican and Swedish, and he and Gabe had connected on their multiethnic identities, working with him was all the best parts of being in a band, with none of the drama. Their partnership made sense. Jabari was focused and intense as he played. Gabe's stage persona was more kinetic. He danced with the other musicians, leaned into the audience, slid across the stage. It was different from how he'd been in Barcelona, singing and strumming his guitar in the courtyard. That was all voice. He was a performer now and he put on a good show.

"It's been crazy," Gabe said. "It's like I go out and people already know me."

He meant girls. Later he told me there were a lot of girls in that halcyon blur of being a breakout indie music darling. He'd discovered— well, he never said groupies. I think he thought he was being chivalrous or progressive by not saying it, but he alluded to the fact that there were many cute, intelligent hipster women who were into dating a successful, sensitive musician.

Yes. That made sense.

The Hungry Hound was on the corner, right on a major street. We were seated outside and every time I brought the fork to my mouth, I bit into a cloud of exhaust. I'd already filled Gabe in on my last four years: I'd been the typical English major, reading all the time, coming up with provocative thesis statements I barely supported just so I could have something interesting to say in class. There were parties, sharing a box of wine with friends, a semester abroad in Paris where I'd learned how to wax cast. Gabe asked if I was still making jewelry. I hadn't really kept it up in college with the exception of the casting class in Paris, but I was thinking more about jewelry lately, probably because I was bored out of my mind in law school.

Now it was my turn to eat as Gabe caught me up on his life. After the band didn't work out in Oberlin, he moved home to Berkeley. He traveled around for a bit, playing in college towns. I knew Separate Bedrooms had performed in Providence my junior year at Brown. I didn't go. Even though it was a concert open to anyone who bought a ticket, it still felt like randomly showing up at an ex's house. Gabe said after traveling around, he made his EP, then he lived in New York with his dad for a year.

I dramatically raised an eyebrow, aware of Gabe's history with Ramiro. "How'd that go?"

He bit into his breakfast burrito. "I needed a place to stay, he let me stay with him. Then he started coming with me to all these open mics." Gabe wiped a strand of cheese away from his chin with the back of his hand.

"That's nice? He was trying to support you?" I had no way of knowing if this was what Ramiro was trying to do, but I wanted it to be for Gabe's sake.

"No, like he would try to participate. Do you remember—did I tell you he can play the drums?" I nodded, thinking back to a night in Barcelona, the two of us talking through some movie we'd seen before, Gabe telling me his dad had wanted to be a professional musician; there was some botched opportunity to make the right impression on the right person; Ramiro talked about it all the time. Together Gabe and I posited that this was why Leora was so resistant to Gabe going down the music path.

"So one time I needed someone on percussion and my dad volunteers. Then after the show, the club manager says I did a great job and he's like, 'You must be so proud.' To my dad. And he's like, 'Yeah, takes after me.' And someone else asked, 'Did you always know he had musical talent?' And he was like, 'Oh yeah, we knew. He was always playing music.' Always? How would he know? As if he had anything to do with me. As if I hadn't only seen him for the occasional weekend and some birthdays." Gabe took a few gulps of his water, emptying the glass. He placed it on the table and absentmindedly spun it as he said, "Sorry, I just vomited out this whole thing about my dad. I've been talking for five minutes straight."

He hadn't been. But I liked that he apologized. I found self-consciousness in men endearing. I had a theory that in Gabe's case his deference was specific to women. He'd spent so much time as a kid at Leora's side as she pontificated that it was now his nature to take the back seat when a woman was talking.

"That sucks," I said. "Him taking credit like that."

"Thanks." He turned his glass right side up. "This is cool," he said, gesturing to the space between us.

"I *know*."

I could tell he meant us hanging out, just talking for an hour. And he could tell I meant yes, especially since we used to do this plus a bunch of other things in a twin bed. I don't think we'd realized how much we missed *talking* to each other.

This is what I know for sure. The thing about me and Gabe was:

We could talk. We could talk about Gaudí, we could talk about music, we could talk about our families. We could chatter for hours, and we could exchange one word and immediately crack up. It was like finding out someone else was fluent in a language you thought you had invented. Like you were the last surviving member of a cultural group with a specific dialect, and then discovered that across the world, someone had spontaneously picked it up.

There hadn't been any stated goal for brunch, but there was a victory nonetheless. We'd recaptured something important. Despite the breakup, despite the time, we could still talk. I could tell he was thinking about how we began then, because it had occurred to me too. Not when we began dating, but in Roberta's kitchen, when we first discovered that familiar ease of ours. When the waitress brought us the check, Gabe said, "We should do this again."

Six months later we met for a hike in Runyon Canyon, and now I, with big changes to report, did most of the talking. I'd left law school, I had a new job working as a brand director for a clothing boutique with a significant online presence (a combination of words I hadn't even known could exist together when I'd thought about what I wanted to be when I grew up), and Eric and I were really, truly over.

To cope, I'd been listening to *Dodger Stadium*. The album was all about Gabe's parents' divorce, a classic breakup album with the twist of a third party, the kid observer. Even if I hadn't been going through a breakup, even if I didn't know Gabe, it would have been impossible not to find my way to Separate Bedrooms that year. Everyone I knew was listening to *Dodger Stadium*. (My favorite song was "Tu Te Quedas, I'll Go." Gabe had combined a traditional Colombian vallenato style, including the accordion, with the tinkling chimes and chiffon melodies of an American sixties folk song.) We would have met up sooner, but Gabe had been on tour.

I stopped by the entrance to the trail to tie my shoe, balancing my right foot on my left knee in a precarious standing figure-four position. "And Leora doesn't mind you writing about the divorce?" I asked, wobbling on one leg. "She doesn't consider it her thing to write about?"

"Well, first, she's written about me too." Leora's most popular book was about her first year as a mother. It was told from his perspective as a newborn. Gabe offered his elbow for support. I leaned against it.

"Right," I said as I tied my laces into a floppy bow that would fall apart again in five minutes. My concentration was no longer on my sneaker. It was on the fact that Gabe was able to touch me without the sensation rippling through my entire body. It was an arm and an elbow. An arm and elbow who had once known each other intimately and were now cordial, friends even.

When I had two feet safely back on the ground, Gabe continued, "And second—no, she's never touched the divorce stuff. She's very good at plumbing the depths of whatever topic she chooses and completely ignoring the other difficulties in her life. I mean, I think she knew it was going to come up. I called myself Separate Bedrooms." He added, "Shira thinks there's going to be all this divorce content coming out. Because our generation will be talking more about the domestic spaces we grew up in." Gabe was dating a writer named Shira who was becoming well-known on the internet for her vicious cultural-commentary takes. They'd met online after she gave Gabe one of her rare rave reviews.

Soon Shira and I became friends too. When we hung out as a group, it was usually me, Gabe, Shira, Jabari, and occasionally Casey if he could spare a moment away from law school. I spent a lot of time with this girl Ali who also worked for the boutique. Then I met my next boyfriend, Brandon, through mutual college friends. We'd been at Brown at the same time but never crossed paths. Though he was also Black, so I'd been aware of him, like I was of all other Black students. And he was hot. I'd noticed that too. Tall, swimmer's body, glasses, the nerd-who-works-out type. He'd worked in consulting after college but had recently decided he wanted to be a cinematographer. "You're so perfect for each other," my cousin Ines said. "You're like the Obamas if they were artists." During this time whenever any well-dressed Black woman and man were together, someone had to comment on how they were like the Obamas.

The next year Rose moved to LA. She wanted to be an actress. She and Jabari hit it off and soon they were dating. By the time my twenty-fourth birthday came around that summer in 2010, Gabe and Shira had broken up, then Rose and Jabari were over, Jabari moved back to New York, and Casey got a job at an entertainment law firm. Rose and I moved in together. During all this, Gabe went on first a Europe tour, then a South America tour, coming back to his LA apartment whenever he could.

When he got back from the South America tour, we met up at The Hungry Hound again. I don't remember what we talked about. There were so many nights and afternoons at The Hungry Hound. When I first moved to LA, I thought I would go to the beach all the time. And I thought I would catch up with my old summer boyfriend once. In my eight years in LA, I went to the beach twice and I saw Gabe all the time. We went to parties in Hollywood apartment complexes, in shared house rentals off Wilshire, in bungalows up hills, in the Valley. We waited outside the taco stand near the auto dealership by USC. We waited inside the Apple store at the Grove. We went to late nights at the Getty and saw *Christian Marclay: The Clock* at LACMA, we drove to Santa Barbara and Palm Springs on the weekends. At first, there was The Hungry Hound, Runyon, only a few places we'd been together. Now if I drove through LA, I could point out all the coffee shops, music venues, trails, restaurants, bars, and the places friends used to live, where, for nearly a decade, Gabe and I spent our lives.

In London, as I walked down Old Street, then on to Shoreditch High Street, my shoulders dropped, my stride loosened. I thought, At least I'm not in LA. This was why I had been taking two-hour drives, six-hour drives, why I'd hopped on a plane. I had to get out of LA.

There is something about a city that isn't yours. Perhaps better than a beach vacation is the trip to a new city, the luxury of walking leisurely through a busy metropolis, observing a hustle that does not require your participation. You walk past scaffolding around a building without any consideration of when the construction work will be completed, how it will affect your commute, if you will benefit from whatever new structure rises. Heading to my hotel, I relaxed, knowing whichever route I took, at least it would be London streets. At least I wouldn't run into Gabe.

ELIZABETH'S RESTAURANT WASN'T OPEN FOR BREAKFAST OR LUNCH, so the next morning I headed out on foot, picking up a tea and croissant from a coffee shop. The air was crisp, cool enough for a light jacket but warm enough to pleasantly shrug it off your shoulders after a brisk walk. What a difference a day makes in September. When I'd gone to college on the East Coast, the sudden seasonal shift had always been a cause for celebration: Tights! Warm drinks! School supplies! But after living in Los Angeles for years, I'd forgotten what a true autumn felt like. I walked around Shoreditch for a bit. My first impression was: quaint English village meets hipster punk. There were many cool shops, but there were even more trees. There were other people walking, but except for the occasional dozen or so pedestrians backlogged as they waited for a light to change so they could cross the street, the streets weren't teeming with people. When I passed an Underground station, I decided I still had enough time to explore and hopped on the Tube. I ended up in the center of London. Now I could barely move down the street. Tourists, commuters, it was like Times Square. I walked to Bond Street, then Savile Row. I left the main road and turned down a quiet side street. A man on a bicycle rode toward me with his dog. He held the handlebars with one hand and the dog's leash in the other.

Somehow the dog kept up with the bike, or the bike kept up with the dog. Either way it seemed like a miracle they were pulling this off. The bike passed a redbrick building with vines of intensely dark red leaves clinging to it like crimson ivy, and a banner hung from the side: HELEN FRANKENTHALER: YEARS OF COLOUR. I knew the name: Helen Frankenthaler was a painter who'd been at the forefront of American abstract expressionism, but I'd never seen her work in person. The art I usually sought out was sculptural, related to my work—Maren Hassinger, Louise Bourgeois, Ruth Asawa. Recently I'd been into Yayoi Kusama's light installations.

Perfect, I thought. There had been so many surprises recently, all heartbreaking. It was a relief to experience something unexpected that would be good for me. The cyclist passed by, maintaining his adroit management of both pet and bicycle. I turned my head away from the sunlight reflected on the bike's chrome. When I turned back, there was a woman standing in front of the gallery. She was wearing a hunter-green jacket over a busily patterned floral shirt, with a canvas tote slung over one shoulder. A book was tucked under her arm. Her profile was familiar, and though her features were imperceptible from that distance, her auburn hair shone like a penny. She went to grab something from her tote, but it fell out and she bent down to pick it up. A pack of cigarettes. She dusted them off, then turned in my direction.

Elizabeth did not see me, but I saw her clearly now.

SIX

She was waiting in front of the gallery as if we'd planned to meet, like she knew I'd be there. But how would she have known that? My London trip was a complete secret, I'd told no one I was going, the plan was to get in and get out before anyone even knew I'd left LA. We were the only two people on the street, there was no crowd to disappear into, I watched her impassive stare in my direction change as my features coalesced for her. Yup, she saw me.

Muscle memory took over and I found that culturally mandated female acquired habit of making everything sweet; the stickiness that binds you to other people but clogs your own system. I said, in an octave higher than I've ever reached, bordering on that falsetto kid in *Sister Act 2*, "Elizabeth! Hi!"

"Julia. Hello." She had to project, we were still on opposite sides of the street, but her voice had a calm, resonant alto quality, nothing like my helium-chipmunk shriek. "I was just thinking of you," she said. "And then I was running errands and I saw an advert in the Tube for the Frankenthaler exhibit, and I thought, Today's the last day, if I'm going to get over to see it, I better do it now. And then here you are?"

Even though I had gone to Fleur Bleue with the purpose of creating a run-in, there was something different about actually running into Elizabeth. Funny how seconds before I was grateful for stumbling upon this exhibit, comforted by a lucky turn of events. It occurred to me how often I pounced on a silver-lining meaning when faced with coincidences. Once Gabe and I became friends and he was in my life—and it seemed he would always be in my life—our Echo Park run-in acquired a sense of fate: we were meant to see each other again, meant to be friends, everything had worked out as it should. But now, thinking of Gabe led me to the conclusion it was all random chaos. I mean, what were the chances that someone would slip in their hotel shower and fall at the exact angle that would lead to a fatal brain injury? Was this the same *fate* that had brought us together in Echo Park, popping up again to place him on that shower floor? My intention was always rational thought—Casey said the most important thing he'd learned from law school was that most people *don't* think rationally—but now I understood how often I'd ascribed cosmic causality to life's surprises. There was no harm to déjà vu, destiny, the Universe working for you *when things were going well*. My parents never went to church, they'd both rejected organized religion. But it turned out I had organized my own religion, one that relied on what I now saw as the seemingly romantic, but ultimately cruel, philosophy that Everything Happens For A Reason. Without this private logic, I was vulnerable; it was a crisis of faith.

Now I watched Elizabeth try to make sense of our run-in. She was thinking of me and then here I was! Like magic! But it wasn't magic. I had come to London to see her. It was an accident, and it wasn't.

"What brings you to London?" she called out.

I forgot all about my cover story. Instead of saying I was in town for work, I yelped, with the desperation of a game show contestant who'd hit the buzzer before knowing the answer, "This exhibit!"

"Really? All the way here for this exhibit?"

"I love seeing art from around the world."

"She's American."

"Exactly!" I pretended like I hadn't heard her. I crossed over to Elizabeth's side and was a few steps away from her when someone yelled my name. I turned around. Caroline, a woman I knew in LA, was headed toward us, waving big. "Julia!"

What was going on? Was everyone I'd ever met converging on this London block?

"I didn't know you were in London," Caroline said. She leaned in for a quick hug. Freckles dotted her light-skinned complexion (mother Polish and Italian, father Black). "We just saw Casey before we left and he didn't mention it."

Of course he hadn't. He didn't know I was here. "Last-minute splurge," I said, glancing at Elizabeth.

Originally I knew Caroline through Casey, her husband worked with him, but we'd also ended up in the same book club. The conversations in book club had become so personal that I felt like Caroline and I were closer than we would have been if we'd had, say, four coffees instead of four wine-filled nights talking about the sexual desires and ambitions of women in 1950s Naples. We'd talked about getting together on our own a few times, but then Caroline got married and pregnant soon after, the book club meetings tapered off, and our friendship never fully launched.

"What brings you to London?" she asked.

Did everyone need to know what brought me to London? I don't know, it's a major metropolis with beloved tourist attractions? Mind your business, people! Aware that Elizabeth was in earshot, I said, "This exhibit here."

"We've been running into everyone on this trip! You read that article in the *Times*?" I shook my head. "It's all about how you have to get to London right now," Caroline said. "It's having a moment."

"Just as of this week?" Elizabeth chimed in from behind me.

"What did she say?" Caroline asked. "Is she talking to us?"

"That's Elizabeth," I said.

"You know her? Let's go over then," Caroline said, pulling me by the arm, like I was a child that needed to be wrangled, *Go ahead, say hi to your friend.* She introduced herself to Elizabeth.

When Elizabeth said hello, Caroline's eyes lit up like two sparklers. "You're British?"

"I am," Elizabeth responded.

"What's the closest you've ever been to the Queen?"

"The closest? In my flat. About an hour from Buckingham Palace."

"In my *flat*!" Caroline laughed hard, delighted as if Elizabeth were a small dog that had just balanced a Frisbee on its nose. "So any tips?" Caroline asked.

"On England?"

"Europe. We're going to Paris and Amsterdam next."

"Tips on Europe!" Elizabeth exclaimed.

Oh God, Caroline.

"This gallery is quite lovely," Elizabeth offered. "They have a garden in the back."

Caroline peered up at the Frankenthaler exhibit sign. "Never heard of her." I didn't like where this was headed. If Caroline joined us, I wouldn't get time alone with Elizabeth.

"She's not for everyone," I said.

"I was just reading something about great female artists and how they often don't have children," Caroline said. I remembered that her conversation topics were usually based on whatever she'd last read online.

"No children," Elizabeth said. "It's the key to getting work done."

"I have a kid." Caroline sniffed.

"And what masterpieces have you created lately?" Elizabeth asked.

In another world, I would have not only laughed, but barked like a seal in delight, and never stopped barking, but in this one, I stifled a smile. Right, she could make a joke. Gabe must have liked that. Caroline did not. She gave Elizabeth a caustic look. "Oh thank God," she said, turning away from us, pointing to a tall white man pushing a stroller around the corner onto the street. I glimpsed the sticky hand of a toddler holding an ice cream cone.

"There's Tim!" Caroline waved to her husband. "Come say hi," she said, and pulled me away toward her family. Oh, I realized, she thinks she's saving me from this rude woman. "Honey, it's Julia!" Caroline said as we approached Tim.

"Julia, it's you!" He doffed an imaginary cap to me. "Welcome to jolly old England, mate!" Tim made everything into a one-man show. Though he had the "mate" thing right.

"Who was that woman?" Caroline asked. I asked if she remembered my friend Gabe. She said, "Separate Bedrooms Gabe? Who just died?" I said yes, that was the one, and Caroline and Tim launched into their experience with Separate Bedrooms. One of their first dates had been at a Separate Bedrooms concert, they were huge fans. Caroline said, "He always seemed like such a nice guy. Was he nice in real life?"

Is he nice? The boring question that everyone always asks about celebrities. Any time I worked with a famous client, that's all anyone wanted to know. Is she nice? As if they would ever describe any of the people they knew as simply nice. Who was, only and always, *nice?*

I said, "He was sooo nice."

Tim asked, "He wasn't twenty-seven, was he?" I shook my head. "That's good because all those musicians die at twenty-seven."

I'd have to let Leora and Ramiro know the greatest tragedy was that their son wouldn't be included in posthumous conspiracy theories.

"He's twenty-nine," I said. Wrong tense. I corrected myself. "He was." Caroline gave me a syrupy look, her eyes thick with sympathy. She touched her hand to her heart. "Anyway," I said. "He and Elizabeth used to date. That's how I know her."

"*She* dated him?" Tim exclaimed. "But wait—Casey told me you dated him."

"A long time ago," I said.

"Catfight!" Tim chuckled. He curled his hand like a paw and batted it at me. I swatted it away and his hand hit his own face. "Ow!" He rubbed his nose.

Caroline turned to Tim. "That's sexist. I was just reading a piece online about 'shine theory,' how women need to support each other, *not* be threatened by each other."

Tim scoffed. "That's for female coworkers, not two girls in a love triangle."

A love triangle? I did not like the sound of that. And as soon as I realized I didn't like the sound of it, I knew why. There were plenty of famous love triangles with two men and one woman, but the only triangles I could think of with two women and a man involved the women teaming up to get back at the man. Brandy and Monica. All the first wives from that club. Maybe because there were already perceptions of catty women fighting over men and we had to undo those stereotypes? Or was it that people didn't want to see women in this way? With two suitors, there would be a victor, which meant there would also be a loser, the rejected one. No one wanted to see a rejected woman. No one wanted to *be* a rejected woman. Desperation wasn't in fashion. It was embarrassing to pine after someone who didn't want you as much as you wanted him. Only Dolly Parton had the courage to say otherwise.

Either way, Elizabeth was not my Jolene.

I told Tim, "It's not like that. I think she's very nice."

It was not convincing. Tim laughed. "Sure you do." Caroline glared at him. He held up his hands in surrender. "Sorry! Julia, if it helps? You're prettier than her. Kind of mannish, isn't she? She's got a strong jaw. You could crack Brazil nuts with that thing."

Tim was repulsive. I felt the need to defend Elizabeth and said, "I like her jaw."

"Nope," he said, as if his opinion was the only thing that could put a definitive end to this debate he'd started. Caroline sent another glare his way, but this one seemed to signal some unspoken marital code that meant *Go over there now* because he immediately said he'd see me around, waved goodbye, and rolled the stroller away from us. I turned back toward the gallery. There was no sign of Elizabeth. Had she gone inside? Had she left? Then what would I do? Show up at Fleur Bleue and run into her *again*?

Caroline placed a hand on my elbow. "Look, I know grief is hard." So we'd entered the ladies-only portion of the conversation. *No, Tim, come back, Tim.* "My grandmother died three years ago. So believe me, I get it."

"How old was she?"

"Ninety-seven, we knew it was coming, but it was still a shock."

Ninety-seven. Twenty-nine. There were enough years in between those ages for two adult lives, both longer than Gabe's.

"Julia." Caroline paused dramatically. She looked me right in the eye, then unveiled her wisdom. "Grief comes in waves."

I RETURNED TO THE GALLERY. GREAT, I THOUGHT, ELIZABETH'S gone through the exhibit and out the back door by now. But when I walked in, she was inside the entrance, ending a phone call. "Good, that's sorted. I'll see you," she said.

"Hello again," I said in a tone that I hoped sounded friendly, not creepy.

"Hello again," Elizabeth said in a tone that echoed mine. I decided it was friendly.

She opened her tote. I peered in, hoping for a glint of silver. Inside: the pack of cigarettes, some lip balm, a wallet, and a flower. A real one, a dahlia, I thought. As if it would be that easy. Even if she had Gabe's bracelet, why would she be carrying it around the city? She dropped her phone in her bag. "Just finishing up a call," she said. "I'm chained to my phone. I run a restaurant."

"Oh," I said. "You do?"

SEVEN

What are you reading?" I pointed to the book Elizabeth was still holding.

She held it up so I could see the cover. "Didion," she said. "Everyone keeps recommending *The Year of Magical Thinking* so I'm rebelling and rereading *Slouching Towards Bethlehem.*"

"Wouldn't rebelling be reading . . ." I tried to think of someone who wrote in more florid language, a style the opposite of the cool journalistic distance of Didion, but my mind went blank. The only writer I could think of was Leora Wolfe and I wasn't about to bring up Gabe's mother. Not yet.

"I know what you mean," Elizabeth said, waving her hand to indicate there was no need for me to recall. But then, I could tell, a name had popped into her head, like a slice of bread springing from a toaster. "Anaïs Nin!"

"Exactly."

She tucked the book into her tote. She asked if my friends were joining, and when I said no, she asked if I'd mind if she joined me.

"Not at all," I said. We approached the gallery ticket counter. A young woman with a teeny nose ring greeted us and explained there was only one exhibit brochure left.

"We could share it?" I suggested to Elizabeth.

She took the brochure from the woman's outstretched hand and passed it to me. "Why don't you have it and then you can bring it home as a souvenir?"

"Oh thank you!" I chirped. Like this was a brilliant idea and she was so sweet to think of me. Why had I even suggested we share it? There was no way this would ever become a catfight. Where other women fought, I fawned. I've sensed some aggression, let me see how I can make you like me. Despite being aware of my stress response, I continued to try to please her. Maybe Elizabeth would enjoy some art history facts? As we walked into the exhibit, I offered, "Helen Frankenthaler was young when she started, she invited a New York art critic to her college show."

"Yes, it says so there." Elizabeth pointed to the wall text right in front of us, which included biographical information on the artist, including everything I'd just said. "It says she pioneered this style."

"Soak-stain," I said, not missing my chance to regain some authority. I continued, "She was inspired to paint on the floor, to get down on the ground and use her body instead of painting at an easel."

"Hmm," Elizabeth murmured. I was unsure if this had impressed her. I didn't have a read on her yet. It was strange, we'd fallen into step with each other, entering the gallery together; she was being friendly, completely unlike her behavior in the Berkeley City Club restroom. While Elizabeth studied Frankenthaler's history, I took the opportunity to study her. Her default expression was staid and a bit inscrutable, not unlike the Mona Lisa or a bored teenager, but now as I watched her, it opened up into awe.

"Wow," Elizabeth said.

The first painting of the exhibit had caught her eye. The volume of each color had been lowered, beyond pastel, into an almost watered-down ghost of the original hue. A pink sank under an orange, which reached for mauve, then dove into peach and green and blue. The colors touched but didn't pass through, their borders were distinct. There was something arresting about the bold gestures paired with feminine colors. Like a diva's ballad, it was equal parts power and beauty.

The exhibit included photos of Frankenthaler. We walked over to a black-and-white picture of her laughing on a boat with her husband.

"On their honeymoon," Elizabeth said, reading the label.

"Robert Motherwell," I said. "Another huge artist of the time."

"She's very pretty."

I agreed. "I think that worked against her at times? Pretty pictures from a pretty girl?" I added, "And she was privileged. She grew up in Manhattan. Well-off."

Elizabeth laughed. "Figured that. What with the villa vacations and private boat rides."

Not a rich girl herself then. But what did that mean, specifically, in England? I knew the British class system was complicated—or maybe it was simple but impenetrable. There was something about how your accent could reveal all of this. Elizabeth sounded like what I associated with posh, but was she?

We moved on to the next painting. The gallery was relatively quiet, an older man and woman were two paintings ahead of us.

"I'm not really close with the people we ran into earlier," I said. "Sorry she asked you all those questions about Europe—"

"That was fine. Standard American-tourist stuff."

"After you left she wanted to talk about Gabe," I said, ripping off the Band-Aid and chucking it at the elephant in the room.

"Gabe? Did they know him?" Elizabeth asked, glancing in the direction of the entrance, as if Caroline and Tim were now of interest to her and she might have to track them down.

"No. They were fans, but they'd never met him. She was just checking in on me." I'd brought this up to segue into getting Gabe's stuff back, but it was overtaken by a real annoyance as I recalled Caroline's attempt at a pep talk outside. "She compared Gabe to her grandmother dying at ninety-seven."

Elizabeth nodded, unsurprised. "I've gotten some of that too. No, it's different," she said. She tilted her head to the side. "But a loss is a loss. My father died when I was twelve. Of cancer. And I remember that same week my best friend lost her dog. She'd had him since she was born. We were crying in bed with each other and her mother came in and was furious."

"Did she think you were in some kind of sapphic embrace?" I asked, thinking this was a story of a homophobic parent.

"No. She was embarrassed. For my friend, and herself too, I guess. That the dog was being equated to my dad."

"Did you mind?"

Elizabeth tilted her head to the side again. This seemed to be a particular tic of hers, a physical indication of weighing mental dissonance. But she didn't weigh it for long, because almost immediately she said, "No. It was nice to have someone to cry with."

A loss is a loss. Of course. Now I regretted my exchange with Caroline. Why had I not been kinder? Caroline hadn't said the exact right thing, but it wasn't easy to know the right thing to say. I'd fumbled all over my visit with Leora.

We headed upstairs to the next floor of the gallery. I passed a large photo of Frankenthaler spread out on the floor of her studio, paint, brushes, and canvas in front of her. The next painting caught my attention even before I had the chance to take in its entirety. I slowed down as if approaching a deer in the woods. The other works on display were amorphous expanses of color, whereas this piece was more symmetrical, with a curtain of blue on each side of the painting and islands of green below. In between were yellow layers, in similar but distinct hues: egg yolk, mustard, orange, canary. Shades of the sun. I stood in front of it, dumbstruck. I felt that these colors in a square on the wall knew me, almost like the painting and I had met before. *I recognize you*, my bones said to the canvas. *You too*, it said back.

By 2011, Gabe had gone from opening to headlining. There was a short profile in *Rolling Stone*, a Grammy nomination for Best Alternative Music Album (no win, drinks at The Hungry Hound the next night to celebrate with friends per Jabari's new girlfriend's insistence; I mean, she was right: an honor just to be and all that).

Gabe took to success as well as anyone can take to success. He was kind to fans, modest and genuine in interviews, and he held on to those of us who knew him in the before times. The only problem was the venues. He was playing bigger spaces—not arenas, but large concert halls—and they overwhelmed him. He wanted to play smaller spots again. Kathy and the rest of his management team would only agree to this if there was some kind of angle. That's when he started playing secret shows. Forty to fifty people, a surprise announcement, tickets went up the day of, a password needed at the door. From Gabe's point of view, it created intimacy. From Kathy's, scarcity.

At the end of the year, Gabe put out a holiday album of Christmas, Hanukkah, and generally wintry songs. He played a secret show debuting the album at a comedy club. I don't remember all of Gabe's concerts but I remember that one. I was backstage, technically "backstage" was off to the side of the stage, in the wings. It was not the best vantage point, and when I really wanted to enjoy a Separate Bedrooms concert, I'd ask Gabe for tickets, but I'd brought Casey with me, who was hoping we'd see someone famous backstage. When we arrived, he saw an actor who was on an HBO drama and headed over. I waved to Gabe, who was standing in the wings. It was winter, his skin was paler, he always joked that around this time of year he acquired a completely new ethnicity. He was wearing a dark green hoodie, a black T-shirt, bouncing with pre-show energy. I don't remember my outfit, though I know I must have been wearing Rachel Comey ankle boots. That year a lot of us were wearing Rachel Comey ankle boots. I made a few hand gestures to indicate that I was unsure if he was already in performance mode and it

would be a bad time to say hello, but he shook his head and beck-
oned me over.

He said something to me, but I couldn't hear it. Most of the noise
was coming from the other side of the curtains where the audience
was gathered. If you'd dissected it, you would have heard people
placing drink orders, greeting friends, probably some were singing
or humming Separate Bedrooms songs, taking last-minute calls, everyone already speaking in louder voices because of the setting even
though the show hadn't started. I leaned in closer to hear Gabe. "I
want to do something different for the fake encore," he repeated.

"Oh, when you're like, 'That's it, everybody, show's over!'"

"Yeah. But I go get some water and wait around as the applause
feeds my ego."

"Then when you come back out, you're finally a real boy."

Gabe's eyes sparked. "That's funny. Can I say that?"

"Sure," I said. "Then give a little wink or something," I added
sarcastically.

"Right, that will really play to the back row," he joked, shifting
perspective to an outside observer mocking the musician looking for
ways to entertain his fans. It was Gabe aware of Separate Bedrooms.
And I was doing it too. Separate Bedrooms was a minor phenome-
non, but we could usually disregard that fact, most of the time truly
forgetting about it. Except when Gabe was about to go onstage—
with a crowd of people waiting for him, the anticipation was palpable
and it shifted the energy around him. Separate Bedrooms surpassed
Gabe, ballooning out like an inflatable mattress in a small space.
Barely noticeable before, it now took over the room. Impossible to
ignore, you had to awkwardly move around it. Joking deflated it.

We didn't do this to diminish Gabe, but to shrink Separate Bedrooms so we could *see* Gabe again.

He started the show on the piano, with a song he'd written about Rudolph from the point of view of his best friend, kind of like Ben Affleck at the end of *Good Will Hunting*, but if he and Matt Damon were both reindeer. There were green and blue twinkle lights at the edge of the stage, a kind of nondenominational peace-on-earth aesthetic. By the end of the show, Gabe was wearing a Santa hat. He sat down on a stool with his guitar for the last song—the last song before the whole encore bit. Leaning forward, he said, "Don't tell my Jewish mother. It's just such a beautiful song." He strummed the first notes of "O Holy Night." The audience laughed, and Gabe chuckled. "Actually, it's one of her favorite songs too. Don't tell her I said that either." More laughter. He picked up the glass of water by his stool, took a sip, then started again, this time singing along.

From my position in the wings, I only got Gabe's back or profile, so I usually ended up watching the audience. There had been some dancing, but now with a slower song, they switched to swaying, some of those familiar with the Christmas carol singing along. A woman near the front of the stage, with a wide moon face and freckles, her long blond hair braided to the side, looked straight up at Gabe, mesmerized.

There were people like Elizabeth and Shira, who fell for Gabe after he was famous, and there were friends like me and Jabari, who had been supporting him from the beginning. But there were also people like this woman with the braid. They met Gabe in a song and fell in love with him by the end of an album. That perfect presentation of emotional range without any of the alternating joys and disappointments of time spent with another human. Watching the woman with the braid made me fully understand, on a level I hadn't before, the concept of musicians as idols.

In the final swell of the song, he sang, *"No-ELLLLL,"* hitting the last high note, his voice, in its perfect clarity, like church bells ringing. There was that classical-music-summer-camp training! And the audience loved it, already overjoyed and now recognizing the technical brilliance of what they'd just witnessed, they burst into applause. Gabe dipped his head down. "Thank you," he said. "Thank you." He hopped off the stool. "Now I have to do that thing where I pretend to leave. But I'm just waiting around, getting a drink of water and listening to your applause, letting it feed my ego until I become a real boy."

The crowd laughed. He waved to the audience as he headed backstage. They continued clapping. Once he was behind the curtain, he pointed at me and winked.

Bwahayhay.

In an area off to the side by himself, Gabe paced around, getting back in the zone, making sure he didn't—with that joke to me—slip back into his human form. One of the club's employees handed him a new glass of water. The applause grew. People stomped and howled; they cheered. The walls were coming down.

When Gabe walked back onstage, casually, as if the thought to return had just occurred to him, the crowd, which seemed to have already reached its sonic peak, hit new decibels. The blond-braid woman burst into tears. Gabe noticed her then.

"I told you I'd be back," he said. "We still got one more song. Don't worry, baby."

So corny. But it worked. I thought she was going to combust after that. I thought how funny it would be if I had her reaction when Gabe entered a room. I was a Separate Bedrooms fan, but I would never be a fan like her.

As Gabe sang his last song—the actual last song—Casey came over to me, finally taking a break from selfies with celebrities to join me in the wings. He whispered, "Is it true there's no after-party?" I shook my head. No after-party. Casey poked me. "Are you and Gabe going to get together or what?" Clearly Casey had been enthralled by Gabe's performance too. He'd joked about this before but in the way that all twentysomethings run through the list of single people they know, considering all couple permutations, like pulling dolls at random out of a large bag and smashing their faces together. Now he seemed to expect an actual answer from me. "He's cute," Casey prodded.

Gabe had grown into that kind of charming, bedroom-gaze straight man who doesn't appear to take himself seriously. People go gaga for that. I understood the appeal of his image. He was a good-looking guy, I had always known that, and the money and management had given him the best products, an excellent facialist, the right hairstylist. But that's not it, I wanted to tell his fans. That's not why you should want him. The real reason was . . . something I couldn't put my finger on. I didn't feel any particular urgency in locating this unmapped territory, more important was that I'd been there first. Smug satisfaction was my reward. So you're into Gabe? So was I. Like a decade ago. It was the equivalent of liking a band before they became cool—it was almost exactly that—and a surge in popularity curdled your interest.

I wasn't going to explain all that to Casey because it didn't feel particularly kind to talk about Gabe like he was a used CD from the Tower Records bargain bin, so instead I joked, "Wait, the indie rock star is cute? How did you find out? Who told you?"

"Okay, okay." Casey waved me off. "But—" I could see the attorney in him coming up with a rebuttal.

I countered before he could present it. "He has a girlfriend." They'd broken up for a bit, but Gabe and Shira were back together.

"He always has some girlfriend. He's a *musician*. Get in there. You could make him have after-parties at least." So there it was: I could wield my influence as a partner to benefit Casey. The man was celeb obsessed. It was always clear why *he'd* chosen a law school in LA. In the end, the only reason he hadn't gone into entertainment law was because he'd have been required to keep any gossip he acquired confidential. "C'mon," he said, slinging his arm over my shoulder and swaying us back and forth. "Don't you think we'd be good for him?"

"Too good for him," I joked.

"Fine." He exhaled. "I have to get back to work anyway."

"It's eleven P.M., Casey."

He waved his phone at me. "Yes. That is my job."

I started to make a joke about *this is why I left law school*, but he saw it coming like I'd seen his romanticizing of my friendship with Gabe, and he shook his head at me, telling me not to go there.

But I *was* glad I'd left law school. And I was glad I wasn't dating Gabe. In general, I felt happier with my life than I ever had. Earlier that year, I'd made Rose a ring for her birthday. A gold signet ring with ornate latticework at the center. A few weeks later, she told me,

"Everywhere I go, people keep asking me where I got this ring. They wanna buy it." I made more. People did buy them. As soon as I started getting orders, I knew this was what I wanted to do. Probably what I had always wanted to do, but now I had customer validation and Rose cheering me on. Rose was instrumental. She knew people, she knew actresses (she'd moved to LA to try acting), she understood social media in a way that would eventually become required for entire generations, but she got it instinctively before most of our peers. We built a My Grandmother's Collection website, started selling rings direct to consumer. Soon I was working days at the boutique and spending nights fulfilling orders. I was exhausted and *so happy*. It had been a hard year, but a good one. As the last round of applause crested, I threw my own enthusiasm into that wave of sound, experiencing a high on a different level than Gabe's, but still a high, and loudly cheered.

Gabe bowed, waved goodbye, and bounded offstage. He handed his microphone to a member of his crew. Dripping with sweat, he walked over to me and Casey and said, "Hungry Hound?"

A FEW NIGHTS LATER, GABE WAS DRIVING US HOME FROM MY FRIEND Ali's white elephant party in Culver City. A fire truck pulled in front of us. Gabe slowed down, but there was no siren and the truck's lights were off. Riding on the top was Santa Claus. We waved at the man dressed in a large red-and-white suit, with a hat identical to what Gabe had recently worn onstage. The Santa waved with both arms and threw his head back in a jolly *ho ho ho*. Clearly some holiday event had required a fireman to dress up and now this relaxed, off-duty Saint Nick was enjoying the view from his perch. The truck made a wide turn onto the next street. We were supposed to continue straight, but I said, "We should follow him."

Gabe grinned and took the turn, right before the light changed. We tailed the truck, waiting to see where it would end up, but it kept going, straight down Pico Boulevard. Other drivers took notice, a few honked. Santa waved to all of them. Gabe and I settled into this turn in the night's events, a Mariah Carey Christmas playlist on as we drove.

I asked him how things were going with Shira. They'd been on, then off, then on again. Gabe said he'd invited her to the concert to try to repair things, but now they were once again off again.

"Shira and I . . . our relationship is like a video game I keep thinking we can beat, but we can never get past this one level."

"You should use that in a song." (He did.)

He said, "But I think this time, it's really over."

I could tell it was. There was a finality in his voice. The same one I'd had when Brandon and I threw in the towel the year before. We'd been talking about moving in with each other, but when we finally went to look for apartments, it felt like he wasn't into it. He said it was because I had such high standards for the place I wanted to live (I wanted some outdoor space and a view, the apartment Casey and I had shared faced a concrete wall). I said I'd go with the next place we saw as long as it had Wi-Fi and a working bathroom. I filled out my half of the rental application, it took him a week to complete his. He's never going to tell me, I thought. So I had to ask if he still wanted to be together. Basically I broke up with myself. We were both pretty bitter by the end, no way that *we* would remain friends. But we had been in love. For a year, maybe a year and a half—that half is questionable, I can't pinpoint for sure when things unraveled. It was the kind of relationship where in the aftermath you don't even consider yourself single, you're just *recovering*. I didn't want to be with anyone. Not like that. I had work and I had my friends. That's all I wanted.

The fire truck turned down a residential street. A festive block. The houses were lit up in full Christmas regalia, the manger and wise men, snowmen, reindeer, rainbow lights, crystal icicle lights, bright plastic snowflakes. Despite all the visual pageantry, the street was quiet. It was only us and the truck. Red lights flickered on the concrete.

I said, "It's not going to, but it would be so perfect if it—"

"Snowed right now?"

"Exactly."

When the truck slowed down, Gabe pulled over to the side of the road. "Makes sense," I said.

"Yeah," Gabe said. "Not sure where else this would end."

We watched as the fire truck pulled into a firehouse.

I wish that night had come before Gabe's concert when Casey asked if the two of us might get together, I would have known exactly what to say. The scene was set for romance: the long drive, Los Angeles quiet, the unique, shared experience. We were both single. Why had it never turned into something more, one might ask.

But that night *was* more. Much more than when we were two kids fumbling around for a summer. The more was the friendship. The more was knowing we would have each other even as the people we dated passed through our lives. We were lucky the way we were.

In other words, it would have been perfect if it snowed that night. But it didn't and it was perfect anyway.

STANDING IN FRONT OF THE FRANKENTHALER PAINTING, I WAS reminded of the stage festooned with blue and green twinkle lights, the fire truck pulling into the firehouse, the spotlight on Gabe, of that week in December, and wondered: What if he returned now? What if he walked right into this room? What if it had all been a brief disappearance into the wings, Gabe hidden backstage, a show trick?

Come back, come back. It can't be over.

Because—and I know it sounds strange—I felt his presence in that painting. It was almost like he was back and I knew that if he had walked up to me at that moment, I would have been exactly like a fan in the crowd, cheering and stamping my feet in relief. I thought about that blond woman with the braid and wondered where she had been when she found out Gabe died and what she had done when he didn't return this time.

EIGHT

I stood crying in front of the painting, aware of Elizabeth watching me.

"Are you all right?" she asked.

"Totally," I said, wiping my cheek with the back of my hand. "Absolutely." I snorted back a sniffle.

Elizabeth watched me. I waited for her to say it comes in waves or something like that, but she didn't. She said, "There's something in this Didion book about crying."

"Oh right, I remember. Someone tells her it helps to put your head in a paper bag. I love that essay."

"Me too."

Didion. Frankenthaler. Gabe.

I remembered what Casey had said about Gabe having a type. Maybe we'd ended up at the gallery *because* we'd both dated Gabe. Maybe we were both the type of woman who would take herself to an art gallery in the middle of the day. A woman with a flexible creative career? A city-dwelling woman who had read Joan Didion, sought out female painters, and found herself attracted to a charming musician? But that described a lot of people. What would I find out next? That Elizabeth was absolutely obsessed with Beyoncé? Did she also have a pair of Rachel Comey boots? Forget about being Gabe's type. We were just a type.

We moved on to the next piece, an intense saturation of red, maroon, and pink. Elizabeth tilted her head, whispering to me, "There's something a bit menstrual about this, isn't there?"

I smirked, a half smile. "Something tells me she would not have liked that interpretation. It's like Georgia O'Keeffe." Elizabeth didn't follow, her eyes requested an explanation. "The whole reading-female-anatomy-imagery into the work," I said. "O'Keeffe flowers. With all these people saying they were vaginas. She said they saw what they wanted to see."

As we walked away from the painting, Elizabeth said, "You know, I can't even picture Georgia O'Keeffe's work. I know she's unbelievably famous."

"Yeah, her *Jimson Weed* was the highest price ever paid for a female artist's work."

"*Jimson Weed* . . ." Elizabeth took out her phone, tapped a few times, then turned the screen so I could see. She zoomed in on the painting of a large white flower, and we leaned our heads in closer to inspect it. She laughed. "That's a vulva, Georgia."

There was something about her that irritated me in that moment. That she didn't agree, maybe? Or, once again, that she was so sure of herself? We continued through the exhibit, drifting apart at times as we each went at our own pace, but always within earshot. I stopped in front of a photograph of Helen Frankenthaler in her studio, a long roll of canvas stretched out on the floor. Her hand held a paintbrush that touched a black line drawn from the top of a painting to the bottom. "I wonder if this piece is here," I said to Elizabeth. "What do you think of it?"

I turned around. Elizabeth was gone. The presence I'd felt next to me was a short white woman in her sixties wearing a tan windbreaker.

"It's all right," she said. "She didn't invent this style of painting. It's not true, you know."

"Really?" I expected her to say another abstract expressionist or someone from the Color Field movement, one of Helen's male peers who'd been given more respect.

"My friend did," she said.

"Who's your friend?"

"Irving."

I had not heard of Irving.

"Irving was doing the exact same thing at the same time in the eighties." She folded her arms across her chest and gave me a defiant look, daring me to contradict her.

Helen Frankenthaler had painted her first soak-stain work, *Mountains and Sea*, in the fifties, maybe the sixties, I wasn't sure. Definitely not the eighties.

"The exact same thing," she said again. I could sense delusion and urgency. Never a safe combination.

"Excuse me," I said. "I have to catch up to my friend."

I hurried past two smaller paintings until I was next to Elizabeth again. She peered around the corner. "No, that's the fire exit. Think we're at the end." She was right. We were at the end. I hadn't asked about Gabe's bracelet, or the guitar or sheet music or Mets cap. I'd started crying and then been distracted by a strange woman.

Once we were back on the sidewalk in front of the gallery, I said, "It was good seeing you." I hoped it sounded sincere.

"You too," she said.

I pointed at the red leaves climbing along the building. "Do you know what this is called?"

"Virginia creeper."

"Sounds like how a tabloid newspaper would describe some philandering senator."

She smiled. I nodded. This was the moment for one of us to say goodbye but neither of us did. I knew why I was delaying my departure. Why was Elizabeth?

She blurted out, "I have to apologize."

"For what?" I asked. I was so focused on my mission that I sincerely couldn't imagine why she would need to apologize.

"At the funeral. In California? I . . ." She searched for a word. "I probably came off a tad rude. It wasn't—it was weird, I'm sorry."

"Oh my God," I said. "You're fine, I didn't even notice."

"Really?" She doubted me. Fair, considering I was lying.

"I mean, there was a lot going on. There's no need to apologize." It felt true. In offering her apology, she now seemed to be a better person than I'd thought, which made her apology unnecessary.

"Thank you, that's really lovely of you," she said. "I didn't even have a call earlier! I was waiting for you in the entrance so I could say sorry for the last time you'd seen me. The whole time we were in there, I kept thinking, Say it, Elizabeth! I should have said it as soon as we ran into each other."

"It's fine," I assured her.

"Okay, good then." She tucked a strand of hair behind her ear. "Would you like to have dinner with me tonight? At my restaurant. It's pretty good. I'm not biased, people do like it."

"Tonight?"

"Yes. If you've nothing else on." She paused. "I've always wanted to get to know you. Gabe spoke so highly of you. I figured you and I would meet eventually."

I recalled my first impression of her. I'd liked her. Now that she had apologized, maybe I was free to like her again. Assuming she'd give Gabe's things back. "I have something I've been meaning to say too," I said.

"Yes?"

I hesitated. I might be warming up to her, but this wasn't about me. I'd made a promise to Leora. I had two options: I could take a chance by forcing the matter now, or I could play it cool and accept Elizabeth's offer.

I said, "I need to know where you got your ring! I love it."

"Oh, this!" she exclaimed, waving the hand with the garnet cocktail ring. "I've been wearing it a lot lately. It's from this vintage shop—"

"I *love* a good vintage find."

"Really? Right, then, I know a store you'd love, it's some vintage, some new stuff, but all that vibe—it's near a bakery Gabe loved— over in Hackney. Where are you staying?"

"Hotel J? Shoreditch?" I said in the tentative tone of a visitor who doesn't know the physical context or significance of the locations around her.

"That's right by my restaurant!"

"Oh, wow!"

"I mean, then, would you like to stop by? Tonight?"

I pretended to consider it, as if I had other plans. After a respectable beat I said, "Sure, why not? Sounds great."

"Fabulous. I'll see you tonight? Eight?"

"Totally. See you!" I headed off, but turned around when I heard her voice calling me back.

"But you don't know where to meet me!"

For a second I thought she knew. Not that I was in London because of her, not all of that, but that I already knew about her restaurant because I'd tried to learn as much as possible about her. "Oh right!" I did my best to play it off as a ditzy, absent-minded moment. "What's the restaurant called again?"

She gave me the address, plus the name of the vintage shop in Hackney and Gabe's favorite London bakery, then headed down the street. I needed to go that way too but instead I turned around and walked in the other direction. Something had happened to me—or almost happened to me—in front of that painting, and I needed to shake it off.

I walked through Piccadilly Circus, allowing myself to be swallowed by the mass of tourists and commuters. Above me loomed scrolling neon advertisements alternating between encouraging and scolding messages. I walked across a bridge, then walked back toward the gallery on a different bridge. I walked until the buildings felt like they were getting too close and I needed to shake them off too.

IN MY HOTEL ROOM, I CALLED MY PARENTS. THEY KNEW GABE, they'd met him once in LA and immediately liked him. He and my dad had talked about jazz and the Mets. My mom thought he had good manners.

"Did you know anyone who died when you were young?" I asked them.

"I can't think of anyone I was particularly close to," my dad said.

My parents are both bank managers. They met at a barbecue, where they discovered they managed two separate branches of the same credit union. "And can you believe we never ran into each other?" I would mouth along with them as they told this story again and again for my entire life. It was a crowd-pleaser. Everyone thought it was so romantic—except for my mom's first husband, Arthur. Over the years, the more I heard the story, and the more I dated, the more Arthur was the person I related to. Two roads diverged in the wood. One was this true love like my parents'; the other was my path, the lonely path, the path of Arthur.

"Wait," Dad said. "I had a cousin who died of cancer."

"That sounds pretty close, Dad. It was your cousin."

"Yes . . . it was." He searched for something. "It was much harder on my older sister and mother than me."

"Right," I said.

"I knew someone!" Mom piped up as if she'd discovered the correct answer to a trivia game.

"Who?" I asked.

117

"A boy in my school. I remember because they changed the rule with the buses after that."

"What rule?"

"Well, there was this boy. Larry Field. He was headed home on the bus when he saw his girlfriend Shelley walking home. And I guess she was supposed to be on the bus too? Or maybe they were going to walk together? Whatever it was, they were meant to be in the same place, but they had missed each other. This was before cell phones."

"Right."

"And he leaned out the window to wave Shelley down and didn't even see the pole coming. It knocked his head completely off."

"What?" I screamed.

"Diane," Dad muttered.

"Well, the force of hitting the pole decapitated him."

"Diane!" Dad said again.

"And he died."

I snorted. "Yeah, Mom, I guessed that. What, did you think I was on the edge of my seat about whether this decapitated boy is still alive? Like it was an Ichabod Crane situation?"

My parents crowed in unison. Their laughter was comforting. My first, and easiest, audience; a huge reaction was typical from them, but it still always felt good to receive it.

"You asked if I knew anyone who died!" Mom protested, but I could tell she was now amused by her own ridiculousness.

"Right, this is on me," I said. "Wait, so what was the new bus rule?"

"The windows could only be lowered an inch, so you couldn't fit any body part through it."

"Oh," I said.

"Because of the decapitation."

"Diane, stop saying decapitation."

"That's the correct term, Donald. And they didn't want any other children losing parts of their bodies."

"That's awful," I said.

"I know," Mom said. "It could always be worse."

Yes, it could always be worse. That should have been on my mom's personal crest. Nothing was a problem because potentially anything could become a problem, so it was best to move on, saving your energy for when the truly big catastrophe hit. Dwelling was frowned upon. They asked how I was doing and I assured them I was fine. "I'm staying busy." This was what they needed to hear from me. I'm sure I needed to hear something from them too, but I wasn't sure what that was.

I went back out. I browsed the store Elizabeth recommended, I walked to the bakery she said was Gabe's favorite. I liked learning a new tidbit about him. It was never-before-seen footage that kept the movie of his life rolling.

I returned to the hotel to change before dinner. I stared at the shower, unable to step in. No. Absolutely not, my body said. Sink bath again. My third one of the trip. After, I put on the stiff, minimalist hotel robe and lay on the bed with my phone, scrolling. I looked up Helen Frankenthaler, gathering details to fill in her biography. I didn't know she was friends with the poet Frank O'Hara. He died in an accident on Fire Island. (Were these accidental deaths just part of life, happening all the time, and I'd never noticed them?) I read a few Frank O'Hara poems, which made me think about the poet in my life.

I texted Leora. *Will have everything to you soon. No worries! X*

I scrolled up in our conversation. Mostly texts about recent books we'd read. Gabe used to joke that Leora and I had our own little book club and had both read more in a month than he had in five years. There was one photo I'd sent. Gabe on the night of my studio opening the year before. He'd flown in for the occasion, as had Rose and Nneka. For once, all my favorites together. Gabe brought cake and champagne and a vintage Halston beaded-sequin-and-silk jacket, explaining, "Leora doesn't have a daughter and despite my suggestion that I find a way to make it work onstage—"

"You could definitely make this work."

"I *know*. But she wanted you to have it."

As I finished scrolling through our conversation history, Leora texted back. *Thank you dear.*

I had stopped trying to imagine how Leora felt. But now something passed through me. An immense visceral pain, an unsustainable longing. This was the limit of my empathic reach; it had not been enough, but it had also been too much.

By a quarter to eight, I was bleary-eyed but ready to head out.

I was a bit nervous, thinking about how to get back what Leora needed, wondering if Elizabeth knew anything about Gabe's missing bracelet, but even with all that, to my surprise, I wasn't dreading dinner. Since I'd heard about Gabe, I'd been dealing with a paradox. I didn't want to be alone. I didn't want to be around other people. There was some kind of impossible divide between me and the world. Not only clueless people like Caroline and Tim, but friends like Casey and Will. My parents. I couldn't bring myself to call Rose and Nneka because I feared it would be exactly the same with them, and then I would feel truly alone. For some reason, it was different with Elizabeth.

And it had been nice to see the bakery where Gabe went. Maybe she knew more little things like this about his time in London. I'd return to California with his belongings *and* a few stories. So I found myself looking forward to dinner with her, this woman who was basically a stranger, if not, as Tim had suggested, a rival.

I completely forgot that she'd asked *me* to dinner, that this was something she wanted. When I tell this part of the story now, I'd like to think I offered some resistance to walking onto Elizabeth's turf. But no, I jumped right in.

NINE

I was back in line at Fleur Bleue but this time I knew I'd get in. It was later than when I'd arrived the day before, with a slightly different crowd; no after-work rush, past the point of drinks with acquaintances and I'll-give-it-an-hour first dates, it was now into the part of the evening when people are invested in making a night of it together. Ahead of me were two women around my age.

"I found something to replace smoking," one of them said. Both were wearing scarves piled high under their chins and large gold hoop earrings.

Tuning out the rest of the line, I tethered my ear to their conversation. "Breathwork," she confessed with pride. "I do breathwork now. It's the same thing! Inhale, exhale. That's why so many people are addicted to cigarettes." She twirled her hand, lassoing the air to indicate the many addicts among us. "A smoke break is the only time in the day we have to take a breath!" Her friend laughed. "Fill your lungs with toxins if you want, or you can fill them with, I don't know, the air? From Earth?"

Had anyone ever felt as passionately about anything as this woman felt about breathwork? Saints and poets were amateurs compared to wellness converts.

"Start from here. Like this," she said. "Expand as you breathe in."

Quietly, so they wouldn't notice me, I attempted the long inhale and slow exhale they were practicing.

"I feel it!" the woman's friend said, and the woman clapped her hands. "See? Didn't I tell you?" Meanwhile my breath was trapped higher up, near my clavicle. I wanted to release it, but I couldn't. When I tried, I thought of a mouth gulping in water, a goldfish out of a bowl, a man on a shower floor.

"Julia!"

Flowers were calling my name. "Julia!" A large bouquet of roses approached. "Sorry!" I heard them say. The flowers marched closer, then veered downward, revealing my dinner companion. Bright red lipstick and sparkling gold boots. A trench coat, open, showcasing a pink ruffled blouse and trousers made of some fabric that made them shine, so instead of light brown, I thought of a caramel in wrinkly cellophane. She was a shimmering modern Dalloway. My stomach dropped. Elizabeth looked beautiful, and while it's not like I felt envy exactly, or unsure of myself, what I craved was indifference, and it made me sad that I couldn't find it.

"Sorry I'm late." She laughed. "What are you doing? Why are you in the queue?"

"There's a line," I said as she linked her arm under mine and pulled me forward. I noticed the women ahead of me staring.

"I love your boots," the breathwork devotee called out to Elizabeth.

Elizabeth paused at the door. "Oh, thank you."

"And I *love* the restaurant. I love what you've done with the space," she continued. Other people in line bobbed their heads in silent adoration. Of course. They'd looked up the restaurant and read the same articles I had, and now here was the lovely florist turned restaurateur in the flesh. Celebrity was relative, it wasn't always the totality of the sun; it could be local and concentrated, a single ray shining through a keyhole.

Inside Fleur Bleue smelled like rose, honey, and some grounding scent I couldn't quite make out. Something like cardamom but earthier. White-and-amber tile on the floor. Three walls were plaster, that kind of natural limestone texture. Across from the tables was a bar with rows of glasses hung from above, wine and spirits behind two bartenders wearing black shirts and jeans.

"Give me one moment," Elizabeth said. She rushed ahead. Her coat billowed out behind her as she let it slip off, catching it midair. She tapped each spot on the bar, dropping her index finger next to small jars containing yellow flowers, as if checking their placement off a list. She went behind the bar, opened her bouquet, and began cutting the stems off the roses. They were a variety of soft, delicious colors: white chocolate, strawberry ice cream, crème brûlée. Elizabeth replaced each jar's yellow flower with a rose.

"Floral emergency?" I joked when she returned to my side.

"Someone posted a photo, I saw it on my way here, it wasn't— chrysanthemums weren't right." She adjusted her irritation, adding, "It's no one's fault."

"If it's not right, it's not right," I agreed.

She looked thankful that I got it. She led us to a table for two near the window, a tea light at its center. "This isn't the best table," Elizabeth said, subtly leaning her head to indicate that the best one was next to us, right in front of the window, where two men were sitting. Her hand rested on the top of my chair. Her fingernails were painted bright red, matching her lipstick, complementing the garnet ring she was once again wearing. "I have to give that to paying customers. But from here, you can see the whole restaurant and the bar. Is it all right?"

"Elizabeth!" Before I could answer, someone called her and she headed off again. A man stood up from one of the tables, they hugged, then she stopped at each of the other tables, greeting the guests. "No, don't get up!" she said to an older woman who was dining with a teenage girl. "You can get up!" Elizabeth pointed at the teenager and they all laughed. There were three tables pushed together to form a six-top. The women seated there were all already very drunk, thrilled to be with each other. When Elizabeth passed them, she made some joke I couldn't hear. Something about hens. It pushed them all into immediate hysterics. Fleur Bleue was a joyful place and Elizabeth was at its center, some combination of maestro and show model.

When she returned to our table, she remained standing and asked, "Is wine all right? Or do you want beer? I know it's having a moment."

Beer was having a moment. London was having a moment. Fleur Bleue was definitely having a moment. I felt like I should excuse myself as the only one not having a moment.

"Wine works for me," I said.

A waiter appeared next to us. When he said hello, I could tell he was French. And from his skin and features I could tell he was African. If Nneka were there she would have been able to tell which part of Africa, confirming or ruling out Nigeria immediately and then speeding through the rest of the continent until she landed on the correct answer. His hair was buzzed short. He wore a cartilage piercing and two studs in one ear, a lone stud in the other.

"Louis, this is Julia Hendricks"—she pronounced his name *Lou-EE*—"my very special guest for the evening. She's a beautiful American jewelry designer, so I put her right by the window so everyone passing by can admire her sparkle." Louis nodded as if this description fit me perfectly.

Elizabeth clapped her hands. "Okay, so we'll start with the pétnat and then the red we're always—yes, you know the one!" She spoke more to Louis than to me. "And the bread with absolutely everything. Oh!" Elizabeth turned to me. "You like oysters?"

I said, "When they're salty."

Elizabeth and Louis burst into laughter. Louis explained, "We have French oysters." Seeing that this explanation meant nothing to me, he kindly continued the lesson. "French oysters are known for being especially salty."

"Okay, perfect!" I said. We smiled at each other.

When he walked away, as Elizabeth took her seat, she said, "He was flirting with you."

I said, "I think that's his job. To be nice."

"No, it isn't, I hired him. Here the waiters do not have to be nice to the customers, the customers have to respect the waiters."

She placed her napkin on her lap. "Okay, I'm here now," she apologized. "You look lovely."

I'd worn a navy off-the-shoulder bodysuit with high-rise jeans and backless loafers. I'd seen, on my first night, that Fleur Bleue was a bit of a scene. I wanted to fit in, without giving away that I was anticipating a scene.

"Thank you," I said, forgetting to compliment her in return. Though with all the praise she'd received as we entered, she had to be at capacity.

Our table jostled. I looked down, Elizabeth's foot was tapping against it. There was a bit of her calf visible between the gold boot and her pant leg, pale skin with a few stray brown hairs. The boots were made of a papery material. They seemed out of place. Not in relation to the outfit, that was working fine, but they seemed out of place on *her*. At the funeral, Elizabeth had been in the black wrap dress. Then at the gallery, basic staples. I thought I'd pegged her style—classic, no frills—but the gold boots were bold, they didn't fit my idea of her. Meanwhile with her Hackney shop recommendation, Elizabeth had figured me out. I'd loved everything there.

I scrambled to adjust my mental image of her to include not just the boots but tonight's performance so far, the flurry of energy, her genuine warmth with others, but there wasn't enough information to bring the complete picture into focus.

Louis passed our table, wordlessly dropping off our wineglasses in a fluid motion as if they were flower petals, not stemware.

"A toast," Elizabeth said.

"To what?"

"To your Helen Frankenthaler pilgrimage. And that I got to be a part of it."

I held up my glass before I understood what she was talking

about, forgetting my own lie. "Yes! Definitely worth the trip." Our glasses pecked, we pulled them apart. I drank from my glass, Elizabeth set hers down without taking a sip.

"I'm sober," she explained. Right: Gabe had said something about this. Long before they met, there was drinking, drugs, all in excess. No one had ever been hurt, but she'd reached some personal rock bottom and decided to get clean. "But I love to toast," she said. "You can have mine. Or I'll give it to Paula." She angled her head in the direction of the blond hostess. "So?" she asked, pointing to my glass, clearly expecting a rave. "What do you think?"

"Really good," I said. I tried to think of wine words I knew. "Very full. But not quite full."

"It's this amazing cuvée. We only have a few bottles left after this summer." She spoke quickly, she was still tapping the leg of the table. Was she nervous? She noticed me notice. "Sorry. I'm jiggling it, aren't I?" She pulled her legs back. The table steadied.

I pointed to the roses she'd set up along the bar. "They're so beautiful."

An original take on roses. I was nervous too.

"See the copper ones?" She pointed. "It's called Julia's Rose. Thought it would be fitting."

"Thank you," I said. "You didn't have to go to the trouble." She waved her hand to indicate it hadn't been any.

We smiled at each other, the same tepid smiles. They slipped off our faces as we reached the same conclusion. We'd exhausted all possible small talk before we'd even begun eating.

To break the silence, I said, "I've always thought if I had a restaurant, I would call it Lady of Shallots."

"What?"

"Like 'The Lady of Shalott'? The poem?"

Louis set down a small platter with a round loaf of bread, accompanied by pickled vegetables and olives, with labneh and other spreads. He handed Elizabeth a bowl of honey with an adorable tiny spoon in the center. "Thank you," Elizabeth said. She tore the bread in half, then began shredding the rest. She handed me a piece. I dipped it in the labneh, then honey, which was sprinkled with some combination of seasoning that added heat. I wanted to lick it straight from the bowl.

Elizabeth observed my delight. *"Right?"*

"How involved are you in the menu?" I asked. "Are you ever in the kitchen?"

"Oh no!" She laughed. "We started the restaurant together, but Emmanuel is the head chef. I work with the farms and gardens, help plan menus, provide the changes in ambience for each season. I'm often front of house, but sometimes I'm here eating." She leaned forward, conspiratorially, lowering her voice. "And people like seeing me dine here, it's become part of the mise-en-scène. I think every restaurateur should do it. Makes us feel like a family." She sat back in her chair. "I have my signature dishes, but anything I've created Emmanuel can make better than me at this point."

"Don't let her fool you. Her cacio e pepe is a marvel." A middle-aged man in a chambray chef jacket and black pants approached our table.

Elizabeth chuckled. "Speaking of! Julia, this is my partner, Emmanuel. Our head chef. I wanted to make sure he had a chance to meet you." Emmanuel had a chiseled tan face and thick wavy black hair that curled over his brow. He shook my hand, gripping it strongly. Elizabeth seemed to be pulling out all the stops—the wine, the roses, the compliments and personal introductions from handsome men she worked with—literally wining and dining me. Was it only hospitality? (It was her restaurant, of course she wanted to be a good hostess.) Or did she feel so guilty for her behavior at the funeral that she was desperately trying to prove to me she was a nice person?

"How did you two meet?" I asked. I was making conversation. I knew the answer from digging through her life online, they'd met working a wedding. But she surprised me when she said, "His brother is a friend of mine. We were both donating our services to his wedding."

"Was it a donation? It felt like a demand." Emmanuel laughed.

"They got married so quickly, it was more like an emergency."

This was different from the official origin story, that two professionals joined forces, this version was scrappier, more DIY.

"How are you?" Emmanuel asked Elizabeth, squeezing her shoulder.

"All right," she said in a quiet voice. She patted his arm as if he needed the comfort even though he'd asked her. He said it was a pleasure meeting me and returned to the kitchen. The hostess, Paula, passed him on his way. I turned away, nervous she might recognize me.

"Do you like living in LA?" Elizabeth asked. Her accent made it sound like *El-AYY*, like the *A* was a hot-air balloon drifting up into the sky.

"I do," I said.

"And you moved there to start your business?" Elizabeth asked.

"No, I went to law school first."

"Right, yes," she said. "But then you dropped out."

We were both silent as we considered the reason she knew that. The person we had yet to mention entered the room.

"And your studio's there?"

"Yes. The idea is to open a storefront next." Though some days that seemed farther down the line than others.

"I'm sure you'll have a store. Your designs are fascinating. There's something timeless about them, like something you would see in a vintage shop. Like that piece, with all the stones."

"The Party Ring." It was an intricate ring stretching across three knuckles, like a twisted Slinky sprinkled with gemstones, a confetti burst over barbed wire.

"How'd you come up with that?" Elizabeth asked.

I explained that I'd bought some multicolored Christmas lights for my place one year. After the holiday, I kept them plugged in but would place them in a heap on the floor or on a table. Like a light sculpture. "One day I thought, I'd like to *wear* that. And the structural design, I was inspired by a Ruth Asawa piece. So I kind of put the two together. Thus the Party Ring was born."

"And there's a wait list. Is that by design or . . . ?"

"No, it's real. Only because I have to be careful about the provenance of the stones. The original ring was custom for an actress based on pieces she already had. When other people wanted their own, it became a madhouse."

We talked about our jobs for a bit, sharing similar thoughts about turning a hobby into a career, the stress of running a business. "I had help," she admitted. "Financially. I should say that. Because I know so many people who come from money and they never mention the help they get and it always annoys me. Not that I come from it. But my stepfather does and he wanted to help, so we agreed he'd put in ten thousand pounds."

I knew what she meant and I appreciated it. Most people would have acted as if it were all grit, omitting the financial assistance. My parents hadn't put money into my line, but—having decided business owner was even better than lawyer, my dad truly thrilled I'd found a way to monetize art—they'd helped pay off my law school debt. I shared this with Elizabeth. She nodded as she chomped on a carrot.

We were moving beyond being a "type" and into having real things in common, out of awkward discomfort into somewhat enjoying each other's company. Still, it was slow going and I didn't have months to deepen a bond. I had one dinner, and after traveling all this way, I had to get it right. In a bid for connection, I declared, as if I were coming up with it on the spot, "You know what would be cool? If, next time you're in America, we did like a collaboration. At my studio. Maybe a class. Flowers and jewels."

"Maybe," Elizabeth responded in the same tone you use when someone asks if you want to meet up after work, but you've already committed to a plate of nachos and bingeing a television series. "I have something similar to that. Where I teach a bouquet-making workshop. I have one tomorrow." She took out her phone and handed it to me. "I can add you to the list. You're welcome to come."

"Sure," I said. I typed in my email address. Watching her teach a bouquet workshop would be a great way to get to know each other. But I couldn't let this wait until tomorrow.

Louis appeared again, this time with a large steaming-hot bowl and two plates. Another waiter followed with more dishes. Elizabeth listed the items as they set everything down. "Kale and white beans, smoked cod and cauliflower, bagna cauda tonnarelli, and of course our trademark medley of microgreens and edible flowers."

When he left our table, Elizabeth asked, "Are you seeing anyone? Last I heard, there was some guy, Jarret, was it?"

"We broke up."

"I'm sorry." She gave me a deep, understanding nod as if she'd always known this was exactly where Jarret and I would end up. She must have realized how this looked because she added, "It seemed like that's where it was going. Unless he broke up with you? But I thought it was the other way around because when you called Gabe you sounded like you'd had it."

I tried to think of which call she could be talking about. I'd talked to Gabe, and all my friends, about this particular subject a lot, in the last days of dating Jarret. It was that time in a relationship when you can tell something isn't working. You're reviewing every possibility for why it isn't, except the obvious: the two of you aren't a good match.

Had Elizabeth been with Gabe when I was on the phone with him? I remembered telling Gabe, "I thought that he was sensitive, but he just loves complaining."

"Yeah, I'm kind of having the same thing with Elizabeth," Gabe had said. "I thought she was perceptive. But she's kind of judgmental. Sometimes I think she's a fundamentally cold person."

She definitely hadn't been present for that part of the conversation.

I said to Elizabeth now, "It just didn't work out."

I mean, when did it ever?

In 2014, off the success of helping me launch my line, Rose returned to New York, where she'd grown up, to build her own branding company. The year before, Gabe had sold his house, and he was in LA less and less. It was only me and Casey left and then he met Will and they moved in together. I was single for most of my midtwenties (I hadn't had a serious boyfriend since Brandon), but being on my own only felt intolerable after my friends became unavailable.

I was twenty-eight when I met Kyle, at one of Casey's work parties. He was also an attorney. He was white with light brown hair. He had a big head, a solid, square jaw, and dimples when he smiled. Casey said everyone was always asking Kyle if he was an actor; his theory was this was *why* Kyle worked in LA. For the ego boost of this mistaken identity.

He was a bad boyfriend. Not a criminal one, just simply bad.

An example: Before a work party at the house of one of his co-workers, he stopped me at the end of the driveway, hiding us behind a large family-size SUV. Kyle was thirty-six, older than anyone I'd dated, but he also *looked* like a man in a way that none of my other boyfriends had. He had a straightforward professional haircut and a skincare regimen that left his face supple and gleaming.

"Oh, I meant to tell you," he said. "You don't need to be funny tonight."

"What do you mean?" I asked. "Are they more buttoned-up or something?"

Kyle lifted his foot to the SUV's bumper, looking down with

concern at his leather loafers. He used his elbow to buff out a scratch. "Not at all. Joe loves doing impressions. I'm saying *you* don't have to be funny. You're pretty. You're a jewelry designer. You're with me. No one's expecting you to carry the conversation."

As if a sense of humor was an unnecessary accessory that could be jettisoned. The Coco Chanel theory of personality: before leaving the house, remove your most brazen quality.

Kyle whispered as if he were giving me some much-needed advice, like there was food stuck between my teeth or toilet paper on my shoe, "It throws off the rhythm of the night. You can just sit quietly."

I said, "I'll sit quietly in the car. Right now."

I was only with him for four months but even that seems too long. And why *was* I even with him?

Well, ever since My Grandmother's Collection had taken off, men looked at me differently. Jeanette, Casey's sister, who was always ready with some cringey men-are-from-Mars, women-are-from-Venus line, had warned me this would happen if I went from boutique girl to company founder. But Kyle was older and a partner at a firm. He owned his own home. Unfortunately, in looking for a man who wasn't intimidated by me, I'd overshot the mark and found someone completely comfortable belittling me.

After Kyle, I went on a series of bad dates, each with its own dead end and weak excuses; guys broke promises I didn't even ask them to make.

Several months into this, I accomplished a rite of passage for a young person living in Los Angeles: I dated an actor. Not one you would know. Not yet anyway. His name was Tomo, and his day job was waiting tables at a fancy pizza spot on Abbot Kinney. That's where we met.

Tomo was Japanese, from Hawaii, and he surfed; he would talk about "the waves" as if they were a close family member. Every time we went to a movie, as soon as the lights dimmed, he'd reach for my hand and hold it until the movie ended. When he went down on me, I held the back of his head and felt the gritty granules of sand behind his ears. We held hands at the movies and we had sex and we went to the beach. Basically every physical moment together was lovely. But when we talked—mostly he listened to me talk. He didn't have much to say. That's not a knock against actors, or surfers, or even Tomo. We just weren't a match that way. When I ended it, in typical Tomo fashion, it was the chillest breakup I'd ever had. I said, "The drive to Santa Monica is really far for me." He said, "Have you tried getting off at the 10 before La Brea and then back on at the next exit?" I said I had. He said, "Oh, then yeah, I get it." We had sex one last time, went to a coffee shop by the beach where he talked about the waves, then parted ways. That was it. I never saw or spoke to him again.

But he set a new bar.

He was a cool, kind guy. Which made me think there had to be another cool, kind guy out there.

Who could hold a conversation.

That's when I thought of Gabe.

Honestly, I don't know if it was a thought born from desire or desperation. I went out with Gabe when I was so young, I'd always assumed that my dating experience would continue in an upward arc of one glorious love affair after the next, like a rocket into space, instead of a turbulent commercial-airline descent with a few good snacks and one okay in-flight movie on the way down. And you know what they say. It is a truth universally acknowledged that a heterosexual woman entering her thirties coming off two disappointing relationships and a series of casual flings will eventually consider every man she knows as a potential long-term partner.

Luckily there were still other options. There was no reason to start with Gabe, to go that far back in my history, when there were men I'd met through work, brothers of friends, people I saw every now and then at parties. Plenty of fish. Then I met Jarret. And then I broke up with Jarret.

Yes, Gabe again crossed my mind, but by that point, I hadn't seen him for months.

Besides, he was living in London. With some woman.

ELIZABETH STUCK HER FORK IN HER FLOWER SALAD. "AND AFTER Jarret? Any rebounds?" I shook my head. We were getting a little too close in my sex and dating timeline to the recent events.

"I love your nails," I said, hoping for a lighter topic.

"Jungle red." She held them closer to the tea light so I could see.

I rubbed the sides of my arms as I leaned in.

"Are you cold? The aircon is up too high in here, isn't it? Or are you one of those skinny girls who's always cold? I had a friend in school who used to—whenever she was trying to lose weight—say out loud how cold she was. She called it getting into a thin state of mind, as if she could manifest the pounds away."

One of those skinny girls. There was an edge to her voice. Something was slipping. If pressed, I'd have to say: it took effort for Elizabeth to be nice to me. Which was fine. After tonight, as long as I got what I needed, I'd leave her alone; she wouldn't have to pretend to like me or be a decent host or whatever it was she was doing. But first we needed a reset. I excused myself and headed to the restroom.

On my way out of the bathroom, the wall to the left was in my eyeline. The restaurant was ahead of me; the kitchen on my right. When I'd walked into the bathroom, I'd looked toward the kitchen, waving to Emmanuel as I passed. Now I looked at the wall. It was wallpapered, a pattern of interlinked sapphire and sky-blue hexagons, almost entirely covered by photos in gold frames, record album covers, and original art. Amid all this ephemera, hung on a peg by its strap, was a guitar.

It looked like any guitar. Tuning pegs, fretboard, the part that looked like a teardrop or speech bubble, depending on your point of view. I lifted the brown leather strap, running my hand down until I hit two small grooves, the letters *L. W.* stamped on it. I leaned in closer, the scent of the leather and maple pulling me in. I knew them well, but the rest was missing. The rest was hemp leaves, crisp pear, campfire, and marshmallow. Applause, sneakers stamping on a bar floor, the strap slipping off his shoulder.

It won't bring him back, Will had said.

Bullshit.

I returned to the table. Elizabeth looked up, noticing my face. "Everything all right?"

"The guitar. In the back."

"I should have warned you."

"It's just hanging up there."

"Where else would it be?"

"Did you know that Leora is looking for that guitar? Have you told anyone you have it? I mean, why is it hanging up here?" So much for my careful approach.

"He played secret shows here."

"He played secret shows everywhere."

With a perfunctory nod, Elizabeth said, "And he played some of them here. He liked to play acoustic and he'd sing right over there." She pointed toward the bar.

"But he's not living here anymore."

"He's not living anywhere."

When she said that, it was like my brain was a kitchen drawer that had been turned upside down, the contents scattered, silverware clanging as it hit the floor. A blink, a breath, that's all the time I had to place everything back in the right spot, but I did it. I spoke calmly, looking directly at her.

"I'm sure Leora would appreciate if you returned the guitar to her."

"Leora. Right. That codependent relationship."

"Sure, single mom, only child, it's intense. I'm sure it's annoying. But her world has fallen apart. And if anyone should have that guitar, it's her."

Elizabeth was silent, unmoved. "Why? Because she's his family? I'm closer to most of my friends than I am to blood relatives. You should understand that. You and Gabe were incredibly close."

"We weren't that close." I knew as soon as I said it that I'd messed up. It was how I honestly felt since last month, but of course, as far as anyone else knew, when Gabe died, he and I were still the best of friends.

Elizabeth pounced on this. "Really? Because when I was dating him, you talked a lot. That's what I'd like to know, honestly. What did you two talk about on those *long* calls?" She exaggerated the word *long* in a suggestive way, as if our calls were part of some lascivious sex hotline. She leaned back in her chair, her chin lifted up like she was waiting to see what I had to say for myself. "You two got on so well, why not just date each other?"

She was jealous. This at least was a completely normal reaction, the first thing she'd said since I returned to our table that made sense to me. I could handle this. I spoke briskly. "As I'm sure you know, we did date. It didn't work out, and we moved on."

"What about his vocal cord surgery?"

"What about it?"

"You picked him up."

"Yeah, he needed *someone* to do that," I said, pointedly. "His girlfriend was in Paris."

"I was getting the business underway and he had to have the surgery with his American doctor in LA. I couldn't go. But he could have called Jabari."

"Yeah, Jabari is a musical savant who can barely remember to put on shoes, but sure, make that guy your emergency contact. I think you're looking for someone to blame for a shitty breakup. I get it. I've had shitty breakups."

Her face snapped to attention. "How do you know we had a shitty breakup?"

"Because he told me. That you didn't want to move to America."

"Is that what he said?"

"Did you want to move to America?"

"No, but that's not why we broke up."

"Why did you break up?"

"Because he was an alcoholic, for one."

"No, he wasn't. What are you talking about?"

"He was clearly an alcoholic."

"Based on what?"

"Based on all the drinking."

"He didn't drink that much."

"Maybe not when you knew him."

"I knew him currently."

"There was the beer," she said, referencing the beer found in his hotel room.

"His blood alcohol level was fine. Actual police went over this information."

The detail about the beer had sparked speculation but Gabe's BAC had shown it was just that: one beer. Maybe two, but not a bender or a DUI waiting to happen. People joked about the beer online, saying that that's how they'd like to go out, slightly buzzed, toasting to the haters, pouring one out for the homies. And Casey had said, if there were a drunk musician dead in LA, people would know about it. Gabe had no record, no history. He had one beer. The point was no one was taking it seriously, not the police, not celebrity gossip sites, not even internet trolls.

I paraphrased Casey. "Trust me, if there were a dead alcoholic musician in LA, about twenty-five gossip outlets would have beat you to this news."

"You don't have to be blackout drunk to be an alcoholic." She was insistent.

"Why are you saying this?"

"Because it's true."

A wave of heat crashed under my skin. I'd thought Elizabeth might add to what I knew about Gabe. But now she was taking away pieces, throwing balustrades, drilling into the foundation. She wasn't saying, *Here's something you didn't know.* She was saying, *You didn't know him.* With the same smug confidence she had at the funeral.

Fine, if she wanted to make this a contest of who knew Gabe better, I'd play. He'd been a complete mystery to me by the end, but she was right, we had been close, and I knew him better than she did. I mentally rolled up my sleeves as I dove back into our conversation. "Did anyone else ever tell you they thought he had a problem?" I asked.

"No. But they weren't inside our relationship."

"So your relationship made him drink."

Elizabeth grimaced. "I mean, they wouldn't have had an up-close seat to how often he was drinking. How much it came up in his life."

"He was a touring musician whose girlfriend owned a restaurant with a full bar. I'm sure it came up *a lot*. You said yourself you're sober. Maybe we all look like drunks to you. Do you think I've had too much tonight?"

Elizabeth rolled her eyes, but then, glancing at my near empty wineglass, said, "Maybe."

"I've had two. Almost two, I'm not even done. And you were the one saying it was the house wine that I absolutely *had* to have. Enabler much?" That last part was childish; I was aware I now sounded like a petulant American teenager arguing with a parent.

Louis approached with our dessert. "Chocolate layered baklava topped with burnt rose petals and maple and cardamom ice cream.

It's the best thing on the menu." He glanced at Elizabeth, and she nodded, switching into owner-of-Fleur-Bleue mode. "I agree," she confirmed.

I glanced at the burnt rose petals, then at the roses on the bar, the selection of Julia's Rose now seeming less a gesture of hospitality and more like nefarious manipulation, a kind of bait and switch. She drummed her nails on the table. I imagined one scraping across my cheek. Tim and his misogynistic premonition of a catfight—the thought had been planted and now appeared as if it were my own, like some power-of-suggestion trick in a street magic act. This isn't a competition, I reminded myself. And even if Elizabeth was insisting it was, I could get us back on track.

"Maybe he was drinking too much," I conceded. "I guess we'll never know."

"I guess so." Elizabeth dug her spoon into the baklava. It cracked open, pastry flaking off into the dish. "But what about your eulogy?" she asked.

Every cell in my body lined up in defense.

She said, "You didn't mention you saw him the night he died."

I scooped a spoonful of the dessert, swallowing the ice cream too soon. The cold scorched my mouth. I was stalling, waiting for some inner stability to return. When it didn't, I said, "I didn't see him that night."

Elizabeth scrunched up her face. "You didn't? Was he lying to me? Because I spoke to him that night. And he told me he was on his way to meet you."

I shook my head.

"I mean, he was in LA. Wouldn't he normally see you?"

"When he has shows he doesn't always have time to meet up with people."

"Even you?"

"Even me. Yeah."

"But he told me he was going to meet you. He said he had to go. He had to get off the phone because he was going to meet Julia. You were on your way."

If I spoke, I wasn't sure what would come out. A scream. Tears. Or perhaps it would all remain inside and I'd implode. I shook my head again and said the worst possible thing. The credo of liars. "I don't know what you're talking about."

She took another bite of the dessert, then placed her spoon down. "It was my last conversation with Gabe, so I've thought about it a lot. And I'm trying to get some closure. That's what I was referring to in the bathroom after you spoke at the funeral. I thought, Oh, so that's what was going on this entire time. They were sleeping together. And of course she's not going to stand up in front of everyone and go into detail about *that*. Otherwise, why not mention that you were the last person—the last person who knew him, not a fan or someone who worked at the hotel—to see him alive?"

When I didn't say anything, she placed one finger on the table and pressed down. The skin around the fingernail reddened until it nearly matched her nail color. "So you're saying he lied. Gabe was a liar." The claim was teased out, as if she were beckoning me forward. "That's what you're telling me."

I had a choice. Eat my dessert and let Elizabeth think what she wanted to think about Gabe. Or I could tell the truth.

I couldn't bring myself to do either.

"Yeah, well that doesn't mean he was a liar," I said. "Maybe he had to get off the phone and didn't want to hurt your feelings or something."

"My feelings aren't easily hurt," Elizabeth said.

"Fine," I snapped. "You want to know what we talked about on those calls? He said you were a fundamentally cold person. Which tracks. Because you're sitting here interrogating me, trying to make yourself feel better about how you picked away at your boyfriend until he had to leave your country just to escape you when we should be talking about the fact that you're holding on to a family heirloom so it can give your trendy restaurant some character."

She looked at me with what appeared to be disgust. "I guess I got my answer then. Excuse me, Julia." Her chair scraped across the floor. She stood up and walked away, toward the kitchen.

You might have expected me to feel as bewildered as I had at the funeral. But this time, as I sat alone at the table, I finally felt certain I knew more than Elizabeth.

TEN

W ant to come out to the desert?" Gabe asked. It was August 2016. I was home on a Saturday morning. I'd lost track of where Gabe was, we'd been playing phone tag for months. He told me he'd played a show in Joshua Tree, then decided to hang around for a few days before he joined a touring music festival. If I could have chosen a weekend getaway it would have involved an ocean, but it felt like forever since we'd seen each other, so I put the address into my phone and said, "I'll be there in two hours."

A series of freeways pulled me out of the city; the scenery became a repeating pattern of strip mall, gas station, and tan, tan, tan. I had to give it to the California Tourism Board. They'd concentrated on the beaches and failed to mention the hundreds of miles of blank landscape that made up most of the state. I put on the latest Separate Bedrooms album, his third, *Tuesday Afternoon Flu*. I hadn't listened to Separate Bedrooms in a while and felt I should hear the tracks again before seeing him, like mentally reviewing the names and ages of a friend's kids before you meet up. With Gabe's voice in the background, I drove past windmills, spinning white pinwheels towering above me.

I'd never been to Joshua Tree. Small green shrubs populated the strips of desert on either side of the road, and in front of me, a mountain range blocked any view of the horizon. I passed a saloon with a buffalo statue on top of the building, then a liquor store with a cow cutout on the roof. After the giant clay turtle in front of a strip mall, I wondered what was going on with this place and large-scale animal installations.

Minutes away from the address Gabe had given me, my phone lost service. I drove back to the strip mall I'd passed and tried to get a signal in the parking lot, walking back and forth in the dense, dry heat, holding my phone up in the air like an offering to the gods. When that didn't work, I went into a small grocery store, checking for service as I walked down each aisle, grabbing a bag of air-popped popcorn, a water, and a fizzy orange drink.

The woman at the register, her hair dyed orange-red, observed the contents of my basket and asked, "Road trip?"

"The end of one."

"You're staying in Joshua Tree?" She recommended I go to the Integratron. "It's a sound bath that used to be a UFO station. The guy who built it thought he'd spent time with aliens. It sounds out there, but I'm telling you exactly what they say." She threw up her hands. "Joshua Tree is a spiritual place. People come out here to change."

"Do you know how to get to Sage Tree Road? I lost service and I know I'm close."

She stiffened. "Nope, can't say I do."

"Is there someone else I can ask?"

She seemed to be the only person working. Except for some teen-agers hanging out by the magazine rack, we were the only people in the store.

She ignored my question. "I wouldn't go up there anyway. It's far from town and the streets are unmarked." She placed my popcorn and drinks in a paper bag and handed them to me. I left the store, wondering what to do next. It was August in the desert. There was not a drop of humidity in the air. This was a heat that would burn until you burst into flames. I didn't notice the teenagers following me until one of them said, "She won't tell you how to get there."

"Excuse me?"

There were three of them. All white kids. The boy was the one who had spoken to me. The other two were girls; one of them had the same limp blond hair and dark blue eyes as the boy, maybe she was his sister. I put the grocery bag down on the hood of my car.

"You're trying to get to Separate Bedrooms' house, right?" the boy asked.

Did I know these people? Were they connected to Gabe's back-ing band in some way? Or were they a California murder-cult trio? My confusion lasted long enough for the maybe-sister to come to her own conclusion. "She is!" she cried out.

"We heard he's staying here," the other girl said. "That he stayed after the show last night."

Aww. Gabe had teenage stalkers.

"He mentioned this grocery store and that he was staying nearby. We've been driving around talking to people all day."

"Are any of you getting service?" I asked. They all were. "Can I use one of your phones?"

"Why?"

"Because my phone lost service. I'm friends with Separate Bed-rooms. And if you let me have your phone, I'll call him and he'll come here and meet you."

"And then we'll have his phone number!"

I hadn't thought about that. Oh well, he could always block their numbers. The maybe-sister handed me her phone. When I called Gabe, he laughed and said he'd be right there. It was still so hot. I opened my bottle of water and chugged.

"What's he like?" the maybe-sister asked. "Is he like how he is when he sings?"

I smiled. It was a weird question, but I knew what she meant. "Kind of," I said. "What's your favorite album?"

"The new one," they all said.

I thought it was a bit too poppy, but okay.

Five minutes later, Gabe pulled up. He talked to the kids, signed their shirts and concert tickets. He looked a little heavier than when I'd last seen him, his standard T-shirt fit more snugly than usual. His hair stuck out in different directions as always, but he had new stubble. We said goodbye and they climbed into their car and drove off. We waited until they were down the street and out of sight, in case they were still thinking of finding out where Separate Bed-rooms was staying, then we got into our cool, climate-controlled cars and headed to the house.

We drove up a long driveway. At the top, a fence made of what looked like driftwood encircled the property, with a ram's skull on the gate. The house was one level. It had soft, rounded corners, its walls were painted white. Very adobe. The living room had a large window that overlooked the desert below, with a view of the mountains ahead of us.

"This is your room," Gabe said as he led me down the hallway, pointing to the first room we reached. "I'd already taken the bigger one because I thought I'd be here alone, but we can switch if you need."

I checked it out. Clean white walls, brown leather, a red-and-yellow-patterned wool blanket, it all fit with the rental's aesthetic. "This looks great." I set my phone up with my charger and placed my overnight bag down. Once I was settled in, I found Gabe in the living room, on the floor leaning against an armchair, working something out on his guitar. I rolled my eyes and said, "We get it, you can play the guitar."

Usually he would have smiled at that. He didn't. He held up some sheet music. "I'm trying to go analog. Nothing else is working. That's kind of why I'm here, I'd thought I'd make, like, a writing retreat for myself."

"Soak up the Joshua Tree vibes, spirits of the coyote, all that?"

"Yeah, coyotes are great songwriters, don't you know?"

"I heard they did *Abbey Road*." I sat cross-legged on the floor opposite him. "And when that wasn't working and you were stuck, you thought, I'll see what Julia's up to? I'm honored." I asked, "Is this a general retreat or specific project?"

"It's for the fourth album," Gabe said briskly, a quick indication he did not want to discuss it. "That's why I'm doing festival shows. Until there's a new album to tour."

"You're still working on the fourth album?" I didn't mean it to sound like an indictment, I was genuinely surprised. This was the thing about friendships. Unlike in a romantic relationship, you could disappear for a few weeks, even months, without a check-in. You'd always pick up right where you left off. Knowing this, the problem was you could easily end up going too long without spending time in person. Since he'd moved, Gabe and I heard about each other's lives, but we were no longer *involved* in them, no longer familiar with all the events and players or participating in the weekly ups and downs. Instead we had catch-up phone calls. They were a necessary evil: the conjugal visit of friendships, talking in the car on the way to or from somewhere, or while waiting in line, or during a lunch break, cramming every recent detail into fifteen minutes or less of conversation. It was a perpetual update exchange as opposed to experiencing life together.

"How's London?" I asked.

"I don't know. I don't live there anymore."

"How's Elizabeth?" I asked.

"I don't know. We're not together anymore."

Okay, so there was a lot we had to cover.

"You know that guy who interviewed me for *Rolling Stone*?" Gabe asked.

I didn't remember. Gabe pulled up the interview on his phone. I noticed he had it at the ready.

The journalist had seen Gabe perform before in New York. Then he'd spent a day in the studio as Gabe worked on *Dodger Stadium*. He wrote: "In fact, Wolfe-Martel's vulnerable tenor is his greatest weapon. With another singer, it might sound thin or plaintive, especially considering the intimacy of the songs, but Wolfe-Martel's voice is buoyant, almost plastic. It transforms midlyric. I spent a day with him trying to figure it out. I've listened to the album many times since. The best I could come up with is that there is a willingness there and it is without effort. It leaves you with the impression that we could all sing as well as Wolfe-Martel if only we would, as the kids say, 'open up.' And yet there is a skilled level of control. He is not spilling his guts, but after listening to this album, there they are. How they appeared before you without any grandstanding or mess is a mystery. One gets the sense he is no longer holding back. He has given us himself completely."

"Yeah, it's great," I said. "He summed you up perfectly."

"He wants to interview me again. About the process of making the fourth album."

"You'll figure it out," I said.

"I guess. Anyway, whatever." Gabe's expression brightened. "Happy birthday!"

"What? My birthday was two months ago. You called me."

"I know, but I wasn't there in person—" He held up a finger. "I have a surprise for you."

"What is it?"

He jumped up and jogged toward the bedrooms. "Close your eyes!" he yelled back.

I waited. I heard nothing. Total stillness outside, and whatever Gabe was doing in the house, he was doing it silently. When he returned, he landed on the couch next to me with force. My eyes snapped open. "No, no, no," he said. I closed them again. He smelled like campfire and marshmallows. "Now hold out your hands." He took my hands and flipped them up, cradling them in his palms. I hadn't held his hand in years. They were knotted, solid, warm.

"Okay, open them."

He'd placed something in my hands. I already had an idea what it was, and when I looked down, I laughed. "You're giving me my own iPhone?"

Gabe shook his head. "Check the date."

I opened my home screen. It was my birthdate.

"How'd you do this?" I asked, holding up my phone. "I thought Cupertino controlled the calendar."

"Nope. It's me." He lifted his arms above his head. "I am the new Cupertino."

"The old Cupertino is dead," I said blankly, as if hypnotized.

We found the joke simultaneously and in unison said, "All hail new Cupertino."

Bwahayhay.

He sprang back up from the couch, clapping his hands. He pointed his finger at me as he backed away. "Today's your birthday. Forget about two months ago. The party starts now."

GABE HAD MADE A DINNER RESERVATION AT A BYOB RESTAURANT, so we needed a bottle of wine. He'd changed into a clean shirt, a button-down. I was wearing a vintage white tee with an image of the 1997 Albuquerque International Balloon Fiesta on it, tucked into a high-waisted A-line mini. The skirt had a lilac-and-white gingham print with gold buttons on the side. We drove back to the strip mall grocery store. In the beverage aisle, I remembered an old joke from when we were both living in LA.

"Do Billy Joel." I laughed.

He held up a bottle of pinot noir to his face and sang, "'Bottle of red.'" He grabbed a sauvignon blanc. "'Bottle of white.'"

He lost his grip and dropped the bottle of white. It shattered.

"Man, we're getting old," I said. Now that I was thirty and Gabe was approaching his third decade, we constantly referred to how old we were getting.

The store clerk who came to help us clean up was the same one I'd met earlier. She smiled at Gabe, widening her eyes when she saw me. He raised a questioning eyebrow. I whispered, "She thought I was stalking you earlier."

"She's not a fan," he said to the clerk. "Thanks for looking out though."

Gabe paid and we left. He walked ahead of me. I turned back to the clerk and said quickly, "And I am a fan!"

"Yeah right," Gabe said, not looking back. "You thought the last album was too poppy."

THE RESTAURANT WAS CALLED DESERT SUSHI. THE NAME ALONE concerned me, but Gabe said he'd heard it was good. We walked through wide swinging doors into a Western saloon. Two dudes in their twenties were playing on a pinball machine. At the top of the machine, on one side was a cowboy with a lasso, on the other side was a blue-and-white cartoon fish. It was immediately clear that this was Desert Sushi's *thing*, an intentional mishmash of sushi bar, diner, and the Wild West. It was a theme restaurant, but for hipsters. I'd heard that more people from LA were coming out to Joshua

Tree. Desert Sushi was clearly looking to be the fun, niche place that made it worth the drive.

"Yoke 'em if you got 'em!" the machine's mechanical voice hollered.

We sat at a table in the back. Despite the target clientele, no one noticed Gabe or seemed to recognize him. This was how it was when you were out with him: he could be the absolute center of someone's world, or he could be a random guy sitting in the back of a restaurant.

The idea was "sushi" meant that everything, including vegetables and cooked meat, was wrapped in hand-cut rice rolls. Not all of them had raw fish, though the whole point was to try the ones with raw fish. It was like a culinary trust exercise. Gabe went all-in, I opted for a few pieces à la carte. We handed our menus to the waiter, then Gabe and I pondered the pinball machine. "So he's actually more of a fishboy," Gabe concluded.

I looked at him. The stubble on his face was new. "I like it," I said. Then, concerned, "You're not growing a beard though?"

"I guess not." He laughed.

"A little one might work, maybe. But not that Movember disaster."

"It was for charity." He groaned.

"Any good you did by growing the beard to raise money was completely canceled out by the emotional damage to those of us who had to see the beard."

Gabe rolled his eyes. He asked what was going on with My Grandmother's Collection. It was going well, and more important, I loved it. I even liked the business side of it. Putting all the components together, the design, the team management, the press, the negotiations, was fun. Now I had my studio, I'd hired more employees. What was next? I told Gabe, "A store, I hope."

His eyes became round and bright. He reached across the table and squeezed my wrist. "Julia, that's amazing."

I told him there was no need to congratulate me, I was a long way from a grand opening, but in two, three years, I could see it happening.

"Yeah, of course." His face was one huge grin. "Of course it will happen."

Our sushi arrived and we dug in (Gabe was right, it was good).

"So what's next for Separate Bedrooms?" I asked.

"Next would be to sell out several nights at venues like the Bowl."

"You hate doing large shows."

"Doesn't matter. That's the next thing. Kathy and I have been talking about it."

"When's the last time you played a secret show?"

"I can't only do secret shows."

"But if you like them, you could do *some*."

"I need to bring more people in, not keep fans out. I'm trying to do this for the rest of my life." He took a bite, chewing angrily. "I know you have the same concerns. You *just* talked about opening a store."

"Yes. But those aren't concerns. Those are goals."

He was quiet. I didn't understand why.

"Tell me about the fourth album," I said.

He hung his head, stared at his unagi, then looked back up. "Do I have to?"

"It can't be that bad."

"There's bad, and then there's nothing, and I would choose bad at this point."

"Tell me," I said. I placed my hands under my chin and leaned forward.

"Okay, as long as you're in listening position."

"Yup, who knows how long my hands will be under my chin, you might as well take advantage."

He poured a second glass of wine for himself and then topped off my glass. "So I put everything into my music."

"I know," I said. "'One gets the sense he is no longer holding back,'" I intoned, quoting the *Rolling Stone* article.

"Lately I've been wishing I held something back."

"You think there's nothing left? Is this about the vocal cord surgery? How are you?"

"Better. People are saying it affected my range, like I can't do as much as I did before."

"Are they right?"

"Right observation, wrong reason. I don't know. I got the yips or something."

"Then the surgery is good timing," I said. "Blame it on that."

"For how long? The third album was barely good enough and I let that squeak by, if I go out with another clunker, that's it. *Dodger Stadium* becomes the exception. The fucking dreaded one-hit wonder. They put me in that box and I'm done." I didn't say anything. Sometimes when someone is feeling awful about themselves, you have to let them get it all out and not intervene, otherwise it becomes a screaming match between you and that awful voice in their head. No one ever wins against that voice. "I've had three albums. I'm almost thirty. You don't know how many good musicians burn out. It's so easy, *especially* now, to disappear. Or you coast on the one good thing you made, playing the same songs forever. It's not like I have any other skills to fall back on. I've known exactly what I wanted to do for a long time."

"I remember."

"Don't roll your eyes." Had I? "I'm not saying I'm special. I remember you too." I didn't track where he was going. "You were making jewelry. And you were very good. I still wear this bracelet. You knew you were talented. Then you decided to go a more corporate way, hide out at law school. You were scared."

"Corporate way? Yes, I was scared. It's called needing to make money. I know you didn't go to college, but didn't they cover socioeconomics in one of your private school classes?"

"Julia, don't be a dick. Talk to me like I'm me, not a demographic. You're one of the only people I can talk to about this."

"Turns out you can't talk to me either. Talk to other famous rich people."

"I've tried. Comparing stories. Talking about the industry. But as soon as they start commiserating with me, telling me how hard they have it, then I think, Wah wah boo-hoo. Shut up."

"So you know how I feel!"

Bwahayhay.

This way that Gabe treated his career, as if it were some mythical calling—it made sense when we were young, but still? I could have laid into him about it, but I didn't think either one of us was ready to go there. It was a little too early in the night to go there. It was a little too early in our lives to go there. Instead, I made it a joke by enunciating each word: "You. Are. No. Longer. Relatable."

He laughed. "Fine." Then, "I know it's stupid." His eyes shone, they looked rimless, filling up his face. "But tell me the truth. What did you think of the last album?"

"Giddyup! Yee-HAW!" the pinball machine exclaimed.

I said, "I told you. It was more pop than I expected from you."

"Julia. I want your crit." He was serious. He was asking for the candor of the teenage Julia who'd just met him so she had no reason to protect his feelings.

But now I did know him, so I tried to find the nicest possible way to say it. "They were technically good songs. But if I didn't know it was your album, I wouldn't know it was *your* album." I quickly added, "But that's probably because we're friends. I mean, the average person wouldn't even notice."

"Thanks," he said. He looked like I'd stabbed him in the heart with one of my chopsticks.

"I don't think you wanted a crit."

"Trust me, it's not as bad as what I've been telling myself."

I didn't want to leave him dangling all alone on a vulnerability branch, so I said, "I worry about how my life is going to turn out too."

"Like what?"

I squirmed in my chair, wringing out a moan. I was already so bored with myself, and I hadn't even said it yet. "I don't know. Being alone?"

"You won't be single forever."

I wasn't worried about being single forever. I was worried about feeling this lonely forever.

"Maybe there's more about Shira?" I asked, quickly returning to Gabe's problems, having endured a heroic twenty seconds of my own vulnerability.

Gabe said, "I've covered Shira. Shira is done. You know she's getting married this year?"

"She is?"

"She asked me to perform at the wedding."

"No." I put down my chopsticks. "Gabe. You have got to be kidding me."

"She said, 'You never know if you don't ask.'"

"No! Sometimes you know. Oh my God, Shira, sometimes you *know*!"

"Jabari was saying he has a theory that everyone needs to date that dream person you *think* you want but if you stayed with them, they'd ruin your life. Like for him, it was a willowy-blond fairy-child woman who seems like a free spirit but is actually a flake and kind of dumb."

"Lynne," I said automatically.

Gabe nodded. "Right. He calls Lynne 'the Near Trainwreck.' And now he's marrying Jenny and she's got that hippie thing, but she's grounded, you know?"

"And Shira's your Near Trainwreck?"

"Yes. A supersmart, bookish girl who makes *me* feel smart instead of like the guy who didn't go to college and can't stop using the word *autodidact*."

I guffawed. "You did go through a phase when you said that all the time." I told him my theory about his childhood with Leora making him conditioned to let women do the talking.

He leaned over the table, cradling his head in his hands. "Oh God, that's exactly right."

"That's not bad! Everyone wants a good listener."

"Right. But does everyone want an acolyte?"

"Personally, I adore your worship." I fanned my hands in front of my face.

"Right," he said again. He swayed to a rhythm I couldn't hear. I'd seen that before, the motions of him working out a song in his head. I took a sip of water, then another, and continued until I finished it. When I did, I asked him, "Still working?"

He looked around the restaurant, then turned back to me. "I've been thinking about pulling together those songs I wrote in Barcelona."

"What songs? Like the instrumental stuff you were trying out?"

"No, I wrote lyrics. I was too embarrassed to tell you."

I remembered the pocket notebook he carried around. "You did? About what?"

"About us! What else was I doing that summer?"

Looking for bands to join, as I remembered. "You wrote an album about us?"

"Not a whole album. It would be four songs. Something I could put out. Like, the artist before he was the artist?"

"You could call it *Puppy Love*," I offered. "Ooh, you could put a little puppy on the cover."

Gabe stared at me. "Great, we've got the cover art down." He stabbed his chopstick into a roll and swallowed it in one bite. Then, while digging his chopsticks into another, said, "So you definitely weren't interested when I had the beard."

"What? What are you talking about?"

"What about when I dyed my hair that time?"

"Gabe. You're cute. Are you worried you're no longer cute? Didn't some Frenchwoman recently fall for you?"

"Elizabeth isn't French. She's English and she lived in France."

"Boo! Not as cool." I expected his laughter to join mine, but he looked completely serious when he said, "I think you've looked beautiful every year I've known you."

I was still laughing when I said, "You what? Gabe! I'm sorry. I didn't hate the beard that much."

"Why weren't you interested in me when we first met again? I could tell you weren't."

"No you couldn't."

"Yes. Something was different. I perceived it immediately."

"Perceived? Who are you? Professor X?"

He waited.

"Honestly, it was your haircut."

"I knew it! My haircut?"

"Why are you asking? Do you really think I never dated you again because you weren't hot enough?"

"I don't know!"

"Gabe, we just met three people who think you're so amazing they were driving around the desert hoping to get a glimpse of you."

He shook his head, frowning, his mouth a straight line. "Don't do that. Don't tell me to come back down to Earth and then do the whole 'Oh, who me, Julia? You're the rock star, Gabe.' Don't act like, 'Why would my opinion of you matter?'"

"I'm not. I'm saying don't be so insecure."

Gabe scoffed. "My haircut."

"I was joking!" I wasn't. But of course that hadn't been the only reason. Did he really want to get into all of this?

He stuffed a California roll into his mouth, which made me think that was the end of the conversation, but he kept talking as he chewed. "We had this great thing that summer, completely in love, but the timing was off. And then you see me with a bad haircut. And earlier? The thing with my beard?" He laughed then, tiny bits of avocado sprayed out of his mouth. "Maybe you're a little shallow?" He said, "Exhibit A. Kyle." He brushed his hand across his mouth, sweeping the avocado away.

"Kyle?"

"Yeah, Kyle sucked. You dated that jerk because he looked like some dude from a teen-vampire-model drama."

"That's a show?" I laughed.

"Yeah, you should talk to the casting director. You have the same taste in men."

"Ohh-kaaayyy." I elongated every vowel. "What about you and all the women of LA? The groupies? The year of"—I lowered my voice and did my best clueless-oaf impression—"'just having a lot of fun and discovering people are connecting with my music'?"

"Fucking around is different from being shallow. There were a wide variety of women."

"Cool." I wasn't going to let him get away with that other thing he had said. It almost slipped by, but I couldn't let it. "And we weren't really in love," I said.

"Why do you say that?"

"You thought we were?"

"Julia, what are you talking about? Of course we were."

"Then why did you break up with me?" Great. He had to bring all this up, and of course this was where it led us. We had never talked about this. We'd gone from together, to strangers, to friends, and not once had we looked back. I'd thought we were so evolved for never discussing this part of our past.

I could tell by how long he was taking to respond that Gabe was going to answer me honestly. I braced myself, avoiding his gaze.

He sighed. "Because I thought you would get in the way of my music."

"I got that."

"I mean, that was it. That was the only reason. And it was really stupid of me."

That can't be it, I thought. That can't be all of it. It has to be me. Over the years, I'd carried that with me. It had to be me. Not because Gabe had broken my heart beyond repair but because it hadn't worked with anyone else either. But as soon as he said this, I immediately saw those other relationships differently. I saw Kyle's insecurity, Eric's indecision. Was I too much for Brandon or had we just not been enough for each other? I exhaled. It wasn't only me. It just hadn't worked out yet.

Except one time it *had* worked. Briefly.

"I loved you," he said. "But I didn't want to have to think about anyone else."

There it was again, that thing that had irked me—no, enraged me—all those years ago. How he had broken up with me, out of nowhere, because it was all in service of his calling, this big career that was waiting for him. I know, we were young; at that age, plenty of people take themselves too seriously. But it wasn't only then. I had seen it again and again over the years, pulsating below the surface, every time he talked about a woman. Why had he and Shira kept breaking up? Maybe because he was always on tour and never around? He dropped in and out of my life, but I couldn't imagine that would be fun as his girlfriend. Most recently, it had been Elizabeth. Of course he couldn't move to London and put down roots with her. She had to come to him or it was over. Gabe's self-importance—that was it! As much as he wanted to call it art, or craft, or the road, or whatever the hell suited him in the moment, it was his ego. He may not have partied like a rock star, but he had the ego of one, and it won every time. Ignoring this glaring weakness of his was the only thing that had allowed me to preserve any sense of romance from those weeks in Barcelona. And anyway, it was someone else's problem. Whoever dated him next would have to figure it out.

Gabe continued, "I was seventeen, I didn't know how to handle . . . stuff. Honestly I thought once things had calmed down for me, we'd eventually get back together."

"How?"

He rubbed his forehead. "I don't know, I think I pictured running into each other again, you know? We'd meet each other in our thirties after we'd lived our lives, and it would be on."

"But we met in our twenties."

"And I had a bad haircut." He looked down at his plate, then back up at me. I could tell that he wanted to say something and that it was going to be important to both of us that he got it right. He rubbed a finger across his bottom lip, eyes upward, thinking. Then he looked at me. His eyes stayed on me as he spoke. "I thought seriously dating somebody would slow me down. It would have been completely different if you could have come with me, but you had college. I thought about us. When I was at Oberlin, when I was living in New York. That first tour." Perhaps sensing my skepticism, he said, "I thought about you all the time. I mean, touring is fucking lonely." His eyes circled my face, I guess surveying the effect of what he'd said. Yes, it made sense that touring was lonely. That was a true statement about touring. Though I knew this remark was aiming at something, it had failed to pierce me.

"Do you still feel lonely on tour?" I asked.

"All the time."

I wanted him to say something more. When he didn't, it was my turn to examine his face. There it was. He was heartsick.

"How are you? With the whole breakup thing. You were together for about a year? That's a while."

"Not for most people. A year is nothing."

I understood what he meant. Not for most people, but at that point, a yearlong relationship would have been something for me too. "Long distance is really hard," I said, trying to be helpful any way I could.

"Yeah. But—" He shook something off, regaining his train of thought. "But being with Elizabeth made me see that it was possible to devote myself to work *and* someone else. That I could do it if I wanted."

"So?" I said, moving his story forward.

"I didn't want to do it with her."

My memories of our summer were two young people in an old city, six weeks in a twin bed, long walks down streets where every block was new. They were pretty postcards. And when Gabe left Barcelona, I put them away. Eventually I was able to look at them fondly without any emotions attached. That seemed to be for the best. Besides, I'd gotten it wrong, hadn't I?

Now Gabe was saying: that time was exactly how it felt, your instinct was correct; it was no small ordinary forgotten thing, it was worth cherishing. What I'd convinced myself was a tiny blip was, in fact, as I'd always secretly felt, a mammoth event. And as my understanding of these memories was altered, our conversation caused a fissure in my heart that widened into a canyon, and I could not stop myself. I filled it immediately with all my romantic hopes, all the hope I'd ever had to be loved completely, not even by Gabe, but by anyone.

We looked at each other for longer than we had in some time. A rare silent moment for us. Not a bwahayhay in sight.

Gabe shook the wine bottle, then, seeing it was empty, laid it on its side and spun it. His bracelet banged against the table.

"So. We covered Separate Bedrooms and My Grandmother's Collection, but the real question is what is next for Julia?"

"And Gabe."

"Yes. What is next for Julia and Gabe?"

ELEVEN

ack at the house, I was the first inside. I fell on the couch, slinging my knees over the arm. Gabe dropped his keys by the door. When he walked into the living room, I sat up, scooting over. He sat next to me. He flicked at the side buttons on my skirt. "These are cool," he said.

"They are . . ." Had we time traveled? This awkward fumbling and narrating our actions was classic material from the freshman hookup handbook.

I leaned back against the couch, angling myself so we were no longer both facing forward like we were posing for a family photo.

"Should we talk about this?" Gabe asked.

I shook my head. He leaned forward. I could smell wasabi and wine from the night. Or maybe that was me, we were so close, and my mouth had slipped open, agape in anticipation. The first kiss was familiar. Like it had been loaded in 2004 and left in the chamber, it was unfinished business and fell easily from our mouths. We looked at each other, surprised, unsure if we should be embarrassed. We weren't. I rubbed my hand against the stubble of his cheek. I pulled him in. The second kiss was a slow kiss. *Slow.* I remembered. Our clothes came off so quickly, it was as if they were burning our skin, we alternated between undressing ourselves and reaching to help each other. Every second we fiddled with a zipper or shimmied away from fabric provided an opportunity for one of us to change our mind. Our eyes met several times, each glance a check-in. We didn't pause until I was on top of him. We moved so fast, speeding ahead to find out if this was going to happen, we had to catch up and realize, yes, it *is* happening. We gripped each other, my hands on his arms, his on mine, steadying ourselves.

In the morning, we woke up together in Gabe's bed. When he pulled back the curtains, the bedroom flooded with sunshine. We giggled. We were laughing at how surprising the brightness was, but also at ourselves. We spent the rest of the day indoors, cuddled up on the couch. We resurrected a game we'd played when Gabe was recovering from surgery. Since he hadn't been able to speak, we'd watched movies, coming up with a six-degrees-of-separation game, starting with *Who Framed Roger Rabbit* and then, because Bob Hoskins was in that, went on to *Mermaids*, then *Reality Bites*, also with Winona Ryder, then *Black Swan*. After *Black Swan*, we were too depressed to watch anything else. We'd written back and forth to each other on a mini dry-erase board and joked that if our day had a movie title, it would be *Rabbit Mermaids Bite Swan*. This time, we started with *The Five Heartbeats*, and from Diahann Carroll ended up watching *Paris Blues*, and from there Paul Newman took us to *Butch Cassidy and the Sundance Kid*. Movie title of the day: *The Five Blues Kid*.

We went outside for the sunset. The open vista provided an

unobstructed view. There were a few patio chaise lounges and we pulled two next to each other. Just when I thought we'd gone back to being friends and I'd imagined the night before, he pulled my chair even closer to his and lifted my foot onto his leg. I was wearing a maxi dress and its skirt fell to the side, exposing my calf.

"For a short girl, you have great legs," Gabe said.

Some guy had tried to neg me with that line at a party once. Gabe had overheard it, and we'd laughed about it later.

"You do have great legs," Gabe said. "He was right about that." He rubbed my leg, moving up my thigh.

This time, we took our time. We knew we would not die of embarrassment, neither of us would utter "Eww!" at the worst possible moment, confirming our friend zone. On my back, the concrete warm underneath me, Gabe went down on me. My thighs quivered. He looked up. "I love when you do that." Sighing, I said, "Then keep going."

Afterward—I would gag if someone else told me this, but it's true—we stayed outside and looked at the stars. In our defense, we both spent our time in cities. With all the light pollution, we didn't normally see stars. And yes, we were high on ourselves and reveling in the romance of it all. The temperature had finally dropped, but it was still warm enough to be comfortable. Gabe brought out a blanket from inside and draped it over us. We snuggled together on one lounge chair. It was like being back in that twin bed again.

I rested my head on his chest. I waited, then exclaimed, "Oh right!"

"What?"

"Wrong side," I said.

"Only if you want to hear my heart."

"I want to hear it." I switched to his right side and placed my palm down.

THE NEXT MORNING WAS A BLUR. GABE HAD TO LEAVE BY 7:00 A.M. if he was going to make his flight. While I packed, he went out to get us croissants and caffeine. When he came back, he closed up the house, leaving the rental key in a lockbox by the door. He took my overnight bag off my shoulder and placed it on his. We walked to our cars. Below us the road was dotted with sagebrush and aloe.

"Okay, well," I began, as Gabe said, "We'll talk." We laughed nervously, then hugged.

Weird.

Perhaps sensing this, Gabe grabbed my hand, the physical contact a reminder that things were different. We made out against his car, that kind of ferocious making out I'd thought I'd left behind in my teens, that kind where the next base is not a given. When we separated, slowly pulling apart like taffy, he said, "You should come to one of my festival shows."

"Which one?"

"I don't know? We'll figure it out, whatever works for your schedule."

I nodded, unsure.

We had talked about this. Were we going to date? We didn't use that word, it sounded ridiculous, we'd already dated, we knew each other. But was this *something*? Yes, we thought. It could be. We didn't define it, no. I mean, imagine, really imagine, me asking him,

"Are you my boyfriend?" It made me cringe then and it makes me cringe now. And if he'd asked, "Are you my girlfriend?" I would have pushed him right out of bed.

Bed. That was the key point. We'd discussed all this in bed, in a postcoital glow, alone in a house in the desert, away from our lives and everyone we knew. If someone had told me it was all a mirage, I would have believed them.

We hugged again, with our arms wrapped around each other, for a long time, until it became comical how long it had gone on and we were swaying back and forth, gently rocking as we embraced. Then we high-fived. It was like we'd made some accursed bargain with an evil troll. We could have the giddy rush, the blatant horniness, the aching crush of feelings, all the attendant fervors of first love. But we'd have to take the awkwardness too.

As he got in his car, he said he'd call me after the show.

In the month when I didn't hear from him, I replayed this scene in Joshua Tree many times. I thought of the line from the *Rolling Stone* article.

"One gets the sense he is no longer holding back."

I had certainly gotten that sense that weekend.

I texted the next day. *I was thinking New York.* There was no response. *Ok fine Boston!*

Then later that day: *Obviously don't really care about the city, just checking in.*

I called, scared something might have happened, maybe there

was an accident or he was sick. No answer, despite three voicemails. Nothing Tuesday. Nothing Wednesday, nothing Thursday. On Friday I texted Jabari's fiancée, Jenny. We knew each other socially and had a text relationship primarily based on gifs. I knew she was on the road with Jabari, who was performing with Separate Bedrooms. It would not seem unusual for me to ask her how the festival shows were going.

She responded, *Great!*

How's Gabe doing?

He sounded awesome last night

Okay, but he was a professional. He knew how to put on a show. A good show didn't mean something wasn't wrong. *Clearly something was wrong.*

I texted him one last time. *What the fuck*

Nothing, nothing, nothing. It was nothing.

He'd had to convince *me*. After we'd slept together the second time, I woke up in the middle of the night. I shook Gabe awake.

"What?"

"I'm okay with this being a fluke," I said.

"Why do you think it's a fluke?"

"I don't," I said. "But it can be."

"Julia, I really wanted this to happen. I'd been thinking about it for a while."

"Me too," I admitted.

NEARLY TWO MONTHS LATER, SO MANY MILES AWAY FROM HOME that I was in kilometers, I sat at the table in Fleur Bleue, waiting for Elizabeth to return. I guessed that it had been less than an hour since she left the table, but maybe it had been more. Of course she was right. Gabe was a liar.

And everything she said about me and the night he died?

She was nearly right about that too.

TWELVE

The few customers left in Fleur Bleue sat at tables clear of everything except coffee cups. There were no more menus brought out, only bills taken away. Louis brushed crumbs off our table. He glanced at me. "I'm sorry to hear about your friend," he said. "I didn't realize you knew Gabe too."

"Oh. You knew him?"

"Yeah, we met a few times. Cool dude. Nice dude."

Nice; there it was again. That empty descriptor, that low bar easy enough for a *dude* to clear. Everyone loves a cool dude who's nice to you. How lucky for all of us plebeians that Mr. Most Popular bothered with basic manners.

"You know there's no bill, right?" Louis asked me. "She took care of that."

"Yup. Of course. Just sipping my wine," I explained, as if I often stayed at the table long after my dining companions had left, savoring the ambience. He looked at my glass. It was empty. I turned it over to show him I realized that. A last drop of red wine slipped off the rim onto my napkin. It sank through the fabric: my own Frankenthaler.

I threw a hand up as if I had performed a magic trick. "And that's that," I said, thrusting the glass at him, ending my weird one-woman cabaret.

He smiled, somehow finding this charming. The bumbling, silly American: maybe that was *his* type.

"Are you going to meet up with Elizabeth later?" he asked. At the mention of my plans for the rest of the night, I sat up in my seat. "Or if you want to move over to the bar, I can get you something . . . Julia, right? Another glass? Or a digestif?"

I hesitated. Elizabeth's comment about alcoholism was on my mind. Had Gabe and I had too much to drink that night in Joshua Tree? Maybe that would explain his disappearance? Embarrassed about a drunken mistake? But no, one bottle split between us the first night over a three-hour dinner, then we were completely sober the next night. I was both grateful Elizabeth was wrong and disappointed to meet another dead end.

Louis waited for my answer to his question. He held my wineglass by the stem. He had long hands with clean, tapered nails. There was a scar at the edge of his wrist. Maybe from recent kitchen work, maybe something older.

"Do you have any green tea?" I asked.

"Yes, but that has caffeine in it, you know?" He was lingering, stretching out this encounter.

"I'm fine with being up all night." Sometimes it's best to be direct.

"Oh, you are?" The effete and regimented pose of table service slipped, revealing a brighter, looser side. "Green tea, all right." As he headed toward the kitchen, he looked back at me. I smiled. My full-cheeked, wide-eyed, smitten-kitten smile.

I moved to the bar. He brought out my tea. I slowly sipped from a blue ceramic mug and watched the last customers leave, then a few of the waiters, then the bartenders. Until it was just me and Louis. I watched as he cleaned up. Occasionally our eyes would meet, him watching me watch him. An Otis Redding song playing in the background.

"Hey!" The blond hostess, Paula, popped up at the end of the bar. I jumped. She turned to Louis. "I'll be in the office, let me know when you leave." She looked at me. "Anything else we can do for you?"

"She's Elizabeth's friend," he said. "They had dinner tonight."

"Oh, great to meet you! And you're staying with Elizabeth?" she asked. I nodded, willing to go along with whatever story Elizabeth was telling people about me. "I'll leave you to it," she said, looking between us with that sense of exasperated amusement when you want to say to two people who are flirting and eventually going to hook up: *Get on with it already!*

After she went in the back, Louis explained, "She thought I was picking up a customer."

"Ah, but you were picking up a woman who got a free meal and hasn't contributed financially in any way to the staff."

He smiled. It was just the two of us now. I'd thought maybe Elizabeth would come back, but it was clear she wasn't returning. Otis sang his last notes and the bar playlist moved on to the next track. "Who is this?" I asked.

Louis said a name I didn't recognize.

Good, I thought. Brand-new song. Brand-new guy. I felt a rush of adrenaline and it emboldened me.

"I'll be right back," I said, and headed toward the bathroom. The guitar was still on the hallway wall. I thought maybe it wouldn't be, that when Elizabeth left, she'd taken it with her or rushed to hide it somewhere. I must have gotten under her skin for her to leave the castle treasure unguarded. I reached for the guitar. Would it be this easy? I slid my hand behind its neck and tipped it toward me. It seemed to fall right into my hands. Right, this wasn't the Smithsonian. Someone had tacked up a piece of wood to a wall and hung a strap from it; anyone could lift the instrument off.

I bounded back to Louis, hugging the guitar to my side.

"Whoa!" He reached out his hand to take it away from me.

"No, it's cool." I sidestepped him. "It's Gabe's. Elizabeth knows. We're passing it from friend to friend. We're having a memorial for him tomorrow. That's why I'm in town." I'd never thought of myself as a good liar, but I was turning into a quick one.

"Oh, okay," Louis said. I felt bad for lying to him, so I kissed him.

HIS BED SMELLED LIKE LAVENDER. A NICE TOUCH. IT MADE ME FEEL like I was in skilled hands. I was nervous, but I pushed this aside. For this to work, I had to be devoured. I needed to fully disappear. I slammed my body against his, hoping I would shatter or dissolve. It was not enough. I cupped one of my breasts and offered it to him, and he traced geometric patterns with his tongue. It felt rote, like he had learned a certain rhythm, trusting a routine that had yielded results in the past. It was not enough. I threw back the covers.

I think it was the best blow job I've ever given in my life.

It was not enough.

Louis scooped his arm under me. He pulled me over to him, lifting me up to straddle him. When we were nearing the end, doing what Ines had classified as actual sex, I grew panicked that this really was not going to be enough. "Don't stop," I pleaded. I needed more time. Being devoured wasn't cutting it. My aim was total erasure. Of myself, of Gabe, the entire Joshua Tree experience. I leaned in harder, pushing Louis into the bed, as if I could drive us both into the ground. My senses lifted, and briefly, gloriously, I was without memory.

Louis pulled me close to him. My head rested against his chest. Of course, his heart was on the left side, and of course, I pulled away.

Between the sex with Louis and his lavender sheets, I thought I had a pretty good chance of making it through the night. I had been having trouble sleeping since hearing about Gabe. I stayed busy during the day, but at night I would think about him. Sometimes I thought about that month of no contact.

But mostly I would think about when he finally did reach out.

THIRTEEN

When Elizabeth asked if I had seen Gabe the night he died, I told her I had no idea what she was talking about, but I remembered every beat. I did my best to forget during the day. I was pretty good at it. But every night it came back and I would run through it all again. Every second accounted for. Every syllable under my skin. I knew it by heart.

Gabe texted me the day he died. I woke up that morning and saw a message from him on my phone.

I'm in LA, he said. *Secret show tonight.*

I did not respond.

Then he called.

I didn't pick up.

I didn't have to pick up. He disappeared and then texted me the equivalent of a generic mailing-list blast? No way.

Then came the voicemail.

"It's me. I—I need to explain. I'm not going to do it on your voicemail. I'm in town. I'm in LA and I couldn't be here and *not* talk to you. I, uh, obviously that's on me, I'm sorry. Anyway, I'm doing a secret show, and you know, you were saying in Joshua Tree how I should do that more. I'm staying at Hotel Frank. You should come to the show. I mean, come and meet me after. Or don't come, but meet me after. Please? Any time after ten thirty. Okay. Bye."

I'd had time to think about this and I'd come to the conclusion that Joshua Tree was a mistake. Which was better. What if I had been right about us when I was eighteen? I would have had to recalculate my entire twenties, every move I'd ever made in relationships, my expectations for intimacy, men, and myself *in* relationships—all of it could be traced back to my first go at it. It would have required a reprinting of the facts, like the news that Pluto is not a planet, or the way the classification of brontosaurus is ever-changing. No, it was definitely better that Gabe proved me right.

Not love, never love. Just two idiots.

Two idiots. Final call?

Yes, underline it, print it in a textbook, shrink-wrap it, send it out, put it on the AP exam. That's canon, baby.

And we could have made our mistake, owned it, and moved on. It could have been *our* mistake, but Gabe had disappeared on me, left me alone with it. Now he wanted to show up and mention Joshua Tree, but not what happened there? If this had been the day after we slept together, then I might have played the amnesia game with him, but after weeks of not answering me, did he really think it would be this easy?

Maybe he had. For a cool dude, a nice dude, maybe it was that easy. I ignored the text. I ignored the voicemail. I went to work. I went out to dinner. I came home. I sat on my bed looking out the window. It had been another long summer day in LA, but now it was after nine and dark. Tonight was here. I took out my phone and texted Gabe.

I'll be there. 10:30

I stood up. I opened my closet, picked out jeans and a blazer. I took a shower and got ready to go out again. But I couldn't do it. I sat down on my bed, slowly peeled off my clothes. I washed my face. I brushed my teeth. I put on my pajamas. I turned off my phone and watched a cooking-competition show until I fell asleep. Ha, I thought, let's see how he likes it.

I HADN'T TOLD ANYONE, NOT EVEN INES, THAT GABE REACHED OUT. I couldn't talk about it. I was angry, angrier than I'd ever thought I could be at someone. I didn't want to feel anger, truly I didn't. I wanted to mourn, to be purely and simply in mourning. I wanted to sob loudly and uninterrupted, instead of it leaking out when least expected: while soaking in the tub, or in front of paintings, or as I was waking up next to the Frenchman I'd slept with the night before.

It was morning faster than I expected. With the aid of sunlight, I checked out the room I'd only been able to get a sense of when I'd entered last night. It was more or less what you'd expect from the home of a single man in his twenties. A lot of brown and navy, dark greens, the black chrome surface of various electronics. Though it was surprisingly tidy.

Louis stretched his arms above him, letting out a yawn. He rolled over, his long eyelashes gently fluttering as he half lifted his eyes to peer up at me. He looked completely different. Still gorgeous, but less like the lead of a French romance and more like a man who'd just worked a ten-hour shift.

"Hey," he said with a questioning look. I knew that look. The post-hookup look. The universal sign for: What did I want from him and was it going to be more than he could give?

I replied "hey" just as he had. Before Gabe, I'd been keeping it casual for the last year, I could go right back to it. And it was fine, I didn't want anything more from Louis. He smiled, kissed the top of my head, and rolled out of bed, an unspoken exchange complete: we'd had a great night, and that was all it would be. It's almost as much a reason for celebration when two people agree they don't want a relationship as when they do.

The door to Louis's bathroom was open, I caught a glimpse of pristine white tiles, a bathtub and sink that glistened.

"Wow, you have a spotless bathtub."

"Yeah. I scrub it every day. I'm very clean that way. It's embarrassing."

"No, it's great," I assured him. I needed to seize the opportunity to take a real bath and not just a standing sink bath. The fact that I was still unwilling to take a shower, even after having sex (I mean, that's just nasty, I thought), was all I needed to know this shower fear was serious and I should do something about it. But I'd have to get to it later. "Would you mind if I took a bath?" I asked.

"Sure, I'll get you a flannel."

Louis went over to his closet, I tiptoed naked into his bathroom. The cold tiles were a refreshing jolt. I ran the bath, finding the right temperature, then hopped in.

Louis knocked. "Come in," I said.

He walked in, holding a washcloth and towel. His eyes dipped toward my body, then back up. "Is this a sexy bath? You want me to get in?"

"No, it's a regular bath."

"Oh. Okay." He remained in the doorway. "You can use the shower too if you want, it works."

"Oh yeah, thanks, I'm good."

The skin between his eyebrows drew together, he dragged his hand over his face. He nodded, getting it. "My friend died in a motor accident last year."

Quietly I said, "I'm so sorry."

"I look both ways *twice* when I cross the street, I cannot stop doing it. I never used to do that, but now I think: Remember Riad." He walked over to the tub, placing one hand on the edge and offering the other, open-palmed, to me. I rested my hand in his, then returned it to the bath.

After I'd bathed and dressed, I texted Leora: *Got the guitar!* At least I had good news for someone. I joined Louis in his kitchen. He was sitting at the table eating a bowl of cereal. There was another bowl, the box of cereal, and some milk next to him. He pointed at it. "Help yourself." I had taken bites of every amazing thing served to me last night, but I didn't feel like I'd really eaten. I'd been too nervous.

"What are you doing today?" Louis asked as I prepared my bowl of cereal.

"Not much. I should probably stop by the restaurant to talk to Elizabeth." I hoped I didn't sound as unexcited by that as I felt. I glanced over at Gabe's guitar, leaning against Louis's refrigerator. Not my best moment, taking it off the wall. And it wasn't going to help anything. I still had to find out if Elizabeth had the rest of Gabe's things. Which would be hard to do once she found out that I'd not only insulted her, but stolen something that, though I did not agree, she clearly considered hers.

The restaurant was closed, I couldn't put the guitar back. But if I could talk to her before she noticed it was missing, maybe I could smooth things over.

I asked Louis what time Elizabeth would arrive at work.

"She's not coming in today."

I leaned forward, attempting to be casual. "Really? Are you sure? How do you know?" Three questions in a row is never casual.

"Because she's the boss," he said. "We all know when she's going to be in."

"Why? Is she like, one of those nightmare chefs who's always abusing their staff?" That would make me feel better about last night.

Louis laughed at the thought.

"Do you have her number?" I asked.

"You don't? Aren't you friends?"

That had been Elizabeth's lie, not mine.

"Oh yeah, of course," I said. "I was thinking of the number for the restaurant."

"But she won't be there." Louis looked at me, trying to get a read on whatever was going on.

"Right, you said that," I said.

"I think she's teaching that flower class today."

185

I gasped. "Oh yeah!" Elizabeth had invited me the night before. I showed him the confirmation email—to get help with directions to the location, but also to prove I'd had some form of correspondence with this woman he thought was my friend.

He didn't seem to care about that part, only saying that if I did want to make the class, which was back in Shoreditch, I'd better hurry. When I asked where we were, he said a name I didn't recognize. It would be an hour Tube ride and a brisk twenty-minute walk; no time for stopping at my hotel to change. "Maybe run," Louis suggested.

FOURTEEN

A woman in a large sun hat with a clipboard stood in front of a group of fifteen people, a brick building behind them. "Are you here for the class?" she asked.

"No," I said, and passed them as if I knew exactly where I was going and it had nothing to do with them.

On the other side of the building, hidden from the street, was a garden. Next to it, a smaller building with a wooden sign hung from the door, ELIZABETH THOMPSON'S FLORAL ATELIER in green calligraphy. Inside, workstations were arranged like a high school chemistry lab. Each station had a vase, shears, and an assemblage of flowers. At the front of the room, Elizabeth was picking up shards of a broken vase from the floor.

I waited at the door. Last night she'd nearly caught me in a lie. Though it had felt less like a *lie* and more like one of those self-protective animal reflexes, a turtle retreating into its shell, a pill bug curling up. If there was any way I thought she'd understand, I would have told her it was nothing personal. There are certain things you can't even reveal to yourself. I took a breath—not a deep one, it was still stuck, currently somewhere around my breastbone—and arranged my face into that of a woman who had nothing to hide.

Elizabeth looked up, she took in my outfit, the same one she'd seen me in last night. She was wearing a white shirt and orange apron, her hair up. Her face displayed shock, then intrigue, before settling on complete bafflement. "What are you doing here? And why do you have that?" She pointed to the guitar.

"I'm here because of the guitar. I took this last night." Before she could object, I added, "Which I shouldn't have done before talking to you." I placed the guitar on a chair, slowly backing away from it while keeping an eye on her, like I was negotiating a hostage exchange.

"You can leave the guitar, but I'm a little busy here. As you can see, I just broke a vase. Now a student won't have anything to take their work home in." She went into the closet.

"Can you use your demonstration vase?" I asked.

She emerged from the closet, a broom in hand. "Already was because I was down one anyway." She turned away from me and began sweeping.

"Do you have any ribbon?"

"Yes."

"Take away all the vases, except one for you. At the end, ask: Who wants a vase and who wants a ribbon bouquet? Once you make it their choice, I guarantee someone will want a ribbon."

She stopped sweeping. "That might work." She pushed the last of the vase debris into a dustpan. I heard a street musician outside begin the first notes of "Isn't She Lovely."

"We weren't having an affair," I said. "I didn't see him the night

188

he died." She considered this, and me. I continued, "And I'm not in London to see art. I told Leora I would get Gabe's things back from you. I was going to email you, but she'd already tried that, so instead I took a flight. And here I am."

Her jaw locked. I pressed on, hoping the volume of information would subdue her. "It's important to Leora. We've looked everywhere. Otherwise we wouldn't be bothering you. She tried emailing, but you didn't get back to her. For weeks."

"I could have not gotten back to her for months."

"You could have, but why would you?"

"Because it's in my right who I choose to have correspondence with. And how long it takes me to reply to someone is my business. It doesn't require an ambush from a foot soldier."

"If you let me finish—"

"What does she want?"

"We have a list."

"Great, excited to hear your demands." She walked over to her worktable and grabbed a pair of shears. I stepped back, then relaxed as she began cutting flower stems.

"The guitar—" I began.

"No. The guitar belongs in the restaurant."

"Someone's going to end up taking it anyway. It's just on the wall, there's no protection."

"Someone did take it."

"Someone else, someone who wants to sell it or something."

"I am keeping everything he left here exactly where he left it."

"While he toured Europe! He didn't have a house! He didn't know he was going to die." She started to interrupt again, but I continued with the list. "And a Mets cap, and sheet music for 'I Left My Heart in San Francisco,' and his medical bracelet."

She seemed to be trying to figure something out. "Oh my God. The gallery. You planned that? I cannot believe—"

"No! That was a coincidence."

"*Right*. This whole time you've been greasing my wheels to get what you want."

"I wasn't, the gallery was a random thing, I swear. And it's not what I want, it's what Leora wants. And she's entitled to it."

I didn't mention that I was the one who was looking for the bracelet. If this became about us, about the ex-girlfriend and the girl friend, it would turn into something else, a tug-of-war, with the spoils going to whoever was declared the winner. It wouldn't be fair to Leora if it became about that.

Elizabeth snipped off another flower stem, too short I thought, and she seemed to also realize that, tightly squeezing her eyes closed in frustration. "I have a right to something," she said.

"Leora has a bunch of concert shirts."

She put down her shears. "Concert shirts. Are you kidding me? Would you want a bunch of free merch? Is that what you'd accept as a token of your time with Gabe?"

If I were her? "I'd take the shirts."

"His things are here because he lived here. With me. And do you know I wasn't even invited to the cemetery?"

"Why would you be?"

She reared back, like I'd slapped her.

"Look, I'm sorry," I said. "I just don't get it. You were together for, like, a year? I'd understand if you fell deeply in love, but you've made it clear that you think he's some kind of asshole. And a drunk. So if he was just some awful ex to you, then why come to America for his funeral, and why invite me to dinner? Why won't you answer his mother or give me the guitar? If you're already over him, then what are you holding on to?"

"I honestly thought you knew. When we first ran into each other. But then you never mentioned it, and I realized, wow, so he had enough respect for me not to immediately tell you." She gestured her hands off to the side as if the rest were obvious. "I'm pregnant."

"No you're not." I scanned her figure for confirmation. In response, she pulled her apron tighter so there were no gaps between the fabric and her body. The outline of a slightly protruded belly appeared. She let the apron go and it billowed out again, the belly disappearing. Now you see it, now you don't.

"I thought you broke up."

"We did. And then I realized I was pregnant."

Neither of us spoke. Outside, footsteps approached along with the indecipherable din of multiple conversations at once.

Elizabeth said, "They've opened the exterior doors."

"When—"

There was a knock.

"I'm four months along. People are here. I rent this by the hour and I'm responsible for being out before the next class. Excuse me." She brushed past me and opened the door. Her students filed in. I walked past them in the other direction, squeezing between them.

She'd misunderstood me. When I asked *when*, what I meant was: When did Gabe know?

The next fifteen minutes were a year and a second.

How did I get back to my hotel? Slowly planting one foot in front of the other, like a zombie. What was I thinking? Nothing. A void, white noise. Everything. A printer spewing a hundred pages directly on the floor.

In the hotel elevator, I was alone. I scrunched into the corner, taking up as little space as I could. My cheek touched the mirror. The glass was cold. Louis's place didn't have a full-length mirror and it was the first time I'd taken in my entire reflection since I was in this elevator the night before. I'd looked better.

In my room, I washed my face, brushed my teeth, and changed my clothes. I thought if I could physically pull myself together, a mental clarity would follow. When it didn't, I took the classic path of millennial disassociation and checked my phone. A few work emails. No more condolences. So that part at least was over. There were a series of texts and calls from Casey, I'd missed a suit-shopping appointment I'd said I would join for, it had been in my calendar for months, he'd waited for me outside my apartment, which had made him an hour late, forfeiting his time slot.

I texted back *Sorry*

I'm in London

The admission felt like defeat. At least he was asleep. I didn't need any follow-up questions.

I had a few other texts, but the only one I paid attention to was from Leora.

Miracle worker!!! ♡ What about other stuff? Any luck?

Fuck. I'd forgotten the fucking guitar.

I lay down on the bed. I was motionless, but I didn't fall asleep. It was more like I'd been knocked out by a tranquilizer, like my body had simply said "no more," in some act of pathetic surrender.

FIFTEEN

The hotel phone rang. I looked at the nightstand clock. Only an hour had passed. The front desk concierge said, "Yes, Miss Hendricks, your guest is waiting in the lobby and would like to know when you will be downstairs."

"My who?" I looked around the room as if the answer to this question would reveal itself from behind the curtains or under the bed.

A muffled sound, the phone covered by a hand. I heard them ask, "Sorry, what was your name?"

And then the unmistakable raspy alto.

"Yes, I'll come down," I said. "I'll meet her in the . . ."

"The office?" the concierge offered.

The office was the hotel's workspace but it felt more like a lounge. There was one long communal table with low, deep velvet armchairs on both sides of it. Not at all the ideal ergonomic setup, and the hotel was blasting techno-pop from speakers at every corner of the ceiling, so I didn't see how anyone would be able to get any work done here. Though there were a lot of people at these tables in the classic office posture, hunched over laptops. One man was speaking loudly into his cell phone as he quickly scrolled through a spreadsheet. Maybe *office* was a state of mind, a portable attitude for maximum productivity. I thought about the work emails I'd seen earlier, still waiting for me.

All the seats except one were taken. I sat down next to two girls who were sharing a chair, asleep, curled up like kittens. They smelled like fruity liqueur, which made me think of college. They looked around that age. Under the chair, two pairs of high heels were knocked over onto each other, fallen dominoes. While I was waiting for Elizabeth, they woke up, yawning big and dramatically. One whispered in the other's ear, then they slunk out of the chair and headed over to the photo booth. I imagined their conversation: *We just woke up in this hotel lounge. First things first: Coffee? Breakfast? Photos!* I love these girls, I thought. I wanted to be them, having their morning, instead of the reality I was experiencing.

Elizabeth speed-walked toward me, carrying a reusable coffee cup. She held a large white bucket by the handle in the crook of one arm, with a dozen or so small dark maroon flowers left over from her class. Her tote bag was on the shoulder of the other arm. She sat down in the seat the girls had just vacated. "I wouldn't have shown up here, but I didn't have your number."

The light from the photo booth flashed, then a *clunk-clunk* sound.

I said, "I showed up unannounced at a private workshop you were giving, so I can't really fault you for showing up in a public hotel lobby."

"Right." Elizabeth shifted in her seat. "Look, I want to choose my words carefully." She paused, doing just that. "Since I've been sober, my aim is to always be honest. I've learned that it's not worth it to stifle myself. If something pops into my head, I find it's better to just say it, you know?"

Not really. And certainly not recently. If Elizabeth had no filter, I was one of those fancy air purifiers with three layers of filtration I consider buying after every major California fire.

"But I shouldn't have told you about the pregnancy."

This was the second time Elizabeth was backtracking, asking me to allow her to rescind something she regretted saying. It felt less genuine the second time, more like she was someone who liked to do as she pleased, asking for forgiveness later.

"When did Gabe know you were pregnant?" I didn't know why she was here, but since she was, I couldn't spend another minute talking about anything else.

Another *clunk-clunk* from the photo booth.

"August. But that's what I'm trying to say. I shouldn't have told you," she said. She was getting to her point right when I wanted to get back to mine. August? Could she be more specific? "Obviously, I know you and Leora are close, but I was hoping that you could keep this to yourself? Until I'm ready to share the news."

"So why did you tell me?"

"I don't know." She reconsidered. "That's not true." But she didn't say what the truth was. Maybe she was experimenting with a filter.

The two girls passed by, nearly tripping over Elizabeth's bucket, but she pulled it back just in time, adding it to the mountain of things she'd lugged over. I noticed one thing was missing. "Where's the guitar?" I asked.

"I don't know. You have it."

"No I don't."

"You have it. You brought it to my class."

"And then I left it there."

Considering we were two intelligent women, this went on a bit too long. What we discovered was: neither of us had the guitar. I didn't get to ask exactly when Gabe knew, Elizabeth didn't get to find out whether I would tell Leora, and though we both desperately wanted these bits of information, we knew if we didn't hurry and get back to the garden as soon as possible, the guitar might not be there.

SIXTEEN

The demonstration room where I'd left the guitar was locked, but Elizabeth was able to track down the woman with the clipboard by phone. Apparently she had building access, but it wouldn't be of any help to us. She told Elizabeth she'd seen some street musicians who were playing songs in the garden earlier leave with the guitar, she'd assumed it was theirs. "She doesn't know where they went, but she said she's seen them play the market on Sundays."

"Which market?" I asked.

Elizabeth hesitated. "You've already told Leora, haven't you?"

"No." And I wouldn't be talking to her until I found that guitar. I slumped onto one of the garden's stone benches. "I can't believe I lost it."

Elizabeth sat down next to me. "Let's not fall apart immediately. We might still find it. Besides, Gabe had a lot of guitars."

"This one was Leora's. She's had it since college."

"Oh. I didn't know that." She looked skyward. "I *love* that guitar."

We were quiet. I followed her gaze. A flock of small birds flew above us. From below, they looked more like butterflies.

"Though if it was Leora's to begin with, I can understand that," Elizabeth said. She tipped her head back down. "Do I need to hold on to a baseball cap or some sheet music?" She answered herself. "No. That's ridiculous." It was a swift judgment, as if she'd attempted to rationalize her behavior, but ultimately it failed some personal logic test. She took her phone from her tote bag and started texting.

"What are you doing?"

"I'm WhatsApping my mates to see if they'll come over and help us search my flat. Maybe Gabe left something there."

The first good news in hours. "Are you serious?"

She stood up. "I can't guarantee of course. He was always losing things. For all I know this Mets cap is on a bus somewhere in Stockwell by now." She dropped the phone back in her tote, then grabbed the bucket she'd placed on the ground. "And if I help you with this and you don't tell Leora, maybe this can be a little exchange." She chuckled nervously and headed out of the garden.

She was joking. Right? I rushed after her.

"Wait, when you say keep this to myself, you mean until after another trimester when you start telling people or . . . ?" We walked briskly down the sidewalk.

"No, I told my mum and some friends last week. But I'm not ready to talk to Gabe's mum." We stopped at a crosswalk, waiting for the bright green man to appear on the pedestrian signal.

"But you will tell Leora at some point? You're asking me to keep this to myself, but do you mean, like, for a few days, or until the kid is ten?" I imagined returning to Berkeley and telling Leora, *Here's your son's stuff. How was the trip? Oh, nothing of interest to report! Fingers crossed you find out you have a grandchild one day, but you won't be hearing about it from me. Peace!*

Elizabeth shook her head. "I honestly don't know." The light changed. She crossed the street, leaving me behind on the curb. A better negotiating tactic might have been to promise me whatever I wanted so long as I kept my mouth shut. It was only because she didn't do this that I thought maybe I could trust her; maybe she might be as honest as she claimed to be. Seeing this quality, I seized an opportunity. Not for Leora, for myself.

"Wait!" I hurried past two other pedestrians who'd walked between us. I caught up to Elizabeth. "I won't tell Leora, but first can you tell me something?"

"What?" She continued walking. I kept up.

"When exactly did Gabe know you were pregnant? You must have some idea."

"I could probably pinpoint it. I texted before I called to tell him, to see if it was a good time to talk."

"Can you look it up?"

She stopped. A man wearing large headphones nearly collided with her. "Sorry!" she called out. She turned to me. "Why?"

Why? Why would I need to know the exact timing of this news? And why should she tell me? We were on Old Street, it was the same route I'd taken to return to my hotel after Elizabeth said she was pregnant. We'd passed two murals, one looked like a Banksy, the other was elaborate neon-colored graffiti. I must have walked by them earlier but had no memory of the artwork. Because all I'd been thinking was when. *When* did Gabe know? Elizabeth had said August. It could not have been before Joshua Tree. If it was before Joshua Tree, I would never forgive him. I felt two sharp pinches under my arms, a squeeze of sweat. I stepped back from the street and stood under the awning of a clothing store. Elizabeth joined me.

"What's going on?" she asked.

I told her that without him here to tell me himself, every detail was important. I don't think the exact words mattered, it wasn't what I said to Elizabeth, but how I said it. We were standing close enough to each other, I'm sure she could feel my desperation. And I didn't even try to cover it up. Which made it the most honest moment we'd shared.

I took the flower bucket from her so her hands would be free to get out her phone. "And you swear you won't tell Leora?" she asked. I could see Gabe's name on her screen. Her finger hovered over their conversation history.

"I swear."

Angling the phone away from me, Elizabeth scrolled through their texts. At one point, she pressed her lips together and blinked as if holding back emotion. I looked away. I glanced back at Elizabeth. She was still scrolling. There must have been a lot of texts. After Joshua Tree, it was like he'd dropped off the face of the earth, but of course he hadn't. He was only ignoring me, he was still available to everyone else. Including Elizabeth.

She looked up. "It was August eighth at three thirty-five."

I quickly converted the time. The day we left Joshua Tree, 7:35 A.M. Not just the day we left, a half hour after.

"Good?" Elizabeth took the bucket from me.

I blinked. "Yeah."

"Great," she said, heading down the street. Over her shoulder she called out, "C'mon, Tube's this way."

SEVENTEEN

I knew Elizabeth had a dog but I didn't remember I knew until we were at her flat. As she unlocked the door, I heard paws slipping and skittering across a hardwood floor, then frenzied staccato barking.

"Yes, yes, I'm home," Elizabeth said to the small dog jumping at her shins. We squeezed by it, into the entryway. Elizabeth closed the door, bent down to greet the dog. Having welcomed her back, it immediately switched its attention to the stranger in the home, and—still barking—ran concentric circles around my ankles. It was the barking I'd heard a few times when I was on the phone with Gabe.

But of course we'd never formally met. I squatted down to the floor to rub behind its ears. "Who's this?" I asked.

"This is Laurent." Elizabeth hung her tote bag on a pegboard by the door. "He's my stepsister's. I've been temporarily slash permanently dog-sitting, it's a long story." She dropped her keys on an entryway table.

"Is he a Jack Russell?" He was white with brown spots and short-haired.

"Partly, he's a mix, we don't know the rest. Maybe beagle? According to my stepsister's psychic, there's a strong Chihuahua energy. But that could also mean he was a Chihuahua in a past life." She rolled her eyes.

Elizabeth and I had been silent on the Tube. On the way to the flat, we'd made small talk, I'd never been on the Overground line, how much of the Tube was aboveground? What was mass transit like in LA? But we'd gotten all we could out of the subways-of-the-world topic, so I was grateful for Laurent. I could mindlessly chatter about dog breeds, nodding along, while inside I processed what Elizabeth had told me. I was still reviewing the facts.

Fact: the day Gabe left Joshua Tree, Elizabeth told him she was pregnant.

That was it. There was one fact.

But it was a significant fact. It was context. Gabe had received surprising, life-altering news. Of course he'd had to focus on that instead of checking in with me. On the Tube, this had felt like a cause for celebration. After stumbling in the dark, here was a burst of light. From underground to overground. As the buildings of East London flickered by, I reveled in the crucial intel Elizabeth had provided. Who knew the clarity a time-stamped text history could bring? And what if I hadn't come to London? There was that possibility. What if I were still in my house working on my own dead-end theories about what had happened after Joshua Tree? But instead I'd ended up here with Elizabeth. And look what I'd found. Finally I had a reason why Gabe had disappeared. I felt immense relief.

This lasted for one stop.

Because—I thought this as I descended the stairs of the Tube station—a reason was not an excuse. Yes, Elizabeth's news would have been jarring. And I could see needing a day or two to get his head on straight. But after that, why not just tell me? *I got this woman pregnant before we hooked up, so let's put a pin in changing our relationship.* I wouldn't have blamed him. As Elizabeth said, it had happened when they were still dating. Before Joshua Tree. Which made the pregnancy an issue of timing, not betrayal. It would have been an awkward conversation for Gabe and me, but not one that needed to be avoided for a month.

Elizabeth headed into the flat with Laurent traveling behind her. I followed. There was a short hallway directly ahead of us, with three doors. One was open and I could make out an unmade bed, the edge of a bureau, and some clothes on the floor. Elizabeth led us to the kitchen. "Do you want anything?" she asked. "Water? Tea? Coffee? Obviously I don't have alcohol."

"Obviously I don't *want* alcohol. It's the middle of the day." I could tell what she was doing. Making some inference to me being Gabe's enabler, or implying that if he was a lush, I must be the same. "Water's fine."

She shrugged, then took out a glass from a cabinet over the sink. She filled it with tap water and handed it over to me. I looked around for Laurent but didn't see him. The only sound in the room was me slowly sipping my water. Finally I gave in to her insinuation and asked, "Did Gabe drink during the day when he was here?"

Elizabeth shook her head. "Not to my knowledge. If we were at a pub with friends or something like that, but not at home." I thought this proved my point, but she gave me a triumphant look and said, "So I've got you thinking."

"You've got me thinking about what *you* said." I set my glass on the countertop. It was important to clarify that this was not the same as thinking Gabe was an alcoholic.

Elizabeth shrugged again. She opened one of the lower cabinets and said, "Feel free to make yourself comfortable. I've got to feed Laurent." With the mention of his name, Laurent trotted in.

When I entered the living room I understood why Elizabeth had needed to bring in her friends. The kitchen was clean, orderly, but the living room was a mess. Not that it was dirty in a sticky-surfaces or crumbs-on-the-floor way; though there were a few water glasses and mugs left out, a bowl on the coffee table with some left-behind grape stems. It was that things were out of place: an unrolled yoga mat on the jute rug, mail, magazines, and catalogs piled high in front of the television stand. Next to it was a record player on top of a console, the shelf below it full of records, and below that there were more on the floor. Less in an artful stack, more in a forgotten pile.

I didn't care whether Elizabeth's home was cluttered or organized. Her place was fine. Actually, I liked it. There were plants everywhere, the space had a verdant, alive quality, and there was a tall brass lamp with a tangerine shade in the corner of the room that I immediately loved. The mess only stood out because it made me think, Oh, this isn't the type of apartment where everything has a place and is returned to that place. Things could (easily) disappear here. Which I knew meant Elizabeth hadn't been stonewalling me. She really didn't know if the rest of Gabe's things were in her flat. Which also meant: maybe they weren't.

Elizabeth came into the living room with a vase and the dark maroon flowers from the bucket. She pushed aside the mail on the coffee table, set the vase down, then dropped each stem in one at a time, both casual and precise. "I'm going to change, clean up a bit," she said. "We'll start going through everything when my friends arrive." She headed down the hallway.

I walked over to the record player, glancing at the albums on the floor. Elton John's *Tumbleweed Connection*. Lou Reed's *Transformer*. Marianne Faithfull's *Live in Hollywood*. Separate Bedrooms' *Dodger Stadium*.

The *Dodger Stadium* cover was a black-and-white aerial shot of the ballpark. The grainy silhouettes of three figures on the field were intentionally barely visible. I turned the album over to the image of Gabe at a piano, a guitar propped next to his feet. I stared at the photo. Why didn't you just tell me, I thought. Is that why you called me? Were you going to tell me at the hotel? Gabe's head was facing the piano, away from me, and I imagined this small image of him turning around and looking at me, filling me in on everything.

Of course the tiny piano Gabe didn't turn around. He couldn't tell me. If I had gone to the hotel, then maybe I'd know. If I had gone to the hotel. That was a possibility that gnawed at me, and if I didn't keep moving, it would devour me. If I had gone to the hotel, everything about the night would have been different. If I had gone to the hotel, he wouldn't have slipped. And if he hadn't disappeared in the first place, I wouldn't be thinking about any of this, everything would be different.

That was enough for me. I was tired of trying to figure out what Gabe was thinking. I placed *Dodger Stadium* on the shelf with the other records. Then I took it out again and peered into the sleeve, just to see if maybe, somehow, the sheet music for "I Left My Heart in San Francisco" had been slipped in. It had not. I put it back, then I went through the other albums on the floor, checking each of them for the sheet music. This is the reason I'm here, I reminded myself. I'd already lost the guitar, I owed Leora the Mets cap as well as the sheet music. Not to mention the bracelet I still wanted to find for myself.

Elizabeth reappeared, wearing leggings and a tank top. The leggings hugged her body in a way her other outfits had not. Now knowing what to look for, I could see signs of the pregnancy. Though it wasn't much of a bump. And I'd never met her, so would I have known what were curves and what was gestation? She held her phone in her hand. "My friends just messaged. They're here," she said. She walked to the door, then paused. There was a long gray cardigan hanging on the entryway pegboard. She threw it on, once again concealing her bump. "I haven't told everyone yet," she said in a warning tone. I wanted to say if I wasn't going to tell Leora, then I for sure wasn't going to tell Elizabeth's friends, but she didn't wait for my response and instead opened the door.

The first to arrive was a couple. Jeremy and Sungmi. Elizabeth introduced us. Jeremy was a musician. "Orchestral," he added. "You haven't heard of me." He was English, white with brown hair, dressed in a very trim, neat way, with his shirt tucked into tailored pants. Sungmi was Asian, and I guessed by her name she was Korean (Casey had a cousin named Sungmi).

"I love your necklace," I said to her.

"Oh, thank you." She swept her long black hair over her shoulder, away from the brown leather cord around her neck. At the center was an Elsa Peretti–style jug charm. I noticed the absence of a British accent. She was American too. Jeremy made a joke about how Sungmi would have someone to discuss Oregon state politics with. This was a joke for him and Sungmi, and it was barely a joke for Sungmi. She rolled her eyes and said, "I don't know why Jeremy thinks the word *Oregon* is so hilarious."

Next to arrive were Elizabeth's friends from university: Tasha, a tall white woman with short brown hair, and Divya, a petite Indian woman with that feisty energy people often expect us short women to have. *Spunky*, a word I lived in fear of, was the perfect description of Divya.

She took charge right away. "Okay, Julia, what's on the list?" She clapped her hands and turned to me, like she was an elementary school teacher calling me up to the front of the classroom to give my presentation.

"Well, his guitar. Which we—"

"Not the guitar from the restaurant?" Divya balked. "But it's part of Fleur Bleue history!" Elizabeth waved her hand in the air, as if to say, *Leave it.*

I continued. "And then there's also some sheet music. 'I Left My Heart in San Francisco.' A gift from his mother. A Mets cap. From his father. And his medical bracelet. That he wore all the time." I didn't need to get into the origin of the bracelet. Divya already had it out for me.

"Right, okay," she said. "We take everything out, empty every cabinet and shelf. Then we each take an area and go through it. When you're done with your area, let me know." She directed us to different quadrants of the flat. Sungmi and Jeremy would cover the living room and kitchen, Divya, Tasha, and Elizabeth would handle the bedroom and bathroom, and I, odd woman out, was given the hallway closet. Before we could start, more friends of Elizabeth's showed up. Emmanuel from the restaurant arrived next with trays and tins of food. "Sustenance for the search," he declared. His wife, Gloria, followed. She was a plump woman, stunning, with the same complexion as Emmanuel, and she was wearing a dramatic plum lip color. She looked so familiar I almost asked if we'd met before. Then I realized it was her social media profile I'd used to search for Elizabeth.

The next knock at the door was Paula, the hostess from the restaurant, with a man I recognized as one of the waiters at Fleur Bleue. And Louis.

He kissed me once on each cheek. "Hello, how are you?" His post-hookup-etiquette game was smooth.

"Oh fine," I said. "You?"

"All well here." He had sleepy eyes. The night before, I'd thought he was tired. But no, those were just his eyes. I liked them. And he seemed like a cool person. I didn't have any regrets about going home with him. That didn't mean I was happy to see him.

"I didn't know you and Elizabeth were close," I whispered. Meaning I wouldn't have hooked up with you if I knew you were.

"We're not really. Joel invited me." That must have been the name of the waiter I'd recognized.

Louis looked around the room. "So this is the memorial you were talking about?"

I'd forgotten I'd said that. "Oh no, I don't think the memorial's going to happen."

"Was this supposed to be a memorial?" Emmanuel popped into our conversation.

"No, no," I said. "We were thinking about it, but it didn't come together." True-*ish*. The royal *we*. And it hadn't come together.

Emmanuel blew right past this. "It's a brilliant idea. None of us were able to make the trip to America. We absolutely should do it."

"We should get looking," I said. "I'm sure Elizabeth doesn't want us here all day."

Emmanuel puffed air through his nostrils. "Of course she does. She doesn't want to be alone. Why would she need eleven people to look for one man's belongings?"

I agreed Elizabeth didn't want to be alone, but I was pretty sure it was being alone with me that was the issue.

"Excuse me." I ducked between them. As I headed to search through the closet, Louis mumbled, "There *is* a lot of rubbish to get through in here."

TWO BROKEN UMBRELLAS, ONE WORKING UMBRELLA THAT OPENED midsearch and nearly stabbed me in the throat, a deflated yoga ball, and a lot of old coats.

But nothing from the list. I'd essentially spent a half hour organizing Elizabeth's closet. No one else had any luck either. But we did locate other things Gabe had left behind. Divya found two hoodies in Elizabeth's bedroom, Sungmi spotted a music memoir on a bookshelf, and Jeremy retrieved a small electronic keyboard from a kitchen cabinet. It was his keyboard, he told us; he'd loaned it to Gabe. He seemed relieved, and I imagined he had been looking for the right time to ask Elizabeth for it back and was grateful he wouldn't have to stumble through the discomfort of the request. Minus the keyboard, we piled the Gabe detritus on the kitchen table. I was putting everything I'd taken out of the closet back when Divya shouted, "Found it!"

EIGHTEEN

Divya waved a blur of blue and orange as the rest of us crowded into Elizabeth's bedroom. "We got the Mets cap!" she yelled.

"Where did you find it?" Sungmi asked.

Elizabeth blushed. "Behind the bed. It must have tipped off his head one morning."

As if we didn't get the point, Divya giggled. "We also found a bra and a pair of knickers."

I pointed to a T-shirt on Elizabeth's bed. "What's that?" Though I already knew.

"Oh, we found this in here too." Elizabeth held up the shirt. It was white with green letters that spelled out BARCELONER. I was there when Gabe had bought it in Barcelona. Ironic tees were very big at the time, as was indie emo culture, and when we found something that combined the two, we were so pleased with ourselves. The T-shirt was old, nearly falling apart, it had been worn to pieces. Elizabeth folded it. "Leora didn't ask for this, right? I'd like to keep it."

I wanted to snatch it out of her hands. But I had specifically suggested she take a T-shirt as a consolation prize and the bracelet was still up for grabs. "Of course," I said. "Why not?"

"Great!" Elizabeth handed the cap over to me. "One down."

I took it wordlessly. Elizabeth placed the shirt in her bureau. I followed everyone else out of the room. As I did, I glanced back. On top of the bureau was a jewelry box. Had it been searched? And if it had and the bracelet was there, would anyone tell me? If I hadn't noticed the T-shirt, would she have mentioned it? Could I trust her, or her friends whose allegiance was to her, to tell me everything they found?

After that I continued to search, but I also kept tabs on everyone else's progress. I skulked around, looking over people's shoulders, ostensibly with encouraging remarks or to offer my help, but actually making sure they disclosed what they found. And when I was sure the coast was clear, I went back to Elizabeth's room, straight to the jewelry box. I lifted the lid. It was tiered, with many drawers and compartments. On the first level was a jade ring in the same style as the garnet one she wore, a few gold chain necklaces tangled together, several single earrings missing a match, and a silver locket. I opened the locket. It was a picture of a man who shared Elizabeth's jawline. From the warm hue of the photo and the ringer tee he was wearing, I could tell it was from the seventies, and that it was her father. This part wasn't any of my business, I knew that. Every bit of my usual self, my normal instincts, said this was Elizabeth's personal space. But I wasn't my usual self. I wanted to find the bracelet, I wanted to know why Gabe took it off. I glanced at the door, then gingerly lifted the first compartment.

"Need something?"

I jumped. I turned to see Divya stepping out of Elizabeth's closet.

"Just checking," I said.

"I already checked there."

I had one of those moments when you suddenly shift away from yourself and land in your mother's perspective. I imagined how my mom would see this: I was in an apartment in England with strangers, seconds away from getting a reputation as the Black jewelry designer who stole instruments from restaurants and rifled through people's personal items.

I closed the lid. "Sorry." I smiled at Divya. "Didn't realize you already checked."

I stepped into the bathroom to have a second to myself, but that was the thing with an apartment-wide search; there were people everywhere. When I opened the door, it bumped against something. Elizabeth was on the floor, clearing out the bottom cabinet under the sink. "Great, this will go faster if I can hand stuff up to you."

It was a small bathroom. I squeezed in through the door and wedged myself against a wall. Elizabeth handed me an economy-size bottle of color-safe shampoo. I glanced down at her roots. No sign at all that she'd need this shampoo. I placed the bottle on the edge of the sink. She passed over some small paper cups, I placed those on top of the toilet. Of course I felt weird going through Elizabeth's things. She was still a stranger, but I knew she colored her hair, she couldn't seem to throw out an umbrella, and her dad had crinkles around his eyes when he smiled.

"This is empty," Elizabeth said. She pulled out another shampoo bottle. She twisted off the cap and the smell of campfire and marshmallow filled the tiny space. I froze. I recognized the scent. Gabe. Or Gabe's shampoo. The label said *Maple Cedar.* I took the smallest inhale and I think Elizabeth did too. Then she tossed it in the trash.

Her face contorted, her nose wrinkling a few times before her features relaxed. "Sorry," she said, noticing that I noticed. "Nausea." She pointed to the bottle of shampoo in the trash. "You know, I used to love that smell. Now I think I'm going to be sick." She took a deep breath. "There, it's passed."

I recognized these facial gymnastics. From our dinner the night before. "Is that why you jumped up from the table last night?"

"Yes. Morning sickness isn't only in the morning." Then she added, "But I could have come back after." She stood up. "This room's done."

After our initial boon with the Mets cap, there came a dry spell. We found Gabe's guitar case, but with no guitar to put in it, it was a hollow victory.

Everyone was quiet as we put Elizabeth's flat back together again. Was that it? Were we done? A group gathered in the living room, waiting for Divya. She was the captain who'd given us our orders and she'd have to be the one to call it.

Emmanuel stood up. "Could I have everyone's attention? Divya, could you come in here?" We all turned, hopeful, as she walked in, but she was empty-handed. She shook her head.

"All right then," Emmanuel said. "I just want to say, while we're here together at this London memorial for Gabe . . ."

Elizabeth raised an eyebrow. Oh my God, I thought, I've accidentally organized a wake.

216

Emmanuel continued. "So Gabe was a piano player. And a guitarist. And a singer. All these things. I mean, I'm just a chef. I do one thing." Emmanuel glanced at Gloria. She had a look like, babe, you need to wrap this up. Listen to your wife, I thought.

"I'm getting off track. What I mean is . . ." He looked up at the ceiling, exhaled, then back at us. "He could do all that. But he also had this other talent, this ability with people. You know, he reminded me of Gloria, in that she can be in a room and know exactly what's going on with everyone in it. We'll go to an anniversary party and I'll think that was so nice, what a lovely couple. And after we get home, Gloria says, 'Oh, couldn't you tell they're about to get a divorce?' Gabe was like that. Always checking on everyone in the room, making sure each person had what they needed. He would have been a great host. Sometimes when he was in the restaurant, I thought he was coming for your job, Paula."

Paula laughed. "Me too." Next to her, Elizabeth smiled.

The guy who'd walked in with Louis, I couldn't recall his name (Jack? Joe?), said, "Remember when he—"

He didn't even get the words out. They all started laughing. Elizabeth said, "Bringing out the slices of pie . . ."

Paula joined in, waving her hands. "And I'm saying, we don't *serve* pie, I've never *seen* pie here, that's not our *pie!*"

Even though they didn't work at the restaurant, Jeremy and Tasha seemed to know the story too. I waited for the laughter to die down, chewing on my cheek, feeling like I was a kid who'd been tagged out and was waiting to rejoin the game.

"Right, right," Emmanuel said. "And with his fans: If I were him, I would tell these people, get away, leave me alone, I played for you, can't you see I'm eating? But he would say hello, answer questions. I thought, Okay, when does he turn it off, when does he replenish? Not when he was alone. I watched him, and he was always listening. To others, maybe to the music in his head. And then as I get to know him, I see he does replenish. With one person, he can be himself, he can complain, get upset, cry and laugh as big as he wants." He paused. It's almost too embarrassing to admit, but at first, I thought he was talking about me.

"With the woman he loved. Elizabeth." Emmanuel placed his hands together, kissed his fingertips, then threw his hands forward, sending the kiss in Elizabeth's direction. He finished with, "This is how I remember Gabe. Loving you. And loving all of us. Even though we knew him so briefly, he gave so much, it was enough for a lifetime." Tasha and Sungmi were crying now.

When we met, I'd felt an immediate ease with Gabe. But Emmanuel had tapped into something—Gabe was someone who put *everyone* at ease. I'd been one of the beneficiaries of this, but not the only one. Same tour, different cities. Now I felt nauseous.

Jeremy's keyboard was on the floor in front of him, he pulled it onto his lap. He tapped two notes—plink! plink! Then, as more notes followed, I recognized the song. I'd probably heard it a hundred times, it began with a long instrumental intro, Gabe playing the piano for about a minute. I watched as the others placed it. By the time Jeremy reached the vocals part, everyone knew he was playing "Pencil and Paper" by Separate Bedrooms. Sungmi and Paula sang with him.

> *They said you won't have a calculator in your pocket*
> *So, son, don't take the easy way out it*

Tasha joined in, as did Emmanuel and Gloria. So much for the British stiff upper lip. Elizabeth's friends didn't seem to have that condition at all. Elizabeth and I were the only ones not singing, but then Gloria put her arm around Elizabeth, and I guess something about the physical connection to someone already singing made her add her voice to the group.

> *Mom's a quadratic equation, Dad is fumbling at the door*
> *They tell me it's not working*
> *Have they ever even tried?*
> *Not to take the easy way out it*

It turns out it's difficult to resist a sing-along. Especially when it's a song you love. I fell in with them on *easy way out it*, my voice wobbling. I will not cry, I told myself. I will not cry at this slapdash wake. I cleared my throat, then tried again.

> *Some people just don't have the brain for this*
> *Some people just don't have the heart for this*

We were heading into the chorus. It was the type of song that built up with an inevitable crescendo. Gabe took you on his emotional journey: his parents helping him with his math homework, urging him not to use a calculator and take the easy way out; the painful irony that at the same time, they were breaking up, refusing, from Gabe's perspective, to figure it out. You took this climb with him, up, up, further, then by the time he got to the apex of his emotion, you were right there with him. You had to belt it out. We tossed singing aside and yelled.

> *You'll use this when you're older*
> *You'll need this when you're older*
> *You should've given me something I could use now that*
>   *I'm older*

Laurent, excited by our voices, barked and ran around the room.

"Pencil and Paper" had become one of those anthems for people our age, like the Outkast song about love or the Arcade Fire song about growing up in a pre-digital age. All those songs were saying the same thing: When I was young, I thought life was going to be like this. Then it turned out it was something else.

By the end of the song, we were spent. The room was hot. Emmanuel unbuttoned the top of his shirt. Tasha and Gloria opened a few windows. Fresh air swept into the room, mixing with our collective sweat, a condensation filled the space.

"Guess we needed to get that out," Elizabeth said. She wiped at her eyes.

"Hear hear," said Emmanuel, who had apparently appointed himself master of ceremonies for the afternoon.

We shared sheepish looks. After completing this radically communal act, we were returning to our own bodies.

THERE WAS NOTHING MORE TO DO. WE'D SEARCHED, WE'D FOUND the Mets cap but not the sheet music or bracelet. I'd lost the guitar. I still didn't have the bracelet. Elizabeth and I followed her friends to the door. They apologized they couldn't be of more help.

No, I thought. This can't be the end of the search. "Where did he play basketball?" I asked.

"Basketball?" Elizabeth shook her head. "He liked baseball."

"Yeah, he liked baseball. He liked sports," I said. "It's pretty hard to get a whole baseball team together, but he'd play pickup basketball sometimes?" I hesitated because I'd recently learned a lot I didn't know about Gabe. Maybe he didn't play basketball anymore. But then Emmanuel interrupted. "Yes! He did. I joined them once. They let the old man play. I have the email list. From when we were figuring out a time. I'll reach out."

"Oh," Elizabeth said. Her face flushed. "Thank you, Emmanuel." She turned to me. "Like I told you, I have no idea. His things could be anywhere."

"Maybe check David's?" Paula suggested to Elizabeth.

"Oh right, David and Alice." Elizabeth explained to me. "They're regulars at the restaurant. They're an older couple, they have a boat on the canal. David's a retired session musician. He and Gabe would play together sometimes. Could be worth a try? And maybe someone could check with the owner of that pub he went to?"

"On it," Divya volunteered.

"They live on a boat. It's quite small," Elizabeth said to me, "so I think it will just be you and me going. And Laurent. He needs to get out."

I gave a quick nod. We thanked everyone as they left. I hugged Emmanuel. I gave Louis the same double-cheek kiss he'd given me when he arrived. I was grateful for our night together, but it was easy to let him go.

When it was just me and Elizabeth, she grabbed a dog leash from the pegboard by the door and called out, "Laurent!" He bounded over. She leaned down to attach the leash to his collar, then ran her hand over one of his ears. He pushed his short black snout into her knee. She sprang back up. "Shall we head out?" As the door closed behind us, I noticed Elizabeth had also placed some of the dark maroon flowers on a table by the door. She said, "Chocolate cosmos, of course." Then, when she saw my confusion, added, "Gabe's favorite flower."

I nodded, like I knew Gabe had a favorite flower. Clearly it was a detail formed out of his relationship with a florist. Like the dog and these London friends. And the baby.

At the bus stop, when the bus arrived, Elizabeth asked if I wanted to sit on the top deck. "It's your first time in London."

"Sure, why not?" We climbed to the upper portion of the bus. Maybe we were both emotionally spent from the day so far. Why not play tour guide and visitor?

It wasn't too crowded, so we were each able to have two seats to ourselves. She sat on the aisle of her row. I took the window of mine. I checked my phone. Another message from Leora following up. I ignored it. When I had everything, then I'd text her.

The bus stopped and a few more people got on, Elizabeth gave her seats to an older couple and joined me.

"What do you think?" she asked. "Of the city?"

"It's great. And your friends are great too. I understand why Gabe liked it here."

"And when you had just me to go on, you couldn't see why he would stick around?"

She had a point. As we'd searched her flat, I'd understood there was something all the objects we'd found so far had in common. The fact that they were in London, with Elizabeth. Why would Gabe leave the most important things he owned with another girlfriend of the week?

Because she wasn't.

When Gabe and I talked about our relationships, it was mostly to vent or complain. I assumed, when I didn't hear much about Elizabeth, that she wasn't important. It was the opposite. Who needs to constantly update their friend when their partner is making them happy?

And even if she had been just another girlfriend, she wasn't anymore. They were having a baby. Or Elizabeth was having a baby that would have also been Gabe's, past tense.

There was Gabe, and there was me and Gabe. And now Elizabeth was mixed in too. Not like in a bouquet, where you could add a stem here, switch out a rose for a dahlia there. It was more like a painting where, once the colors merged on the canvas, it was done, they dried that way. There was no altering it without destroying the whole thing.

I didn't know much about Gabe and Elizabeth. It was too late to ask Gabe. But I was here in London with Elizabeth, she was right next to me. I could ask her. So I did. And this is what she told me.

NINETEEN

I met Gabe on a shoot. I used to pick up extra money as a food photographer, styling cakes and roasts for friends' cookbooks. So I was called in—it must have been a last-minute thing, I don't know why they thought of me—for this "Men in Music" spread. And the idea was that they would hold vegetables. Like, *Look what's fresh: this bloke's music and also turnips!* It was the strangest shoot. I was assigned Gabe. And a tomato. And I kept getting up close to the tomato, setting it up for the most flattering shot—yes, tomatoes have their good sides too—and when I showed Gabe the previews on my camera, he said, "I don't mean to be an asshole, but I think they want to see me too." Of course they did. I wasn't used to photographing humans! Which I told him. And he said it was fine, he would just have to make himself more vegetable. He could grab some green paint? Or we could go by a grocery store and buy some large lettuce leaves? I could not stop laughing. It was ridiculous. I don't know why they sent me to that job. My mum said it was so I could meet Gabe. But she's a nutter. Anyway, we did go to the grocery store after that. Then I made him some soup at my place. A light vegetable soup. And Gabe went right for it. The soup and me. And it seemed like a fun one-night kind of thing to tell friends. I mean, he was American. He was a musician. He was seven years younger.

I said right away let's keep this casual. We hung out when he was in town. If I had a free night, we'd give each other a ring. I was busy going from Paris to London, getting the restaurant ready, juggling both businesses. And then . . . he came to my pop-up in Paris. That's when I thought, What's going on here? This doesn't feel casual. I'd forgotten I was the one who'd drawn the original boundaries. So I asked him out. Properly, like on a date, and it went from there.

He told me about the secret shows and that he'd never done one in a restaurant, so pretty soon after it opened, we organized one for Fleur Bleue. It was fantastic. People would come in expecting a new place to eat and then Separate Bedrooms would be there playing a secret show. It was so secret that people didn't even know they were going to the concert. The password was: Are you willing to pay for dinner? Yes? Right this way! Also my new boyfriend, the professional musician, is going to serenade you. Eventually word started to get out, so we pulled back and made it a special-occasion kind of thing. But those initial dinners were lovely.

And I told him up front when we started dating that I wanted a baby. That was the next step for me. It was still early days, we didn't discuss it again for a while, but eventually I had to bring it up. I said, 'I could see myself with you. This is serious. I want a child. Could you be in?' He said possibly, down the road. Which was fine. I could wait. It was going well. I wasn't going to push anything. We were already moving fast.

He started working on his next album and we thought, Why not stay here for a bit? He properly moved in. I was taking care of Laurent by then. Temporarily. It was during my stepsister's divorce. They had just gotten him and then the marriage went south and my flat was the closest thing they had to Switzerland. It was Gabe who said why don't you keep him? Poor Laurent, I just realized he's been through two breakups. Two broken homes. There's a good boy, you're all right, you're a good sport!

Okay, so where was I? I mean, it was fine. We were together sharing a lovely little life. It was all peachy. And then it wasn't. It was like having a sturdy hammock that's swinging in the breeze and then one day you realize, wow, this is sagging in the middle, I'm not sure how many swings it's got left in it? And then next thing you know it's collapsing.

There were times when his age really showed. He always wanted to laugh things off, before we'd even had a chance to get *into* things. He made me feel like such a shrew. Like an old shrew wagging my finger. I'm not that woman! I was wasted most of my twenties. I'm sober but I still know how to have fun, I'm up for a laugh. That makes me sound like someone who does not know how to have fun at all, but I do. But then I adjusted to make up for him. If he wasn't going to take anything seriously, I had to take it doubly seriously.

Sometimes when we got into an argument, he'd sing his apology. He'd *sing*, Julia. I couldn't stay mad of course, his voice would melt me. It was so manipulative! But you know, I did the same thing. I just kept feeding him. To get out of a fight. And we were fighting a lot.

I don't even know about what. *Everything*. It was like he'd never fought with someone before. Always testing to see what he could get away with. Can I raise my voice? Can I scream? Is this allowed? It was. I'd rather have it out, I don't care. But it seemed like it wasn't even about me, he just couldn't believe he could yell at *someone*. I mean, I've listened to the first album. I know he didn't grow up in a yelling house. He grew up with two parents coldly stalking around him, he didn't know what the hell was going on with them. I mean, that song we just sang? It's like, okay, then what happened? What'd you learn from all this? What was their problem in the end? What was *yours*? Stop blaming your father and trying to please your mother and step into your own life. Where's the growth? I know I sound like a typical sober person on their high horse. But it's true. You have to do the work.

It was tiring, having to show him how to have an adult relationship. He could be such a baby.

Which I kind of fell for—for a bit. I mean, I wanted to be a mother, I wanted to care for someone. But then I thought, Wait, no, Elizabeth, not this kind of baby. My mum said this is what you get for living with a man under thirty. Exactly, she was all gung-ho at first, completely charmed by him, then she acted like she'd known all along. Then there were our schedules. At first, I thought it was great that he was always working and touring. I had work too. But if we were going to have a child together, I needed to know he was going to be there and that we could communicate. I had thought about having a child alone. I was prepared to do that. I didn't need a half partner. That seemed worse than going at it on my own. And so I asked if he had thought about it. He had and he wasn't ready. He wasn't at that point in his life. I mean, I understand, he wasn't even thirty yet. And I still stayed with him. Honestly if that was our only problem, we wouldn't have had a problem. I mean, I don't think I could have stayed forever, but it would have been different.

Then one night we really got into it. We were in St. Ives. It's a beach town people go to. Not the South of France, but it's convenient from here. There's a museum there you'd love, actually. We were staying by the water, near this little boutique hotel. They'd commissioned me to do floral arrangements. He'd figured out a way to do a secret show there, but I had work the next morning, figuring out the floral delivery for the hotel, the placement of everything, so I didn't go. You know, it's great to see him perform, but I had seen it before and needed to work. The next morning when I woke up, he was sitting at the kitchen table, completely hungover, face in a coffee cup. This is after I'd already brought up that I thought he was drinking too much, and he'd told me I was making a big deal out of things. And it was like, do I have to babysit you to make sure you take care of yourself?

And he said, "Elizabeth, when we got together, you said, 'I'm sober, but you don't have to be.'"

I said, "That's because you were a social drinker! I'm not going to stop anyone from having a glass of wine with dinner or a pint with mates. But this is beyond."

"So now you're asking me not to drink?"

"Yes. I'm asking you not to drink. But not for my comfort. See if you can go without it. If you don't have a problem, then it won't be hard to stop."

"I'm not the only musician who drinks."

"You want to play the tortured-artist card? Look at Amy Winehouse."

"You're bringing up Amy Winehouse? Are you serious right now?" He said I was behaving like I was in an after-school special, but I said yes, I was fucking serious and that becoming an addict was not going to make him a better artist.

He was stuck on that fourth album. I think everything had come easy to him so far, and when it was time to put in real work, he didn't know how to do it. He had no idea how to motivate himself and it terrified him.

And I tried to tell him I understood that. I said, "Look, I make art too."

He said, "I wouldn't call what you're doing art. You put flowers together. They're already beautiful, they're *flowers*. You didn't *make* the flowers, Lizzy."

He knew I hated when people called me Lizzy.

And then he said I was coming up with reasons not to move to America with him, and I said there were loads of reasons not to move to America with him. He said he wasn't going to spend another minute in my soggy country. And then we went round and round about all of that. You know, telling you now, it's so clear it was over right when he called me Lizzy, but it took us a few more hours to realize. I told him it was over and he could get the hell out. We didn't see each other again. Then, weeks later, I found out I was pregnant. And eventually I told him.

And that's been a lot. We were still figuring things out and I hadn't had a chance to get my head on straight about all of it. I wasn't ready to start communicating with his mother about his things when I didn't even know what I should be hanging on *to*. I mean, this child will have a right to some memory of its father. So I wasn't ready for Leora. I needed time. And I think it was incredibly pushy of her to assume we would all be on her timeline. I really wasn't trying to be a bitch. But when you came into my workshop, telling me this is how it has to be and I have to do this and that, it made my blood boil. It made me think of him and how when we were together, just because I wouldn't go with *his* flow, then I was being difficult. And it was happening all over again. I know what you must have thought. What type of person would not answer a grieving mother? But I'm grieving too and I'm going to be a mother and I just needed time. I needed some time.

TWENTY

Elizabeth looked at me, scanning my face for a reaction. She'd talked through the bus ride, as we reached our stop, and continued while we walked a block.

I didn't know what to say. There was an immediate obligation to take Gabe's side, the instinct to take any friend's side. I would have felt the same way if Nneka's husband or Rose's boyfriend had complained to me about them. I wanted to say, *Weird, that doesn't sound like him at all.* And it didn't sound like Gabe. Not quite. Though it sounded *enough* like Gabe for me to know Elizabeth was telling the truth. There was something about the way she described him. How he spoke, how he flirted, how he fought.

And there was a certain etiquette when hearing about a breakup. The same when offering condolences for any loss.

I said, "I'm sorry."

"Thank you." She said it quickly, with a rush of gratitude. Then, surprised by her own response, she made a little embarrassed noise that was somewhere between a throat clearing and a closed mouth chuckle.

According to a sign we passed, we'd reached the entrance of Victoria Park. I smelled fresh bread and coffee and saw there was a café up ahead with people in line. Others were milling about nearby on benches, stretched out on the grass, eating their recently acquired orders. My stomach rumbled. Laurent pulled at his leash toward the food and I related to the instinct, but Elizabeth pointed out our path, in the opposite direction. We walked away from the café, through the park. Big yellow leaves were scattered along the grass.

She took out a pack of cigarettes, then, noticing my shock, said, "Don't worry, I'm not going to smoke. Sometimes I just take out the pack. I like the smell." She put the pack to her nose, then sighed. "Honestly, what I really want is a drink." She chuckled at my surprise. "I'm not a prohibition nut! I see the benefits of alcohol, it just didn't work for me. There were pros and cons. Like anything. There were good times, with Gabe, obviously," she said. "You only remember the worst at the end. That's how you move on, you know."

I did. Me, Gabe, Elizabeth, Jabari, everyone I knew, we were all so brutal about our exes. In a way we'd never talk about anyone else. There was something so cathartic about post-breakup critique, as if you'd just been released from an NDA and had to immediately hold a press conference revealing your former partner's flaws.

I nodded. Elizabeth looked skeptical. "Though *do* you know? How were you and Gabe able to become friends after you dated? Do you do that with all the men you date? I mean, I am friend*ly* with some of my exes, but not like you were, not close like that."

"We were young. It was short, it wasn't really anything. The St. Ives of relationships."

Why do you keep saying that, I could hear Gabe say.

Because you disappeared, so looks like I was right, I argued in my head.

Maybe I was coming back.

Maybe maybe maybe maybe. Too late now.

We descended a flight of concrete stairs, meeting a dirt towpath at the end. Right beside it was a canal. I'd had no idea there was a canal in the middle of London, or technically, the eastern part of London. Laurent strained at his leash, pulling Elizabeth toward the small boats on the edge of the canal. "Okay, Laurent, stop. Sit. Sit here." Laurent froze exactly on command. He *was* a well-trained dog. There were other people on the path, a woman in a windbreaker briskly walked past us. A man and a woman, also out for a walk with their dog, a poodle, followed. The poodle and Laurent briefly sniffed each other before they were pulled apart.

Elizabeth pointed at one of the docked boats a few yards away, it was red with *Betty* written on the side. After she tied Laurent to a post along the path, we walked over to the boat. A couple in their seventies greeted us at the door. Elizabeth introduced us. David, American and Black, wearing an Alice Coltrane T-shirt with the sleeves cut off, revealing the lean muscles and sagging skin typical of a sinewy older-man frame; and Alice, English, with an ethnic heritage I couldn't place. She had a deep tan complexion, frizzy red hair, with crinkles at her eyes and lips. Elizabeth and I stepped into the boat. It rocked back and forth with the addition of our weight.

"Julia!" David exclaimed. "Great to meet you! 'Julia, seashell eyes.' 'Our youth got me to play the part, and I was trimmed in Madam Julia's *gown*.' Diahann Carroll in that nurse's uniform; *my girl!*" He said this all in a rhythmic tone, holding the note on certain syllables, like a spontaneous spoken word ode to me. He finished off this introduction by whistling the *Julia* sitcom theme as he threw his arms into the air in an operatic flourish. He had what Gabe called drummer's energy. Not always drummers per se, but always people who seem to be frantically in search of a beat. They speak with their hands, leap from one subject to the next, calling up a file of facts you most likely didn't ask for but that in the end are fascinating.

"Hello, Julia," Alice said. She had the opposite energy of David.

The boat was one narrow room with a small kitchenette setup at the front and then in the back, a dining banquette. They led us to the banquette. Elizabeth and I squeezed in with David. Alice said, "I'll get us some tea." She only had to take a step backward to be in the kitchen again. Most of the space went to instruments. There was a trumpet, a trombone, two guitars; an upright bass was leaning against a corner, and then next to that a piano (how had they gotten a piano in here?). It was a jazz club on water.

"We can't stay long," Elizabeth said. "I wanted to know if Gabe left anything here. Specifically some sheet music. 'I Left My Heart in San Francisco.' I thought because you played together?"

"Might be." David stood up and opened a cabinet above the banquette. The cabinet was filled with sheet music. Some pages were crumpled at the bottom, others were damp, or ripped and torn at the edges. Given the condition they were in, I hoped 'I Left My Heart in San Francisco' wasn't there.

I noticed Elizabeth had only mentioned the sheet music. "And his bracelet," I said. I spoke almost in a whisper. Elizabeth studied me. I shifted away from her. I cleared my throat and spoke louder. "The silver medical one he always wore."

"Yes of course, we know it," Alice said. "He never took it off."

"He did at night," Elizabeth said. "Before bed."

She was thinking of his watch. The bracelet stayed on. But it wasn't the time to be a stickler about accuracy. Her eyes were still on me.

Alice said, "Was he not wearing it when he . . . ? Is that how he . . . ? Why he . . . ?"

"No, no, no," Elizabeth and I said in unison, rushing to put that thought out of her head.

"Though there are strange things like that." Alice rubbed her neck. "Objects keep us safe. I believe that. My nan wore a cross around her neck all her life, it was given to her on her wedding day and she never took it off, and then one evening, she places it on the kitchen counter and walks into her bedroom. The next morning, she's passed. She wasn't even sick. My great-aunt thought it was because she was ready, she knew it was her time." She quickly added, "But that's not what happened to Gabe, of course. He was a young man."

"I don't know," David said. "Eartha Kitt told me herself that there was one day where she went to see James Dean, and she could tell from hugging him that something was wrong and then the next day, bam! He was dead."

Alice responded, "Then sounds like Eartha's the one who knew."

"Someone knew." David swiped his hands across his pants, then closed the cabinet door. "It's not here," he said. "Honestly I didn't think it would be. We never played that one here. I would have noticed too. I have a system."

Elizabeth and I looked at the cabinet, then at each other. "Clearly," she said.

Alice passed me a cup of tea. "And how's My Grandmother's Collection? Have you finished your friend's wedding gift? What was his name?"

"Oh!" I exclaimed, momentarily thrown back into my life. "Casey. Yeah, not yet, still working." David and Alice continued with more questions. It was amazing what they knew about me. It was nice to hear that while Gabe may not have been telling me about his life in London, he was still telling people in it about me.

As we were leaving, David asked, "Have you talked to Wilhelmina?"

Again Elizabeth and I glanced at each other. She looked alarmed, but I couldn't tell if she was thinking what I was. She had no idea Gabe and I had slept together, but she'd had her suspicions about us. And now there was someone named Wilhelmina? Not a third woman to add to this mix?

Maybe David saw the look on my face—or Elizabeth's—because he said, "Strictly professional situation. She's a harpist. I know Gabe met her and her brother because he wanted to explore a harp sound. I don't know what came of it. I have her number if you want it?"

Elizabeth took out her phone. "Sure, we'll take it."

Alice said, "How awful for you girls, going around collecting these things. Have you thought about leaving it for a bit?"

"*I* certainly have," Elizabeth said, not even trying to hide the annoyance in her voice.

"I'm so sorry for you both." Alice hugged Elizabeth, then me.

"Wait!" David exclaimed. He tapped a drum roll on the table, then paused for his big reveal. "We got a new storage unit."

It was unclear how this information was relevant to our conversation.

"Gabe helped me pack it up." He touched his arm. "I just got chills. Alice, did you?"

"No, dear."

"He helped me bring everything over there too. My back is shit, I needed help."

Alice clutched David's arm. "That's right, he did."

"His bracelet could be there," David said.

I was right there with him. I could see it. Packing up a box, the bracelet slips off. Even if he wanted it back, he might not have had the chance to ask David about it. It wouldn't have been an emergency either, he knew where the box was. Though even as I hoped this was what had happened, I also thought, But how would the bracelet slip off? Gabe was at his heaviest when I last saw him. But it was possible, I needed it to be possible, so we agreed to meet David at the storage unit tomorrow.

Once we were back outside on the towpath, Elizabeth bent down to untie Laurent. "The bracelet isn't on Leora's list, is it?"

"No."

"It's on your list."

"Yes," I said.

She looked up at me, still kneeling next to Laurent. "I could tell. Your face when you asked them about it." She considered this. "I understand. It was for his condition, right? So he must have worn it as long as you've known him."

"Nearly. I gave it to him."

She paused, then slowly stood up, wrapping the leash around her hand. "You gave it to him?"

"I made it for him. In Barcelona, when we were dating."

"Wow, that explains a lot."

"Like what?" I asked.

"I bought him a new one last year. And he never wore it."

"Yeah, he was probably just used to the old one."

"Maybe," she said, but she had that same look she had at the funeral, like she already knew something.

Back in the park, we paused to let Laurent use the bathroom, Elizabeth quickly texting Wilhelmina. From where we were, I could see a different angle of the man-made lake. An abstract sculpture was placed as if floating on the water. I checked my phone and saw Casey had texted. *What are you doing in London?* I wrote back *currently watching a dog poop.* When Laurent was done, Elizabeth pulled a small orange bag out of her coat pocket and scooped up his excrement. Her phone beeped. "She's texted back. Wilhelmina. She says to call her." She held the phone to her ear. "Hello? Yes, I'm calling because David Fields gave me your number. My name's Elizabeth Thompson. Yes. Yes, Gabe, exactly. I'm with a friend of Gabe's and we're trying to track down a few of his belongings. We're looking for his medical ID bracelet and the sheet music for 'I Left My Heart in San Francisco.' Oh, all right. Yes, sure, I can wait." She turned to me, covering the phone. "Bracelet, no."

I pressed my lips together.

"Sheet music—yes!"

I gasped. She returned to the call. "A month? Is there any way we could get it sooner? Yes . . . we *could* come to you." She said this as if coming to her was the last thing we could do. "No, she is only in town for a limited time, so, yes, we'll be there. Send me the address, please." She hung up. "So she has it. Or her brother Toad does. It got mixed in with some of their papers. They've had it for months but had no idea. They're leaving for Buenos Aires tomorrow, so we have to meet them tonight. They're playing a show in Norwich, we'll meet them there." Elizabeth frowned.

"Okay?"

"See, you're not from here. That's not the usual response when one hears they have to go to Norwich."

TWENTY-ONE

We caught the train from Liverpool Station. I was revved up with adrenaline, perhaps there had never been a person *more* excited to get to Norwich. But I've always found the steady speed of trains comforting and I slept the whole way, waking up to Elizabeth nudging my shoulder. "Welcome to Norwich, city of your dreams."

It was raining, lightly, like the mist setting on a garden hose. A wet static. From the train station, we walked to the concert center. Norwich was an old city. As in medieval, cobblestone streets and cathedrals. There were lots of people, but no crowds. It felt like a college town. I liked it. But I understood what Elizabeth meant. It's not like Norwich would have been on my travel bucket list. But what about this trip *was* on my travel bucket list?

In front of the concert center, I exclaimed, "It's flint!"

"Who?" Elizabeth asked.

"It's flint. The material." I pointed to the building. From afar, it looked like salt-and-pepper brick. The material itself was mostly silica, naturally derived from chalk.

"Are you a bit of a nerd?"

"Imagine if there were a flower you loved to look at in pictures or books, and once in a blue moon you saw it in person."

"I didn't say I wasn't also a nerd. Just learning more about you."

We walked in. An orchestra staff member directed us to the musician dressing rooms. The door to Wilhelmina's was already open, a white man leaning against the doorframe. His brown hair flopped into his eyes. He pushed it back. He did this two more times before we reached him.

"That was fast," he said. "What'd you get on, the first train out of London?"

"That's what we said we'd do," Elizabeth responded.

We headed into the dressing room with him. There was a mirror bolted to the wall, below that a table. "I'm Toad, this is my sister, Wilhelmina." He pointed to a woman with a pinched face sitting in a folding chair next to the table. Wilhelmina's dark brown hair was pulled back and it made her look even more severe. She didn't get up when we walked in. Toad sat on the only other chair in the room. Elizabeth and I stood across from them.

"And how do you two know Separate Bedrooms?" Toad asked. He had the clean, dull look of someone whose features fit nicely, though blandly, together. Some might call him handsome but he would never be charming. He brushed his hair out of his face again.

"They dated," Wilhelmina said.

"You all dated? The three of you?" He laughed, finding his joke hilarious, then looking to each of us to see if we did too.

Wilhelmina pointed to Elizabeth. "No, just her." Toad gave me an up-and-down, then shrugged and smirked at me, like hey, I wouldn't kick you out of bed.

A thin man with a headset, who I assumed was some kind of backstage manager, tapped on the door. "Just wanted to make sure you were all set for tomorrow." His eye went to a wrapped sandwich and large soft drink on the table. "Don't even think about eating that in here. You know we have mice."

"Don't worry, we won't." Toad waved him off. Then, as soon as the man walked away, Toad handed the sandwich to Wilhelmina. She lifted a corner of the wrapper. The pungent smell of tuna and some kind of pickled vegetable took over the room. Elizabeth's face blanched. "Could you maybe not?" she asked. "He did say not to eat in here."

Toad said, "Oh, he's fine. Don't worry about him. I think he's loving all this mice drama. Gives him a purpose." Wilhelmina unwrapped the rest of the sandwich, its stench engulfed the room. The room was gone and we were four people standing in a smell. Elizabeth moved to the doorframe, she was partly in the hallway.

"So, Gabe," Toad said. "Yeah. Kid was a genius, obviously. Shame about the overdose."

I had to interrupt. "What overdose?"

"Of course the papers didn't say that but rock star dies in a hotel room? I think we know that story." He tapped his nose and sniffed. "Not *judging*," he emphasized. "Whatever gets you through the night."

This is how it's going to be, I thought. He was drunk, he overdosed. Given the location of his death, in a few months, people would be saying Gabe died on the toilet, like one of those awful urban legends about Elvis or Mama Cass. I glared at Elizabeth. She looked at me like, what have I done? Didn't she see she was as bad as this guy? She was part of the rumor mill, that's what she'd done. I turned away.

"Here's the thing," Toad said. "Gabe came to us. Desperate to work with us. He needed a harpist, for one."

"How many harpists are there in England?" Elizabeth interrupted. "Can't be many." I'd had the same doubt of how desperate Gabe could've been to work with these two.

"Quite a few." Toad blew by her. "But there's only one Toad. See, I've got this magic ear. Once I hear something, I can play it back for you. It's how I got the name Toad. When I was young, I used to do impressions of animals. I could do all of them. Cat, toad, bear, cricket."

"Then why not call you Cricket? Or Bear?" Elizabeth asked.

"Or 'the Ear'?" I suggested.

But Toad countered, "Can't choose your own nickname, can you?"

"Right then, good for you," Elizabeth said briskly, as if she were sweeping Toad off a table and into a bin. Now that I'd spent more time with Elizabeth, I was used to her bluntness, I even appreciated it. It reminded me of Ines. And Nneka. When I thought about it, I gravitated to honest women who would tell it like it was. I think I got a vicarious thrill, watching them shoot from the hip while I remained inside my head with all my doubts and ruminations.

Elizabeth tried a slightly more tactful approach. "We'd love to talk about Gabe more, but I know you have a busy day of travel ahead of you tomorrow."

Toad ignored her. He was intent on telling his story. "So we arranged a bunch of things for him. But his producer Jabari didn't like it."

Okay, I was getting a sense of what had happened here. I could see Gabe meeting them and being polite, talking to them about music. He mentions that he wants to incorporate a harp on a song. Toad takes it upon himself to arrange something, hoping to get on a Separate Bedrooms album. Then it doesn't work out for whatever reason. (Toad's and Wilhelmina's personalities seemed like a good one.) Mentioning Jabari's disapproval had been Gabe's way out of an awkward conversation.

Maybe if I'd shown up to the hotel, it wouldn't have been Gabe at all, just a cell phone with Jabari on speaker: *So Julia, Gabe really enjoyed having sex with you, but it's not quite right for what he's looking for moving forward.*

Toad continued. "But Gabe was still *loving* working with us. Obviously since he left his stuff here."

"He left stuff all over the place," Elizabeth said. But then she pursed her lips, quickly glancing to me. This was exactly the argument I'd made to her last night.

Toad said, "We musicians are like that. Home is wherever you can jam, right?" Toad was weird. But not in an accidentally off-putting way; more like he was intent on appearing eccentric and was performing for us. Was this what happened when people who wanted to be onstage never made it there?

"Let's see the sheet music." I spoke in a clipped tone. I had more patience for this guy than Elizabeth did, but not much more.

"Right," Toad said. He leaned back in his chair, stretched his arm out behind him, pulled a briefcase from the floor onto his lap, and took out a file folder stuffed with papers. "We'd completely lost track of this. Didn't even remember we had it until you called." He shared a look of amusement with Wilhelmina. She laughed and looked down at the floor. He handed the folder to me.

Inside were several songs' worth of sheet music. I flipped through, one after the next was music for harp, there were a few for clarinet accompaniment. I nervously glanced up at Wilhelmina and Toad. Did they *think* they had it or did they *have* it? Had they checked? I flipped through faster, searching for "I Left My Heart in San Francisco," passing some loose-leaf notebook paper. I went back to the first notebook page. Something written on it had caught my eye: *Talk to Jabari, add harp and vocals or harp solo?* This was a note from Gabe to himself. I looked at the next page, more of Gabe's writing. Notes from each of his sessions with Wilhelmina and Toad, references he wanted to check with Jabari, a few doodles. One scribble simply said: *Donna Summer + Fountains of Wayne?* Ramblings that would seem strange to anyone unfamiliar with the kitchen-sink mess of the creative process. Next came four pages of sheet music. They were faded, held together with a loose staple. The title at the top: "(I Left My Heart) In San Francisco." Next to that, written in pen: *To Leora, But you left your mother and father in Jersey*. Below it: *To Gabe, My Heart, Love, Mom.*

"Is that it?" Elizabeth asked. I said yes, then showed her the rest of the folder, pointing out Gabe's notes and doodles.

Toad stood up. "That's his handwriting, right?" We both nodded. He took the folder out of my hands.

"What are you doing?" Elizabeth reached for it.

"It looks like scribbles and nothing, but if someone had told me I could have a copy of John Lennon's scribbles and nothing, I'd have sold my left arm."

"You want us to pay you?" Elizabeth asked, annoyed, but also already taking out her wallet.

"I wouldn't bother with that unless you can pay me a hundred thousand pounds."

I said, "Sure, if that converts to one hundred American dollars." I was joking. He was not.

"We obviously aren't going to pay that," Elizabeth said.

Toad shrugged. "I think someone will. If I put it up for auction."

Wilhelmina spoke up. "I've seen celebrity things go for a lot of money. It's helped people. For charity."

Elizabeth turned to her. "Fine. Give it back to us. We can see if his mother wants to auction it for charity."

I took out my phone. "We can call her." Elizabeth stiffened. As someone who was also avoiding speaking to Leora, I understood this reaction. But if this was what was required in the moment, I'd deal with it.

Toad said, "Ah, don't do that." I could tell he meant, *Don't put his mother through the experience of me telling her I'm going to put her son's papers up for auction because that is definitely what I'm going to do.*

"What about just the sheet music?" I asked.

Toad put the folder back in his briefcase. He fastened the buckles. "That's the most valuable thing in here and you know it." Again I got the sense that he was performing. He could have told us when we walked in that he wasn't giving us the sheet music. Instead he seemed to enjoy telling us in person how he'd worked out this plan of his. He was all but twirling a curled mustache.

"Seriously?" Elizabeth balked. "This is *sleazy*. What do you think Gabe would say if he knew you were doing this?"

"I think he would say . . ." Then he spoke in his own version of an American accent, Gabe's American accent to be exact. "Dude, I get it. It's hard to make a living as a musician these days."

It was a spot-on impression. That magic ear.

"FUCK HIM," ELIZABETH SAID ONCE WE WERE BACK OUT ON THE street. We walked toward the train station. It had stopped raining, but it was colder now, and windy. "There was a time—and if I weren't pregnant—I would've kneed him in the groin and ran off with that stupid fucking folder of his." The wind whipped Elizabeth's hair into her face. Some of it got caught in her mouth, she spat it out with force. "I think we'll have to get a lawyer involved. Legally, between me and Leora, one of us has to have a claim."

It was the first time she'd mentioned herself and Leora aligned together. I thought it might be a silver lining I could grab. "Would you like to talk to Leora? We don't have her sheet music or the guitar, but maybe there's a conversation to be had about other things?"

"Maybe I could offer up my firstborn as a consolation prize?"

"No! Sorry!" The wind was picking up. In order to be heard over it, we had to speak louder. "That was wrong, I'm sorry! I'm exhausted!"

"Hungry?"

"I said I'm exhausted!"

"I know! And now I'm asking if you're hungry!"

I'd been hungry since we walked into Victoria Park. How long ago had that been? How long was this day? Had it really started with me waking up next to Louis? I had two more nights in London, and then I was flying home. I thought we were going to end the day with a victory, but I still only had the baseball cap.

We stopped at a hotel restaurant. A wood-paneled room with exposed oak rafters. It looked like it had been there since the sixteenth century. It was easy to imagine ancient marauders eating meat and ale in the same room, and considering where we were, this was likely. We sat at a table in the center of the room next to a man and woman in their sixties, the cutlery against their plates the only sound between them. The restaurant was full of middle-aged couples. There were no single diners, no one under fifty. The menu was traditional English fare and Elizabeth went into a brief culinary history of various savory pies and puddings, coming up with a combination of items we could split that might pair well together. I said I'd go with the fish and chips. She rolled her eyes.

While I ordered for us, she went outside to check in with Divya. When she returned, she told me Divya had talked to the owner of Thistle & Row, the pub Elizabeth said Gabe often went to. As I'd walked around London, I'd noticed this seemingly Mad Libs approach to naming English pubs, taking two nouns and marrying them with an ampersand: Hare & Fish, Rod & Foil, Bell & Wheat.

Thistle & Row was very proud of its twice-monthly-emptied Lost and Found (good pub name), and they told Divya there was nothing of Gabe's in it. "They said he was only in a few times anyway." Elizabeth looked down at the table. She was wordlessly begging me not to say I told you so.

"So maybe Gabe wasn't hanging out at a bar all the time, getting wasted." I couldn't help myself.

"I didn't say that."

"But you've been going around with your theories. Guess you thought Toad was onto something with the overdose?"

"Obviously not. And I haven't been going around. I told you." She paused. "And I mentioned my concerns to Divya."

"Okay, maybe *stop* mentioning your concerns to people and quit acting like some random fan who wants to make this more sensational than it was. Unless you want your kid growing up hearing some really nasty rumors about their dad."

The waitress set down my fish and chips and Elizabeth's potpie. Except she gave the fish and chips to Elizabeth and the pie to me. We switched plates and ate in silence for a moment before Elizabeth responded, "Obviously I don't want that. And having a problem doesn't mean he was drunk that night. We know he wasn't. I wasn't talking about *that* night."

"His vocal surgery," I offered.

"What about it?"

"You can't drink after that. I remember the leaflet he had from the surgeon. Alcohol was forbidden. He had no problem abstaining."

"He may have abstained, but how do you know it was no problem?"

After the search of her flat and our conversation on the way to David and Alice's, I'd been forced to revise my idea of Elizabeth's role in Gabe's life. But there remained points I'd failed to update. For instance, though I'd known him longer, as his last-known address, as his last romantic relationship, Elizabeth had spent more time with him *this* year, more than me or Jabari or Leora had. It was a matter of calculating hours, and he'd spent the bulk of his last ones with her. I set down my fork. "You *really* thought he had a problem?"

She tilted her head to the side. "I can't prove it. And you're right, I could be wrong. But my mother drank. She still does. She's a social drinker, but to her, everything is a social occasion. She's never off, but she's never quite *on* either. It's not like what happened to me. I started young, went hard, and didn't even consider I had a problem until I hit my floor. Smashed right through it in fact. Gabe reminded me more of the kind of drinker my mother is. It's not like there was ever some falling-down-drunk moment. It was more subtle than that. It was developing. But maybe to someone without my experience, it seems alarmist."

"Developing," I repeated. "A burgeoning alcoholic?"

"Right."

"Aren't we all?" I joked.

"No," Elizabeth said firmly. "But we all bring our baggage to things. And who knows what *would* have happened? I can't see into the future." She tilted her eyes up, stopping tears. "Obviously."

Neither of us said anything; this pause in conversation came at the exact moment when the man next to us said, "This isn't going to be the day I try beets, Cynthia." We laughed. The man looked over at our table, clearly pleased with himself that while his wife wasn't amused, he'd somehow delighted these two young women.

Elizabeth stabbed a fork into her pie and shoveled out a layer of ham and peas. She chewed slowly. "Are you sure you don't want a bite of this?"

I chose my words aware of how inappropriate they would sound. "I'd rather die."

We shared a smirk. Which gave me the sense I could ask, "What did Gabe say when you told him you were pregnant?"

Elizabeth was in the middle of a bite. She swallowed. "He came to London. We sat down. I told him I was keeping the baby. He said if I was going to do that, we should get married. He was basically saying if you're going ahead with this, we have to do it this way. Meaning otherwise don't have the baby at all."

"I doubt that's what he meant." I didn't want to defend Gabe, but I had to be honest.

Elizabeth considered this, then said, "You're right. Still not exactly the most romantic moment of my life."

Yes, I understood that. Gabe had spent the weekend with me and then proposed to another woman. I, too, was not seeing much romance here. "What did you say?"

"Oh, I said, sure thing, love, can't wait to lock you down. Whatever it takes for a ring by spring." I motioned for her to tell me what she'd really said. It was taking a while to have this conversation, I think because it was too much for both of us to dive into all of it at once, so there was a bit here, a bit there. "I said we shouldn't rush into anything. Maybe we'd get back together, maybe we'd see each other at airports on Christmas Eve when we switched our child from one parent to the other. We'd have to take our time."

"And that was it?" I asked. "You didn't see him again?"

"He stayed in town for a few more days while we tried to figure things out. He wanted to be part of the baby's life. I wanted that too. We were still talking." She brought her napkin to her face and dabbed at the corners of her lips. "That's why," she continued, "I thought if you had seen him that night, maybe he might have mentioned something. Maybe he asked you for advice."

I imagined Gabe asking for my advice on this after our weekend in

Joshua Tree. If it hadn't been for our weekend in Joshua Tree, he probably *would* have asked for my advice. I wanted that version of events. Gabe confiding in me, the two of us friends without any complications.

Was there anything I could tell Elizabeth that *would* be helpful? What did she really want? If it was what I wanted—and also resisted—it was to learn something about him she didn't already know.

"Have you ever met Ramiro?" I asked. "Gabe's dad."

She shook her head.

"I hadn't either. Until the funeral."

"*You* hadn't?"

"I know. A sign of how close they were."

"I know it was a difficult relationship."

"He thought his dad only wanted to be around him when it was convenient to him. Or only wanted to spend time with him when they were doing something his dad was already interested in. Baseball, playing a live show." I'd heard Gabe talk about his dad so much that when it came to this topic, I could channel him. "And all these things Ramiro was interested in were things he didn't get to do professionally. I can see how, if Gabe was at this point in his career where he felt like he was falling behind, and he could tell he wanted to make music more than he wanted the baby, he'd see that hesitation in himself as confirmation that he was like his dad. I mean, it kind of would have been identity-destroying. Not to put this kid first. To be more like his father than his mother. You know? I could see him really struggling and then overcorrecting."

Elizabeth tucked her hair behind her ear and straightened her neck. "Honestly, that's quite helpful, Julia. And it makes so much sense. I could tell he didn't really want to be with me."

"That's not what I meant." It wasn't.

"No, really," she said. "It seemed unusually old-fashioned, that proposal. I could tell it wasn't about me, but I didn't know what it *was* about. You know? When you just have a feeling something is off, but you can't pinpoint what?" She laughed, relieved. "See, this is exactly why I wanted to sit down with you."

Great. So closure was possible, just not for me.

For the train ride, we bought magazines. *Architectural Digest* UK and *British Vogue* for me, *Red* and a newspaper for her. When we finished, we switched. Elizabeth was studying a remodeled apartment in Cornwall when she drifted off.

I began to make a mental timeline of Gabe's last month. He'd started off with me in Joshua Tree, then flown to Vegas. I knew from the Separate Bedrooms tour list that there had been two more gigs in America that week, which meant he'd flown to London after the performances. Had he and Elizabeth slept together when he was in London? She hadn't said. I wouldn't ask. I wasn't going to tell her about Gabe calling me to meet him at Hotel Frank, and as long as I was keeping this to myself, it didn't seem right to ask more of her. I told myself this was a fair trade. It was easier to think we both had our own secrets. As opposed to the possibility that she had told me everything and I was still holding back.

BACK IN MY HOTEL ROOM, I CHECKED AUCTION SITES. KEYWORDS: "Separate Bedrooms," "Gabriel Wolfe-Martel." I'd thought the worst thing would be to never find Gabe's bracelet, but there was a worse fate: that somehow by searching, I'd alert whoever had found it to

its value, leaving it to end up on the open market for the highest bid-
der. I'd rather it thrown into the Thames than up for sale. I sat on
the ottoman in front of the window, hunched over, scrolling through
Separate Bedrooms fan memorabilia, tour shirts, posters, vinyl. Nothing of value came up, no sign of the sheet music, and no sign of the
bracelet. I plugged my phone into its charger and turned off the
lights. I fell asleep thinking, If we don't find it tomorrow, it might be
time to stop looking.

TWENTY-TWO

The next morning I set out to meet Elizabeth (and Laurent) at Columbia Road Flower Market. On the train, we'd exchanged numbers, and before I left my hotel, we'd texted a plan to meet at the entrance, where the buskers usually set up. It was early on a Sunday, a caesura between the bustling night and the ruckus of the day. It looked like it had rained earlier that morning or late in the night. Everything was sharp and clear, like when I'd put on glasses for the first time in fourth grade. Did London look like this for everyone, or was it an issue of relative comparison? After living in LA for so long, was I used to seeing life through a layer of smog and dust?

Smog & Dust would be the Los Angeles–themed pub I opened in London.

I turned a corner onto Columbia Road, where people were waiting for the market to open. Here was the rest of the world again, popping up like guests at a surprise party. There were families with strollers, women with serious early-morning-errand face, young couples with the self-satisfied look of being young couples out at a

Sunday-morning market. Their conversations mingled with the clatter of vendors opening boxes and setting up wares. My phone buzzed. I took it from my coat pocket. Another text from Leora, following up again. I ignored it. In a few hours, I might have the guitar and she would never need to know I'd lost it.

Elizabeth was waiting for me at the entrance. No buskers yet. We stood around for a bit, but when only a guy with a keyboard showed up, we continued into the market, keeping an ear out. We figured it would be impossible for us to *see* every corner of the market at once, but it was only one block, so wherever we were, we'd be able to hear the guitar.

"I need coffee," Elizabeth pronounced. We were still waking up, slow-eyed and sluggish. Behind the market vendor stalls, a few stores were open. She pointed to a little coffee shop with a black-and-white awning. I ordered a tea and we took our drinks to go. At the end of the street was a store painted millennial pink. You couldn't go anywhere that year without seeing the soft salmon color.

A woman with box braids, a tote slung over her shoulder, and a blond man, in shorts, with hairy calves, passed us. "I can't talk about Brexit anymore," the woman said. Usually I kept up on politics, but I'd turned off news alerts after getting one about Gabe's death.

Current events. A ubiquitous color trend. Both reminders of a life that seemed far away. It was amazing how quickly I'd settled into my new normal as a low-rate transcontinental private investigator.

We reached the end of the block. A tall woman with long brown hair stood in front of the pink store, slips of paper clutched in her hand. Crystals, tarot cards, and little plants in gold-rimmed pastel pots were placed in the window. The door was open, I glimpsed a wall of brightly colored greeting cards. "Let me guess?" She pointed to Elizabeth. "Taurus?"

Elizabeth stared at her.

The woman turned to me. "I'm a Cancer," I offered.

"I've got a Cancer horoscope, here you go." The woman handed me a slip of paper, it looked like what you'd find in a fortune cookie. Would it say, *You will find the bracelet you've been looking for in a storage unit this morning*? I read aloud, "'Today you will choose abundance.'"

Elizabeth said to the woman, "That's more of an affirmation than a horoscope."

"Yes, it can be both!" the woman replied gleefully, missing Elizabeth's critique.

Even though neither of us was particularly interested, it was the kind of store you had to walk into. There was the alternative self-care focus, but also in stock were notebooks, greeting cards, planners, coffee table books, and obviously candles. A birthday-present shop.

"I love this," Elizabeth said, holding up a glazed violet serving bowl.

"Me too," I said.

She flipped it over to look at the price. "Too expensive."

"I bet I could take a class and learn to make it on my own."

"I was thinking the same thing."

By the door there was a display of necklaces. Elizabeth pointed to them. "What do you think about jewelry like this?" The necklaces were thin cords with a single crystal—amethyst, quartz, rose quartz, tourmaline—hung from each one.

"It's nice," I said.

Elizabeth laughed. "*You're* nice."

I lowered my voice. "They haven't really done anything with it, just threaded a string through a crystal. It's the raw beauty of the crystal doing all the work."

"Kind of like arranging flowers? That nature already made beautiful?"

I caught her reference to what Gabe had said when they broke up. "Not like that. You're not just sticking a rose in a cup—" I stopped myself, remembering she had stuck some roses in cups at dinner. But her bouquet for her flower class was different. "There's an art to your arrangements," I said.

"Arrangement*s*?" Elizabeth accented the plural. "Have you seen my work beyond the workshop bouquet?"

"Yes," I confessed. "I googled you."

"How flattering." She traced her finger across her eyebrow, smoothing it. "Of course I googled you too."

Out on the street, we passed the horoscope woman again. "Are you into all of that?" Elizabeth asked.

"No, I'm not really into astrology," I said. A statement that—for an LA woman to make—was akin to Martin Luther nailing his Ninety-Five Theses to a church door. "But some of the stuff about being a Cancer really fits me to a T."

"Like what? Which one's Cancer?"

"The crab. Goes into its shell. And I can close off from people. Retreat into myself."

We were walking down the street side by side. Elizabeth turned her head to look at me, I think trying to figure out if she had noticed this in me. Reaching her conclusion, she said, "It's not always bad to close yourself off to others. As long as you don't do it with yourself." She glanced at her phone. "Oh no, come on now."

"What?"

"David's asking to reschedule. He wants to know if we can come tomorrow."

"No, it has to be today. My flight's tomorrow."

"I know, I'm telling him." She looked back to me. "He says he got a gig." Then down to her phone again. "What time is your flight?" I said early afternoon, and she said it was cutting it close, but we'd make it.

At the same time, we heard it. Someone bleating away on a saxophone. We spun around, searching for the source. Elizabeth strained forward. "I don't hear any guitar, though."

"But they might have it anyway? Just not playing it?"

We headed in the direction of the smooth jazz, but when we reached the saxophonist, it was just that, a solo saxophone player. We stood in front of him, watching, waiting. For what? A special guest appearance from a guitarist? After a while I felt guilty we were standing there and I dropped a £1 coin into his case. We returned to the coffee shop and sat at a table out front. At one point, I went in to order a croissant. Elizabeth walked Laurent to a corner so he could relieve himself. Other than that, we waited in silence, like we were on the world's most subdued stakeout, until the market closed. As the last vendors packed up their stalls, I turned to Elizabeth. "So they didn't show up." I was hoping she'd have a sudden revelation that we were at the wrong market, there was actually a Columbia Road *Farmer's* Market and we were supposed to be *there*. Anything except that we'd hit a dead end.

She looked back and forth down the road. "They might still show up? They might have been delayed?"

I said, "I can wait here all day." But as if on cue, a big fat droplet of water smacked me in the face. Then another. People on the street were unfazed, sauntering slowly. A few took out umbrellas. If this were LA, people would have scrambled for the nearest shelter, shrieking as if they were starring in an apocalyptic thriller. *Rain: The Drizzling.*

We sat in the drizzle for a few minutes, waiting it out. The man at the table next to us calmly packed up his things. Elizabeth pointed to Laurent. "I should get him home." She stood up. I didn't move. I was still holding on to hope. If we moved, that would be it. We'd walk away and miss any chance of spotting the guitar, or we'd walk away and there was no chance anyway, but we'd never know for sure because we'd left. Laurent shook water off his coat, a futile effort. Noticing that I wasn't coming along with her, Elizabeth tried again. "It's not like anyone's going to be busking in this. We don't have to make a run for it, but we can't just sit here either. You can wait it out at my place if you like, I'll make lunch."

"Fine," I said. I didn't want to be alone with my guilt and failure. I couldn't avoid Leora forever, but I could delay the inevitable a little longer.

We walked quickly down Columbia Road, the market behind us. Already it seemed like it was raining less. Should we go back? When we stopped at a crosswalk, I looked back at the market, but there was no market, the vendors had left, the saxophonist was gone, it was a quiet street again.

Elizabeth gasped. I looked in the direction of her shock. On the other side of the street were four kids, about college age, a tall white guy with long brown hair wearing a ridiculous velvet bucket hat, two Indian girls with short mod cuts who looked almost like twins, and another guy, Black, squat, with cornrows. Yes, they made a unique group, but I didn't think it was polite to point at them. I placed my arm over Elizabeth's, pushing it down.

"No, Julia. Look." The guy with the cornrows was carrying a guitar.

She waved her arms back and forth. "Hey! Hey!" They waved back, laughing like we were all playing a funny game. As soon as the light changed, Elizabeth charged forward. I ran after her. "Are you okay?" one of the girls called out. They thought we needed help. Which, in a way, we did.

"That's our guitar," I yelled.

We met them on the curb. Elizabeth spoke quickly, explaining, "You found this by Boundary Gardens? It was ours, we left it."

"This is your guitar?" the white guy in the velvet hat asked. He looked us over, skeptically.

I tensed. They were going to take it. It would be just like Toad, they'd yell finders keepers and run away. Then I'll run too, I thought.

One of the girls said, "Women play guitar, Alvin."

"Check for the initials on the strap," I said. "*L. W.*"

He held up the strap, inspecting it. "Oh yeah. What's *L. W.*?"

Elizabeth was already reaching for it. "Yes, that's me. Lucy Wembley. Thank you." He handed the guitar to her, then she passed it to me. It was such a quick, efficient game of hot potato, there was a slight delay before I realized that was it, it was done, I had the guitar back. "Thank you," we both said at the same time.

They said it was no problem. And I could tell they meant it, it wasn't. They were young, they were in a band, later they'd probably have an argument about women guitarists, the band would stay together or it would break up. Someday they'd be talking about this time in their lives and one of them might remember when they fostered a guitar for a day before returning it to two strange, panicked women who'd rushed through the rain and traffic to get to them.

We watched them go, and as they headed off, the girl said, "You should probably get it out of the rain."

Right. Elizabeth pulled a sweater out of her tote bag and threw it over the guitar, I tugged off my cardigan and wrapped it around the sweater for extra protection, hugging the entire thing close to my body. She picked up Laurent, and we ran as fast as we could. We got into the first black cab we spotted, but only once we had the guitar safely inside her flat, the door slammed behind us, did we turn to each other and scream in celebration.

TWENTY-THREE

Elizabeth brought a stack of towels into the living room. Once we got the guitar dried off, we moved on to ourselves, wiping down our hands and faces. She said, "I have some extra sweaters and sweatpants, we can dry your clothes. Have a shower, if you like?"

"Or a bath?" I suggested.

"A bath? Do you want me to rub your tummy and find you some jammies too?"

"Ha, right," I said. I paused. "I haven't been big on showers. Since Gabe."

"Have you not taken a shower since . . . ?" She looked me up and down.

"I mean, I'm *clean*. I use the sink at the hotel. And I used a tub . . . recently."

"You will have to shower eventually."

I nodded. Yes, I knew that.

"Do you want to have a shower here?" Elizabeth pointed toward the bathroom down the hall.

I told her it wasn't necessary. I had a shower at my hotel.

"And you're terrified of it."

A fair point.

"And at your hotel, you'll be by yourself. At least I'll be here to call emergency services. In case you do fall and die, leaving behind all your friends and family."

"Fine," I said. She led me down the hall to the bathroom, took a towel and washcloth from her linen closet, handed them over, then gestured for me to go in. I closed the door behind me. I reached a hand into the shower and turned on the faucet. I placed one foot in the tub. I took it out. I squatted down. I stood back up. I turned on the shower. I stepped out of the shower. I put one leg into the shower.

Elizabeth pounded on the door. "I'm coming in!"

I shrieked, jumping forward, hitting my knee on the soap dish. But I was in.

"I'm not coming in," Elizabeth said from outside the door. "Just wasn't sure if you were getting in or worrying about getting in."

That's exactly what I'd been doing.

"I'm in!" I called out.

Elizabeth pushed the door open. I heard the toilet seat close. She was sitting down on the other side of the shower curtain.

"How's it going?"

"Bad." I was in the shower but standing perfectly still, as far away from the water as I could get. Only my feet were getting wet.

"Are you scared of falling?" Elizabeth asked.

"No," I said, surprising myself. Now that I was in the shower, I could tell it wasn't about that. I inched forward. "I think it's what you said. Being alone in here."

"You're not alone right now."

She was right. So why was I still terrified? I didn't understand myself. I stepped forward again, now I was fully in the stream. I picked up a bottle of Elizabeth's body wash, used the washcloth she'd given me, and lathered up. Water pooled around my feet, then swirled down the drain.

It wasn't *only* because I'd be alone in the shower. It was that *he* had been alone. It was the idea of him being alone, dying alone. Especially when instead, he might have been downstairs at the hotel bar with me.

Something was happening. It had started here in Elizabeth's flat with the impromptu memorial, and it had only gotten worse on David and Alice's boat. I could see Gabe again. Not the moments when I was most upset or conflicted about him, but all of Gabe, fully. Which even for a brief moment I could not take.

I threw the shower curtain open.

"Oh!" Elizabeth exclaimed. "Hello!"

"Sorry, I have to get out."

She turned away, shielding her eyes with one arm, grabbing a towel with the other.

I took it from her and wrapped it around my body. "I need a moment."

"Absolutely," Elizabeth said. She closed the door behind her.

Once I was safely toweled off, I changed into the sweatshirt and pants Elizabeth had left out for me. While she took her shower, I waited in the living room. I took the guitar case from the pile of Gabe's things we'd gathered and put the guitar in it.

At least I had the guitar. Which meant I could get back to Leora.

I called, but her phone went straight to voicemail, the outgoing message explaining she was on sabbatical. I was ready to launch into the good news, but then I thought of the other news I couldn't tell her, about Elizabeth being pregnant. I paused, unable to speak, then hung up.

Elizabeth returned, dry and wearing a long-sleeved shirt and flannel pants. "Are you all right?"

"Yeah. Better now."

"I can make us toasties," she suggested.

"What are toasties?"

"Like grilled cheese."

"Then absolutely."

In the kitchen, Elizabeth took out an onion and began chopping. "Can I help?" I offered.

"You can take out the green beans I have in the fridge. Should be second shelf. And you can chop some parsley, just this bunch," she said, pointing with her elbow to a few sprigs on the counter. The parsley reminded me of a Passover seder hosted by Leora at Gabe's house when he was living in LA. She kept saying it was not your traditional seder. Earlier Gabe had mentioned to me that Leora was seeing someone, it was casual and, according to her, not your traditional relationship. As I passed through the kitchen, I heard Gabe say, as he tossed a tray of glazed salmon into the oven, the Pyrex clanging against the rack, "Mom, you don't have to add 'not your traditional' to everything. We can just assume that if you're doing it, it won't be traditional."

"Point made, Gabriel," she responded in that weary tone parents have when they've given in, but also want to make it clear they're indulging us.

But I guess his point was made. Leora had tried to make his funeral *not your traditional* funeral, but she hadn't announced it. Though, with the concert tees for example, an announcement would have been helpful. I acknowledged this to Elizabeth. "It must have felt like you were being excluded."

"Don't worry," she said. "I'm not still crying over not getting to wear my Spice Girls tee with the rest of the cool kids."

To make up for this, I didn't bring up telling Leora about the pregnancy again, I focused very hard on chopping the parsley perfectly, no stray stems. I showed Elizabeth the cutting board for inspection. She nodded her approval.

"Do you need anything else?" I asked.

"That's it, I've got it, thank you." She squeezed a lemon over the green beans, threw in the parsley, then four spices, adding just a touch here and just a touch there, sometimes a sprinkle, other times a flurry. She was all business in the kitchen and I realized I was watching someone *work*. There were probably people who would have paid three figures to have this experience. Fleur Bleue in Elizabeth's own home, from the farm to *her* table.

When she served the toasties, as soon as I bit into one, I said, "Okay, this is much, much better than any grilled cheese I've ever had."

Elizabeth didn't respond to my compliment. She was watching me.

"What?" I asked.

"I shouldn't have dropped the pregnancy on you like that."

"Oh. Well, I did badger you into a corner."

"Yes, but that's not why I told you. I wanted to say, 'Nah, nah, I know something you don't know.' I was hoping to hurt you. To tell you something Gabe hadn't told you himself. Then when I saw your face after I did, I thought, My God, now why did I do that to her? I immediately regretted it. I thought, She's just a person, really. But I'd built you up in my mind, you were almost mythic. How could you be hurt by me?"

I knew what she meant. What I had said at dinner the first night, about Gabe calling her cold. It was unnecessary. I'd lobbed it over without thinking how it would feel to receive it. But we were in her gorgeous restaurant, she was so sure of herself. "I built you up in my mind, too." I winced.

"It's embarrassing to admit, isn't it?"

It was, but now that we had, it seemed like a thickness in the air between us dissipated.

"At least we're not alone in that," she said.

"My friend's husband who you met at the gallery predicted this would all turn into a catfight. Because I dated Gabe."

"Ah yes. You were the first, I was his last."

"I was not Gabe's first girlfriend. He was my first boyfriend, I was a late bloomer. But he'd always been . . . Gabe."

I expected her to laugh, but she said, "I meant first love."

I felt like I had in the shower, trapped. But unlike in the shower, I couldn't just hop out of the moment. I considered telling her everything about me and Gabe, including the real answer to her question about his last night. We were clearing the air, revealing things we'd been keeping to ourselves. But then I thought about what she'd said about wanting to hurt me. I didn't know a way to tell Elizabeth that wouldn't seem like I was trying to hurt her. And I couldn't find a way to tell anyone that wouldn't hurt me.

I took the long way back to my hotel, meandering through

Shoreditch with the guitar case slung over my back like a traveling troubadour. The bookstores, the Indian restaurants, the pubs. I passed Fleur Bleue. All familiar spots now. I hadn't expected to care one way or the other about it, but with its crisp air and lush parks and quaint little canal boats and mates outside the pubs, the way I could walk out of my hotel and immediately step into the fray, this was the surprise of the trip. I liked London.

And it sounded so corny to think, but it was true, I felt the same about Elizabeth. I was glad I'd gotten to know her. Maybe that was something to take from all of this? No, I had to stop myself. I was veering into "everything happens for a reason." Now I understood why people said it. It was so tempting to reach for any possible comfort. To say Gabe may have been gone, but—

I stopped, right at the edge of the street, not because of my desperate platitudes, but because I was certain I'd triggered some kind of superstition, jinxing myself. Gabe, gone. That was the problem right there. Thinking Gabe could be gone. Because wasn't it always the same with Gabe? The plaza in Barcelona, finding him again in Echo Park, Joshua Tree, the voicemail. It was never goodbye. I was wrong every time I thought he was out of my life. He would always appear again.

WHEN I WOKE UP, I KNEW SOMETHING WAS WRONG. I WAS SUPPOSED to meet Elizabeth at David's storage unit in the morning, so I'd set my phone alarm, but it felt like I'd been asleep for only a few hours. It was dark in my hotel room. Even though the curtains were closed, I could tell it had to be night outside. I waited for my eyes to adjust, the shapes of the furniture emerging from the darkness. Had my alarm gone off? I checked my phone. It was 3:00 A.M.

Then I saw why I'd woken up. Missed texts from Casey, interrupting my sleep.

I looked at the first one. Casey had sent a link.

A new Separate Bedrooms album was out.

TWENTY-FOUR

It happened like this. Toad put the first page of Gabe's handwritten notes online to gauge interest. Would people be willing to pay? The internet responded. Some people were interested, but what captured more attention was the fact that Gabe had been writing notes at all, specifically notes for new songs. It led to speculation about how far he'd gotten on the fourth Separate Bedrooms album. Did it exist somewhere? Someone commented that it was unlikely a label would ever release an unfinished album, if such an album even existed. Someone else said if it did, fuck the label, the people deserved to hear it. And then a former intern uploaded the rough versions of five unfinished Separate Bedrooms songs. They'd been sent internally within the label for feedback. They were not meant, in their condition, to be heard by the public.

The working title? *Puppy Love.*

CASEY TEXTED AGAIN. *What the fuck.*

The three bubbles of communication percolated and then:

making out at desert sushi, precious jewel, I was always
such a fool

I wrote back: *what?* But as soon as I pressed send, I realized it was a lyric.

Casey sent another link. It was a blog post about Desert Sushi, media coverage for the new restaurant opening in Joshua Tree summer this year.

Summer THIS YEAR???

I knew eating sushi in the desert would come back to haunt me.

I stared at my phone. I wasn't ready to listen to the album. Instead I checked what people were saying about *Puppy Love* online.

It was the album Gabe had told me about. The one about falling in love in Barcelona. The lyrics were already up on a Separate Bedrooms fan thread. In the songs, I was "you" or "she," and fans had taken it upon themselves to name Gabe's object of affection "Barcelona Baby," a moniker I would never have chosen for myself.

I knew, from Casey, that the part about Desert Sushi was in the last song, "Missing the Tracks." What else was in there? I was sure it was nothing I'd want to find out from a fan forum, so I clicked on the album and skipped ahead. In my ear, Gabe growled, "*Westward bound . . .*" As I was listening, Casey texted that I had to call him immediately. I didn't. My phone rang and I answered with, "No comment."

"Will already told me everything."

"What? He can't do that!"

"He's not an actual therapist! And everyone's going to know now. It's straight from Gabe's mouth."

My mind went to Elizabeth. Did she know the album was out? Had she listened to it yet? "There's no proof that's me," I protested. The song wasn't even accurate. I pointed out that we hadn't kissed *at* Desert Sushi. "Songwriters pull together a variety of references and experiences. You only think that because you know me and Gabe," I told Casey.

"You were with him in Joshua Tree, he talks about jewels, you're a *jewelry* designer." He asked about the next line. Gabe sang,

Ruby lips, diamond hips, she wants this to work so bad
It ain't me, it's just something we've never had

Casey wanted to know what it meant. "Because in track three, he hears from someone else that Barcelona Baby"—that was really catching on—"says I love you. But she never tells him herself. Did that really happen?"

"Yes. It happened. When we were teenagers." Yes, Roberta told him I was in love. But Gabe said nothing, he told me nothing. "What are you saying?" I asked Casey. "That it's my fault that I didn't come right out and say how I felt years ago, so I deserved to be ghosted?"

"No, I'm not saying that it's your fault. But that doesn't mean that it's not how Gabe felt. Or at least how he felt when he recorded this song," Casey argued. He paused. "Can I say something?"

"Sure."

"You can be hard to read. I always thought because you were so close, it was different with Gabe."

"It *was* different with Gabe."

"I mean, I can't always tell what you're thinking."

"I can never tell what anyone is thinking!"

"Have you asked them?"

"Have you asked *me*?"

"A lot of the time, it seems like you don't want me to know. Like you sleeping with Gabe and not telling me for example."

"I was trying to figure things out for myself first."

"Sounds like what Gabe was doing."

"I'm hanging up."

"Okay, okay, I'm sorry. Devil's advocate. Professional hazard. But what did you want?" he asked. "I mean, did you want to be in a relationship with Gabe or did you want to stay friends?"

That first morning in Joshua Tree, I'd been nervous, unsure if we'd made a mistake. By the end of the day, I thought we'd made the right choice: it was new but we could make it work. That version of myself seemed so far away. I believed her, I believed she'd wanted that. But then Gabe had disappeared, and when I found out there'd been an accident, it was like my brain exploded. Since then I'd been trying to put everything back together. And even that weekend, when I thought, Okay, this is happening, I'd never been completely sure we weren't ruining something, that we wouldn't have been better off as friends.

I was thinking of that last morning in Joshua Tree again, but instead of going over what Gabe had said, his movements and gestures, I wondered how I seemed from his point of view.

I slept with him.

I played it cool.

I was all in.

And I could imagine it not working out.

I was lonely. I wanted someone.

I missed him. I wanted him.

I hated Casey for introducing this new angle of the footage and told him I didn't want to talk about Joshua Tree.

"Okay. What did you think of track three?" he asked.

"I haven't listened to every song yet."

"You *haven't*?"

"When would I have done that?" I yelled. "You just texted me and told me to call you immediately!"

I LISTENED TO THE REST OF THE ALBUM, THEN RETURNED TO THE internet, searching *Puppy Love* + my name. There was nothing about me but I found some theories. According to early listeners, "Missing the Tracks" stuck out like a sore thumb. They guessed correctly that it referred to a time after the other songs because in it Gabe referenced touring, his failure to make a fourth album, and even recent secret shows from that spring; the Desert Sushi lyric was placed after a reference to the show in Joshua Tree. It wasn't an exact timeline of Gabe's last days. There was no mention of London or Elizabeth. Or maybe there was and I'd missed it. It's why, I think, I kept scrolling through all the fan opinions. And there were plenty. Because *Puppy Love* was his last album, they wanted to soak up everything they could from it.

There were a lot of Big Theories: Separate Bedrooms was being retired, and Gabe was going to start recording under his own name, this album was his goodbye to the moniker; the true opus would have been the fifth album, and this was Separate Bedrooms clearing his throat to prepare us for the real shit; no, it was about the role of men in music, the fragility of the male ego, *did none of you get the Dylan reference.* And still another corner of the internet thought it was just your standard breakup album, the last song included to show that he'd moved on from Barcelona Baby and found someone new. Because Barcelona Baby was all about infatuation. *And this relationship with the woman in the desert is about real partnership. Like she's just this plain regular woman, but to him she's a jewel.*

Another claimed Gabe wasn't dead and had released the album himself. I put my phone down after that one.

I texted Jabari.

> **What is this?**

> *Yeah it wasn't meant to get out.*

I called him. "You were with him when he recorded the last song, right?"

"Yeah."

"So you knew that we had hooked up."

"He mentioned something about it."

"And?"

"He had some other things going on, I think."

"Yes, I think he did." I bit my lip. The way Jabari said it, I could tell he knew Elizabeth was pregnant. But I couldn't confirm it. How long until she told people? How long would I have to hold on to her secret?

He said, "He just thought if he got something out, just get in the studio, record, he'd know what to do. He couldn't think straight until he made the album."

"And?"

"Well, we didn't finish, Julia. I mean, we spent a week in the studio day and night."

And there was the last chunk of the timeline. I laughed out loud as I paced the room. *Of course.* So this was where he'd been while he was trying to figure things out. Gabe hadn't been thinking about me or Elizabeth. He was consumed by his music. That fucking asshole. I walked into the bathroom and kicked at the shower. And then I slipped.

TWENTY-FIVE

J ulia? Julia?!" Jabari yelled into the phone.

"I'm okay, I'm okay." I hadn't traveled far, I'd caught myself, so it was more a tumble than a fall, but I'd screamed as I went down.

"What happened?" Jabari asked.

"I slipped in my hotel bathroom."

"Are you fucking kidding me?"

I repeated that I was fine. I sat down on the bed. So Gabe had gone to work on his album. I wanted to be angry, but strangely I wasn't. After talking to Casey, after standing alone in Elizabeth's shower, after staring at that Frankenthaler painting, all moments when I could feel my *friend*, the friend I knew and trusted with my life, I had to consider that there was another possibility, that it was just as Jabari was saying: the only way through his thoughts about me and Elizabeth was his music.

Jabari let out a pained moan. "I can't believe someone fucking leaked this. It sucks."

I wasn't sure if he meant the situation or the album.

Because when going through fan reviews, the hardest thing to read was not what people thought about our summer together, but what they thought about the album. Most people agreed, though many tried to say it nicely, no one wanted to speak ill of the musician they adored, but the consensus was: it was not his best. And they weren't wrong. It was fine. It was just fine. Gabe said it wasn't working and that hadn't been humility. He was right. I remembered Gaudí and La Sagrada Família, his unfinished masterpiece, he'd known even before his sudden death that it wouldn't be completed in his lifetime. But this was no masterpiece. Everyone was listening to Gabe's failure—this incomplete failure—and he would never be able to correct it. He would have hated that. *I* hated that.

At some point I should have put my phone down, but I sailed farther and farther away from that point until it was a speck in the distance. The sun came up. I kept checking to see if Elizabeth had called. Most likely she was asleep, as I had been when Casey texted me, and she'd learn about the album when she woke up with the rest of his British fans. Which would mean even more commentary. That I would also have to read. I rubbed my eyes. The left one twitched. What had happened to me? In all my combing through our past, tracking down the artifacts of his life, examining Gabe's last days, I had become just like these people, an obsessive fan. I had to stop.

But then, a new comment: *did anyone catch the reference to situs inversus?*

I had not. I went back to listen again and caught the line:

> *Maybe somewhere there's a mirror image of me who knows*
> *the right way*

Two fans responded to the new comment and began talking about the bracelet, directing commenters to another thread.

Does anyone know if he was wearing it at his last show?

I was there right by the stage. He wasn't wearing it. That person uploaded photos. There was a zoomed-in one of Gabe clutching the mic with his hands, both wrists bare of any jewelry.

He gave the bracelet to his girlfriend, Elizabeth Thompson, someone wrote. I gripped the phone tighter. No way, that couldn't be true.

Ooh like an engagement gift? Here's a part of me for you?

I scrolled past the speculation to the supposed evidence.

A link to Elizabeth's social media, still private.

A link to Fleur Bleue.

Yeah, yeah, I thought. I've been through all this. I got to the same place, and it was a dead end.

Then a link to a piece about Elizabeth, one I had never seen, an online profile associated with a French clothing-and-homeware brand.

Look familiar?

OH MY GOD!

The article is in French but she's wearing Gabe's bracelet.

It's so romantic, guess he gave it to her, like a wedding ring

Can anyone translate?

Google can lmao

I didn't need anyone to translate. I just needed to see the photos.

THE PHOTOS WERE TAKEN IN ELIZABETH'S FLAT. IT WAS CLEAN, and there had been some considerable staging, her furniture re-arranged with a tall plant from the living room placed in the kitchen. It was a clothing company feature, showcasing the autumn collection, so Elizabeth wore turtlenecks and corduroy in the photographs. It had come out while I was in London, after I'd completed my internet stalking of her, so I had to assume the photos were taken recently. I squinted. No sign of a baby bump, but it's not like I could notice one when standing right in front of Elizabeth either. I scrolled past three photos, not seeing any sign of Gabe's bracelet. Then, just as I'd written it off as an internet scam akin to *I swear I saw Gabe at the laundromat yesterday,* I got to the last photo, an image of Elizabeth arranging red and gold flowers with a mix of autumnal foliage.

There on her wrist, plain as day, was a sliver of silver, a linked chain, with a nameplate. I zoomed in, blinking. I checked for the garnet ring, as if verifying that this was indeed Elizabeth's body. Yes, there was the ring. And there was Gabe's bracelet.

At 7:00 A.M., I took a shower. It would have felt like a victory the day before. The day before, when I was with Elizabeth and she was lying to me. I only had seven more hours in London until my flight. I packed my suitcase. I tucked the Mets cap in, arranging some of my socks inside it to keep the shape. I set the guitar, now in its case, by the door with the rest of my luggage.

On the Tube ride to David's storage unit, I braced myself for seeing Elizabeth again. After listening to "Missing the Tracks," I was worried she'd realized I lied to her. But she'd lied to me too.

When I arrived, David said Elizabeth was running late and that we should start without her. We searched through the boxes Gabe had helped him load. I thought there might be something of Gabe's there, but I knew it wouldn't be the bracelet.

We didn't find anything. Elizabeth never showed up. I texted her.
No luck.

Brief, neutral, no accusations. All she had to do was respond.

She did not.

I returned to my hotel. I told the concierge I'd be checking out soon, but that I'd need the latest possible checkout. I still hadn't heard from Elizabeth, I had four hours left until my flight, which meant, depending on how close I wanted to cut it, I didn't have much time left before I had to head to the airport. I stood against the door of my room, clutching my phone. I was about to text her again when my hand buzzed. Elizabeth Thompson's name scrolled across the screen. I answered. In her signature style, Elizabeth skipped pleasantries and launched right into things. "You told Leora," she declared.

I was prepared for the aggressive energy of this confrontation, but not the subject matter. "Told Leora what?"

"That I'm pregnant, Julia!"

"No, I didn't!" I cried out.

"She's emailed me. Saying she knows that I'm pregnant. Who else would tell her? Divya, while they were having their morning tea?"

"Did you respond?" I asked.

"No. Wait! She just emailed again." I pictured Elizabeth in her bright flat, Laurent on her lap, phone in hand, her finger hovering over Leora's name. "Open it," I commanded. If she noticed the edge in my voice, she didn't mention it.

"She says she found out from the album. Last track?"

That was "Missing the Tracks." I held my breath. I would not speak first.

Elizabeth said, "Gabe's album came out last night."

"I know. A friend in America told me."

"So you've listened to it?"

"Yes." I waited, leaving room for Elizabeth to interrupt. When she didn't, I asked, "Have you?"

"Yes, I listened to it." A pause, silence. "But I didn't hear anything about me being pregnant." Laurent barked in the background. "She just emailed again," Elizabeth said, panicked. She read quietly to herself. Laurent was barking again. I caught bits of what she was saying. "'—caught a flight—since we're so near each other, why don't we meet?'" Elizabeth's panic was palpable even over the phone. "She wants to meet me."

"Of course she does," I said. I knew if Leora found out a grandchild was on the way, she'd be on the first flight to London.

"Can you come with me?"

"You want *me* to come?"

"I don't want the first time I meet my child's grandmother to be this awkward encounter with a stranger. I want someone there who knows us both."

But I didn't know Elizabeth. I'd felt guilty I wasn't being my true self, but she'd done the same thing. I didn't know who I'd spent the last few days with.

"Maybe she can come to me," Elizabeth said.

"She's like seventy. You can meet her. She'll appreciate that."

Elizabeth sighed. Then: "See, this is why I need you. You know her."

My head felt heavy, like I had a sinus headache. I sat on the bed. I looked at my luggage by the door. Then I lay down on the bed, placing the phone next to me, by my ear.

I'd come to London to find a way to get Elizabeth to communicate with Leora. Now they were in touch, but they needed a little help. I thought about my morning, how I'd spent it, bleary-eyed, searching through hot takes on *Puppy Love*. There is a jewelry-making technique called annealing, it's a fundamental in which heat is used to loosen a metal so it's more pliable, easier to work with and shape. When beginning as an amateur, the risk with annealing is that you keep applying heat, missing the moment right before you've gone too far, before the material breaks down, completely liquefying.

It was too much. I sat up on my elbows. I'd had enough. I shook my head, even though Elizabeth couldn't see me. "I don't think I can be your representative," I said.

"I'm not asking you to be my representative. You'd be Gabe's representative."

I was getting the sense that Kathy had been wrong, that what she said at Gabe's funeral about it hitting you in waves was not happening to me, that instead I was slowly disintegrating, breaking down under the heat and pressure. But—I reasoned—I could take it a little further.

The three of us would meet at some London café, I'd facilitate an introduction, then leave as they sat down. I'd stand outside the window, lingering for a moment as they connected, then catch a flight home. I would do this for Leora, and I would also do this for Gabe. I'd come this far and I could see it through to the end. If I owed Gabe anything—and I wasn't sure I did—I could do this for him. I could be his representative, as Elizabeth put it, and find a way to bring his mother and the mother of his child together. I hadn't shown up to the hotel, I could show up now.

And that would be it. I could take a little more as long as I knew this was it.

"Okay," I said. "I'll go with you to see Leora."

"Thank you." Elizabeth exhaled. "She wants to meet as soon as possible."

"Where's she staying? Not Shoreditch?" I couldn't imagine Leora in such an aggressively hip neighborhood. But I must have missed where exactly Leora was and where we would be going because Elizabeth said, "She's not in London. She's in Barcelona."

TWENTY-SIX

I canceled my flight home, an extra expense I'd have to live with. Elizabeth left Laurent with Jeremy and Sungmi. We were on the same flight, but our seats weren't together. As we deplaned I got a text from Elizabeth asking what I thought was the best way to get to Roberta's. This was our only communication aside from a brief acknowledgment of each other's existence in front of El Prat. She didn't mention the Desert Sushi line, I didn't mention the bracelet. Fine. For now we could enter a détente and focus on Leora.

I had not been back to Barcelona since my summer there. As we entered the city, it seemed both familiar and unfamiliar. There were more people, crowds of people. Hadn't Gabe and I walked down an alley together, alone except for a stray cat trailing behind us? I couldn't imagine finding that kind of privacy in the city now. We drove down a long boulevard with several street kiosks selling FC Barcelona merchandise, blue and red stripes on mugs, T-shirts, pennants, underwear. Of course I knew soccer (football) was huge here; I'd once seen a waiter, in the middle of taking someone's order, abruptly run off to the bar next door because he'd heard people yelling and knew that meant someone had scored a goal. The person ordering, a local, wasn't upset at all; they wanted to know the score too. But I didn't remember there being *this* much football stuff everywhere. Of course I'd been distracted. I was young, in love, and had just discovered pan con tomate.

The cab ride was silent until Elizabeth said to our driver, "Excuse me? Can you stop here? Stop here, please." The driver said there was no place to pull over. She was insistent. I wondered if it was her nausea. Was she going to throw up in the car? He turned down a side street. Elizabeth got out and ran back the way we'd come. I twisted in my seat so I could look out the back window. She ran past a phone repair shop, a café, then stopped at a flower stand on the corner. I watched as she spoke animatedly to the man in front of the stand, gesturing to different bouquets.

She came back a few minutes later, sliding into the back seat, holding three bouquets. "I didn't want to arrive empty-handed," she said. As the driver pulled into traffic, she quickly disassembled the bouquets, resting some flowers on her lap, the rest on the floor. She rearranged them, tucking stems lower or higher, every now and then plucking leaves; she took a particularly stubborn one off with her teeth, the refuse went into her dress pockets. By the end she had something worthy of Elizabeth Thompson's Floral Atelier.

Roberta didn't live in the same place she had when she taught me, her new apartment was in the Gothic Quarter, down an alley between two buildings, both with those metal roll-up graffitied doors you see in European cities. She was standing in the doorway when we arrived, wearing a long-sleeved multipatterned caftan. Her hair was white now and cut low into the teeniest Afro. Her face broke into a huge smile when she saw me. There were wrinkles in the corners of her eyes but other than that her skin was smooth. The Black had not cracked. "Look at you," she said. She wrapped her arms around me. We'd kept in touch with emails every now and then, and I'd heard updates from Gabe and Leora, but none of that compared to standing in front of each other.

"It is so good to see you," I said. My head hit her breastbone and I rested there for a moment before stepping back. "You too," she said, lightly patting my cheek. She shook Elizabeth's hand. "It's wonderful to meet you. Come in, come in."

The apartment was bigger than her previous place, nearly three times the size. The living room was decorated in warm colors, mostly browns and yellows, a lot of wood. *Patina* was a word I thought was overused in design. It came up in jewelry descriptions all the time. Just because something was old did not mean it had a patina. But we were in a Barcelona apartment, and not only was it old—as we walked in, Roberta said the apartment still had its original tiles from 1906— but everything had a lived-in feel, nothing was modern, each piece seemed to have a past life, a story of its own.

There was also original wallpaper, Roberta explained. But it had seemed a bit tacky to keep the entire place covered in it, so they'd left it in only one area of the apartment, placing framed art over it to create a gallery wall. "You get the old and the new," she said.

"Very Barcelona," I said.

"Exactly." Roberta looked at me proudly, like she was my professor again. "Ana saw a photo of the walls in a local architect's home and got the idea."

I remembered pictures online of Roberta and her wife on some beach, garlands of red flowers around their necks. Ana was older, also a professor, there was some family money involved. Which made sense. Their apartment was large, expertly arranged. A singular taste was present here, as it had been in Roberta's old apartment. But now there were just so many more *things*, and all these things were very, very nice.

A lot of the artwork was the same as I remembered in her smaller place but now there was also a television amid the framed works. On shelving below the TV were pictures of Roberta and her family. I gasped. "No! Is that Tamara?" I picked up a photo of a teenage girl. "How old is she now?"

"Sixteen," Roberta said.

"*No.* That's impossible." I dove in for a closer look at the photo. If Tamara was sixteen, how old was I?

Elizabeth interrupted, "Excuse me, do you mind if I use the loo? Just to freshen up?"

"Absolutely, let me show you where it is."

Roberta took Elizabeth down the hall. I heard a snippet of their conversation, Roberta asking about the flight, and then they fell out of earshot. Behind me, a door slid shut. Leora stepped in from the balcony. "Hi!" I yelped. She'd surprised me. I rushed over to hug her; she let one arm fall limply over my shoulder. Her hair was wet. She was wearing a similar dress to Roberta's with long flowy sleeves.

"Your flight was late." She spoke flatly, her voice absent of warmth.

"Oh. Sorry. I should have texted." I hurried to the sofa. I'd dropped my stuff down next to it. "I have the guitar. And the cap, it's in my bag." I unpacked the hat and handed it to her.

She placed it on the top of the sofa, then leaned down to the guitar case. She unzipped it and took out the guitar. She strummed a finger across the strings, blending six notes into one. "This is it," she said. Her shoulders dropped, her expression softened. But only for a second. "What about the sheet music?" she asked in the tone of someone who'd just been handed a greasy bag of fast food and discovered it was missing the fries they'd ordered.

"We ran into some trouble with that."

"We? Have you been staying with Elizabeth?"

"No, I was at a hotel. But for most of Gabe's things, we looked together." A door closed. I glimpsed Roberta in the hallway but she left us alone and went into the kitchen.

Leora folded her arms. "How long have you known Elizabeth's pregnant?"

"Not long."

"Is it why you went to London to see her?"

"I went to London to get Gabe's stuff. Like you asked."

"I never asked you to go to London."

Down the hall, a toilet flushed.

"Maybe if you'd stayed out of it, Elizabeth would have told me sooner."

She absolutely would not have, I thought. She might not even have agreed to meet you at all if it weren't for me. But I didn't say any of that. I couldn't start our visit with an immediate character assassination of Elizabeth. I was focused on greasing the wheels so the two of them could get along. After that my work would be done, then I could privately confront Elizabeth about the bracelet, get it back, and *leave*.

"I'm sorry I didn't tell you she was pregnant, but it wasn't really my place to say anything." I sat on the arm of the sofa, adding—defensively I'll admit—"Gabe should have." The shift on her face was minor, but I could tell I'd hit a sore spot. Was it fair to put my gripes with Gabe—the blame that I was in this situation in the first place—on Leora? I wasn't sure. But reviewing our conversation, I *was* sure that at no point had she thanked me.

"Hello."

Elizabeth stood in the hallway at the edge of the room. Leora's eyes widened in disbelief, as if Elizabeth were an apparition. Leora pushed the heel of her hand against one eye, then the other. "Hello," she said. She paused, at first unsure what to do next, but then she threw away her hesitations and rushed forward. "Oh hello, *hello*." She clutched Elizabeth's arms and pulled her in for a hug. Elizabeth was still holding the bouquet she'd made in the car. She gripped the flowers awkwardly in one hand like a prom date at the door as Leora asked her questions about the pregnancy, how far along was she, what were her plans for delivery, had she spent any time in California before and would she like to? Elizabeth was completely overwhelmed, she kept glancing at me as Leora talked. It was so far from the calm she usually exuded. Blinking eyes. A fake, frozen smile. "Sorry, I'm talking too much," Leora said. "I haven't even given you a chance. I just want to say thank you." She held on to Elizabeth's hand. "Thank you." She said this over and over again. "Thank you, thank you."

That was my cue to leave.

I sat with Roberta in the kitchen, on counter stools in front of an island. To the right of us was a small table with plants and a spice rack. "Is that the table you used to have?" I asked.

"Good memory," she said.

It was only a short time that I spent in Roberta's home, but it was significant, I'd taken in every detail. There were probably pieces of furniture in my own apartment I'd spent less time studying. Gabe and I had stood on opposite sides of that table after we met, when he made me a peanut butter sandwich. In the same place, I'd watched Roberta prepare the platter of shrimp she served on the night she accidentally revealed my feelings to Gabe. An old memory, shelved in the back of my mind: Leora and I playing spades, I was impressed by how fast she shuffled the deck.

"How is she doing?" I asked Roberta.

She nodded deeply, the nod an acknowledgment that she'd been expecting this question. "Better since she arrived." Roberta was wearing large silver disc earrings. She adjusted one of them as she spoke. "I'm sure it was hard for her, getting on the plane, but it was the right decision."

"You invited her to come?"

"Me and a few of her other friends, we talked about it, and it seemed better for her to be out of that house. And with Tamara and Ana going to visit Ana's family, I had the room."

"And you have Barcelona."

"Yes. I beat out a walk-up in the Village and a guest room above a garage in Wisconsin. So she gets some sun. We take a long daily walk, there's always something new to see. She swims in the pool."

I looked around. The apartment was big, but I didn't see room for a pool.

"On the roof. This time of year it's more like a tepid hot tub. It's small, but you can float, do a few strokes from one end to the other. Which is all she needs."

"That's good," I said.

"It's the worst possible thing," Roberta responded. Because we were having two conversations at once. Leora was fine. Leora could never be fine.

"How are *you*?" she asked. She grasped my hand. "I know you two stayed close, and how much you meant to him—" Something in me snapped open—my eyes glistened—but it slammed shut again as Leora burst into the kitchen.

"I'm having a grandchild. A girl!" she cried out.

"A girl!" I said, mirroring her, but also exaggerating my surprise so she would see this was something I didn't know. I wasn't ahead of her anymore. Roberta hugged her. I stepped around them and went to find Elizabeth.

She was on the sofa. I sat down on a rattan and curved bamboo chair across from her, it was throne-like and elaborately woven. It looked cool but was uncomfortable.

"How did it go?" I asked.

"Well. Surprisingly well." She leaned forward. "She told me how she knew I was pregnant."

"How?" I'd listened to "Missing the Tracks" eight times on the plane and still hadn't figured it out.

"You'll never guess," Elizabeth whispered. "Gabe used the same phrase she used in her first book about him."

"What?" I asked which lyric it was.

Elizabeth closed her eyes and spoke slowly, carefully recalling the exact lyric. "'Walking down the beam with my bean. A Jack trade.'" Her eyes snapped open. "Does that make sense to you?"

"No." It was a vague reference to "Jack and the Beanstalk," I'd gotten that. The bean was time, people online thought. Or his talent. The reigning theory was that it was about planting something now that would harvest later.

Elizabeth said, "I guess, in her poem, she compared being pregnant to being suspended in the air above the city, leaping into an unknown. She'd really wanted to get pregnant, but she'd had a miscarriage before and she didn't want to get attached this time. She couldn't bring herself to say, 'I'm having a *baby*.' So she called him the Bean. But then eventually she got excited and started calling him by his name. Jack."

"Jack?"

"I know. She said when he came out, he didn't look like a Jack. So they went with Ramiro's choice. Gabriel."

"Wow. And he remembered her line and used it again. Do you think he was going to play the song for her eventually, like as a way to tell her?"

"That's what I wondered." Multiple emotions crossed Elizabeth's face. Calm, a bit of regret. Worry? "I should be so lucky to be that connected to this child." She placed a hand on her stomach, looking down, perhaps making some silent wish that this would be the case. That completed, her attention returned to me. "I'm sorry I accused you of telling her."

"Oh," I said. Yes, I was innocent. But I'd known that. What about Elizabeth keeping Gabe's bracelet? I turned to check where

Roberta and Leora were. How much time did Elizabeth and I have for a private conversation? Not any, it turned out. Roberta stuck her head out of the kitchen. "We're thinking dinner soon?"

Even though Elizabeth owned a restaurant and Roberta was a good cook, no one wanted to make dinner. Everyone agreed it would require a grocery run, not to mention a hot oven, so we ordered pizza. None of us were in town for the tapas.

While we ate, I asked Elizabeth questions Leora would be curious about, I asked Leora questions I knew Elizabeth would be curious about. Aided by me, they covered Gabe's childhood, his friends in London, how often he played at Fleur Bleue, Leora's experience with guitar playing in college, and how she shared music with Gabe. As they talked about the importance of music in early childhood development, I asked Roberta questions about Tamara. I was aware I was the only one at the table not a mother, but it didn't bother me in the specific motherhood sense of it (I had no desire to join their club); it bothered me because I'd become bored by the conversation and I was anxious for dinner to end. What I really wanted to do was grab Elizabeth by the arm, pull her into a private corner of the house, and say, *Look, I may not have his kid, and that's fine, but the bracelet is mine, pony up.* There was no such opportunity. For the rest of the evening, the four of us were together.

At the end of the night, when we were back in the living room, three glasses of wine and a mug of tea on the coffee table, Roberta asked, "You'll stay here tonight?" She and I were on the sofa. Leora was in the rattan and bamboo chair and Elizabeth was sitting on the floor.

Elizabeth leaned forward. "Uh, no. We weren't sure." She glanced at Leora. "We thought we'd see and if we had to, check for last-minute hotel rooms . . ."

"Please stay," Leora said. "Roberta and I go on walks during the day, I'd love for you to join us."

You. Not you and Julia.

I stood up. "I'll head out."

"No!" Elizabeth insisted. "No, that wouldn't make sense because you have your bag, and then there's my stuff as well, we should just keep everything together, shouldn't we?"

I saw what she was trying to do. She wanted it to seem like we came as a pair. She thought she still needed me. She didn't, it turned out Leora was more upset with me than her.

"Yes, Julia, you can stay here too," Roberta said. Everyone looked at me, waiting for my response, Elizabeth subtly nodding her head, indicating how she needed me to respond.

Roberta continued, "You're my guest, I'm not going to throw you back out onto the streets of Barcelona. Unless you really think you'd be more comfortable at a hotel?"

"No, I'm just super uncomfortable *here*," I said, launching into that thing where you make an honest joke about an awkwardness but then, because of that real awkwardness, everyone desperately wants to relieve the tension, so they overcompensate by doubling down on the laughter, like you've just said the funniest thing in the world, and meanwhile the point you were hoping would be made ends up completely ignored. You never know, sometimes people catch on, it's a way to get out of a situation. But not in this case.

Elizabeth and I took Tamara's room. Every surface was either loud purple or fluorescent teal, completely different from the browns and golds of the rest of the home. It was in transition between early and late adolescence. Dolls on top of a bookshelf, along with ribbons and trophies, mixed with textbooks and makeup palettes. A poster of a boy band on the back of the door.

Elizabeth went into the bathroom to get ready for bed. After she finished, she went to the kitchen for a glass of water. I waited for her to return. We needed to talk. But she was gone for a long time. I took a shower and brushed my teeth. When I left the bathroom, Elizabeth still wasn't back. I stepped into the hallway. I heard voices in the kitchen. Elizabeth's and Leora's. I went back to Tamara's room and got in bed. I thought I'd wait her out, but I fell asleep. When I woke up, Elizabeth was asleep in bed next to me. It was a full-sized bed, so there wasn't much room and we were squished together. Her long frame curled up, the backs of her feet hitting my legs.

IN THE MORNING, SHE WAS GONE AGAIN. OKAY, I THOUGHT, SO SHE'S avoiding me. I walked through the apartment, it was quiet. Roberta was alone in the kitchen, drinking coffee. She said I'd just missed Elizabeth, she'd gone up to the pool. I left the apartment and hurried up the stairs to the roof. I couldn't handle another day of sitting—or in the case of last night, lying—right next to each other without discussing the bracelet. The stairwell door banged shut behind me.

Elizabeth was stripping out of a lavender nightshirt, a navy blue bathing suit underneath. She looked up, putting her finger against her lips. "Shh." She pointed to a lounge chair in front of her. Leora was lying across it, asleep, one arm dangling, the other tucked closely against her body. She wore a black bikini (I couldn't help thinking *not your traditional* mourningwear) and her hair was in that half-wet, half-dried state. I wondered if this was the only way she could sleep these days, outside, pummeled by the sun. This was a woman who wore long sleeves and a giant sun hat to get the mail, adamant she protect her skin, something about righting the wrongs of an adolescence spent baking on the Jersey Shore. Her choice to sunbathe on a Barcelona patio seemed less like a devil-may-care, when-in-Rome spontaneous decision and more like a death wish, or at least a complete giving up. My entrance didn't wake her, but it must have disturbed her sleep because she adjusted herself. Her head fell forward, nearly drifting off the edge of the chair. I reached out to gently push it back, but as I did, I noticed something.

Elizabeth clutched my arm, squeezing hard. She saw it too. "Julia? Julia?" She whispered my name a few times. I was glued in place until she pulled me away.

Once we were back in our room, the door closed, Elizabeth turned to me, eyes wide. "What the bloody hell? Did you see?"

I had.

"Right there on her wrist!"

We'd finally found Gabe's bracelet.

TWENTY-SEVEN

Did you know? Did she tell you?" Elizabeth had grabbed her nightshirt as we left, she pulled it over herself.

I didn't, she hadn't. Had Leora been wearing the bracelet when we arrived yesterday? She'd had on long sleeves, maybe it was covered.

"Does she know you're looking for it?" Elizabeth asked.

"Yes. Well no, kind of. I don't know." I peeked out the door. Was Leora still upstairs? Where was Roberta? "I thought you had it," I said.

"Me?" Elizabeth reared her head back, genuinely shocked. "You went through my entire home. I would have told you if I had it by now, don't you think?"

"There's a theory online that Gabe gave you the bracelet," I explained. "There were *pictures* of you with it on a French site." A weak argument when weighed against her being clearly not in possession of the bracelet.

But she knew what I was talking about. "That wasn't Gabe's bracelet. That was the bracelet I bought to replace Gabe's bracelet. I told you. He didn't want it. I couldn't return it. I thought maybe I'd reclaim it, have a buy-the-flowers-for-my-damn-self moment. A bit pathetic, really. But it was in my jewelry box, and when the magazine stylist was here, she went through my stuff, pulling pieces she thought would work for the spread. They do that sometimes."

"I know they do that sometimes," I said, annoyed. Yes, they did do that sometimes. A few of my pieces had ended up in magazine spreads because of that. Jewelry, actress's own.

Elizabeth went over to her luggage and opened her travel bag, then a smaller jewelry organizer. She took out a velvet pouch. "Here," she said, handing it to me. "I've been keeping it with me." She looked away, embarrassed. "I don't know why, just to have it."

I opened the pouch. There was the bracelet Elizabeth had bought for Gabe. There was a little tag with the engraving: medical: *situs inversus*. Then, on the back, *Protect him.*

ELIZABETH WASTED NO TIME. ROBERTA FELT BAD ABOUT PIZZA THE night before and had gone to great lengths with brunch. On the table were scrambled eggs, pancakes, ham, and a bowl of oranges. Leora was the last to sit down, back from a shower, and as soon as she did, Elizabeth said, "So Leora, Julia and I noticed something."

"What's that?" Leora asked. She reached for an orange.

Elizabeth and I were on one side of the table, Roberta and Leora across from us. Leora peeled her orange. She glanced at Elizabeth, then at me. Elizabeth looked to me, silently urging me to grab the baton.

"Your bracelet," I said.

"It's Gabe's," Leora responded.

"Yes, we know," Elizabeth said.

I spoke gently. "I was looking for it, remember? When I came to your house."

"I didn't have it then," Leora explained. She popped an orange segment into her mouth. I was going to say she could have contacted me, but then I remembered that until recently I had been avoiding communication with her.

"Where was it?" I asked. "Where did you find it?"

She chewed, then swallowed. "I didn't, Ramiro did. Gabe sent it to him."

"*Gabe* sent it?"

"Apparently, he left it on a nightstand at this rental and then contacted the owner about getting it back. But he was traveling, so he had it shipped to Ramiro's in Colorado because he was planning to see him when he did a show there. And, of course, it got shipped to the wrong place, I think Gabe got the zip code wrong? It was rerouted, stuck at some post office for a while, but it made it to Ramiro. And Ramiro gave it to me."

As soon as she'd mentioned a rental, a ripple of fear raced along my spine.

"Where was the rental?" I asked.

"Some house he stayed in this summer after a show. In Joshua Tree."

I had to say it out loud. "The bracelet was in that house in Joshua Tree?"

301

"Yes." Leora nodded.

Elizabeth was right. He did take the bracelet off at night. I'd dismissed it, but of course she'd lived with him; she would know. The bracelet was where I'd last seen it. He didn't discard it out of anger or relinquish it because it didn't matter anymore; it wasn't lost and forgotten. He'd taken it off when he was with me. And then he'd tried to get it back.

TWENTY-EIGHT

Leora continued. "I understand if you—if you were hoping that if we found the bracelet, you'd be able to keep it." I'd been hit, thrown off the road, and now here was a Mack truck barreling toward me. "I understand why you would want it. You made it when the two of you were here in Barcelona. But he wore it every day, it's a part of him now. So I'd like to keep it."

I stood up. "Excuse me." The words came out muffled and strange, barely making their way out of my locked jaw.

I went to Tamara's room and sat on the bed.

Minutes passed. They were clearing the table. A door slammed. Someone left the apartment. The bedroom door opened. Elizabeth stood in the doorway, arms folded across her chest. "They're taking their walk," she said. "I asked them to go without me."

I knew what was coming. I could feel it, a shift in the atmosphere. Something fragilely balanced between us had tipped over.

"Desert Sushi is in Joshua Tree," she said.

"Yes."

"And you were there at that house in Joshua Tree with him."

"Yes."

She shook her head. "I knew you slept with him. Even before I heard that song. I knew it."

"Not while you were together."

"Oh goody! What a relief then!" She spoke sarcastically, followed by a slightly maniacal titter. "The reason he kept that bracelet, that *specific* bracelet, was because of *you*. Wherever he was, on the road, onstage, in another country, his precious Julia would be with him. But I guess he wouldn't need it when you were right there in front of him, the two of you secretly fucking in some desert resort. He must have been too distracted, lost in the eyes of the woman he once said was"—she raised her voice—"*and I quote: like a dude to him.*"

My entire body was tight. Like everything had fused together and if I moved a muscle, I would shatter. I spoke slowly, as if each word had the potential of setting off a bomb. "I'm sure I was like a dude to him. Things changed very quickly."

"I bet they did." She paced in a small loop by the door. While I was trying to slow us down, she was speeding up.

I said, "I'm sorry I didn't tell you the truth."

She paused her pacing. "This isn't about me."

"What?"

"This has nothing to do with me. You don't even know me. I just met you. Tell me or don't tell me that you hooked up with Gabe."

I shook my head. "You had the right to know, I could have told you."

"You don't believe that. You've never believed I had a right to anything regarding Gabe."

"It was one weekend in August. And right after, he disappeared. I think because he heard from you about the baby." I saw Elizabeth calculating this in her head. I continued. "And then I didn't hear from him for weeks," I explained. "Until the night of his show at Hotel Frank, he called me. We didn't talk, he just left a voicemail. But I texted. We were going to meet there. I said I would, but I didn't show."

"You said he lied."

"I said . . ." I didn't remember what I'd said. She blinked at me, furious. I stood up. "Listen, I saw your life in London. What the two of you had. I think he was going to tell me that he wanted to make it work with you. And the last time you spoke to him—"

"The last time I spoke to him was a very terse conversation about antenatal care."

"But it makes sense that he—"

She threw up her hands. "Don't you *dare* tell me I was the better option on paper. Surely you know that's not what love is."

"He left me in Joshua Tree. He went back to London."

"And then he came back to LA. To see *you*."

I felt the tears gathering, the same weight of emotions that had nearly consumed me at the museum in front of the Frankenthaler painting, a bullet of shame tearing through the center of my chest. I wrapped my arms around my body as if I could contain it all.

"Does it make you feel better to imagine some little triangle in your head?" Elizabeth asked. "Where it's all about"—she switched to a whiny, girlish voice—"'Oh, which one of us did Gabe like most? Who was his true love? Which one of us would he choose?' Does that actually help you, Julia? So if he didn't choose you, you can just move on then?" She whisked her hands back and forth. "And be done with it? That settle it?"

I walked out of the bedroom, into the hallway.

"Sure, fine," Elizabeth said. She was on my heels. "I'll tell you right now. He didn't like you much. He hated you. That's a decoy bracelet Leora's wearing. The real one he had crushed because he couldn't stand the sight of you. Feel better now? Is that all squared away?"

When I reached the living room and she was still behind me, I spun around to face her. "*What?*"

"I'm genuinely curious. Why are you trying to prove he didn't love you?"

She knew why, it seemed. She had known all along maybe, and now she needed me to say it. "Because what would it mean if he did, Elizabeth? What would that mean? That he wanted to talk and I didn't go? That he needed me, and I was holding a *grudge*? That probably would have *passed*? And then he died and that was my last chance to see him, and I'll never know what he wanted to tell me?"

"What would you have wanted him to say?"

"It doesn't matter!" Why was she not getting this? "He's gone. He's dead."

"It doesn't matter? I think it does. Otherwise you end up walking around with a wound and you don't know how you got it."

"What I know is I'll never know what he would have said, because I didn't go to the hotel. Why would I want to *talk* about that? How do I come back from that? How do I survive that?"

"I don't know how you survive that!" Her voice was raised, nearly to a yell. "How do I survive raising a child without him?

How does Leora survive without her son? We don't get to choose. You can't opt out. You lost him. We lost him." She collapsed onto the couch. She leaned over with her head in her hands. "You are so like Gabe. You are so like him. And I can't believe I'm doing this again."

"Doing what?"

"Trying to help some emotionally stunted child who can't get out of their own way! Listen to me, Julia, this is the last thing I'm going to do, this is the last time I'll try to help."

"Good!"

"Grief—"

"I know, I know. It comes in waves."

"What? No, I was going to say grief is a monster. It's been three weeks since Gabe died. Three weeks. I know it feels like longer because you're in it, but it's not. And yes, it comes in waves. But first you have to step in the water." Then she stood up. "Honestly, fuck the both of you." She stalked back down the hallway to Tamara's room and slammed the door.

TWENTY-NINE

I left the apartment. I walked for blocks. At Parc Güell, there was a long line in front. I joined and waited. My feet hurt. My neck ached. I'd forgotten sunglasses and held my hand over my eyes, squinting. The line moved forward inch by inch. I reached the gates and handed over my entrance fee. There were palm trees in the park, perhaps the cousins of the palm trees back in Los Angeles.

AFTER MANDY TOLD ME SEPARATE BEDROOMS WAS DEAD, I LEFT MY studio and drove straight to the hotel. I called Gabe on the way, several times. He didn't answer my calls, but that was nothing new. And after I'd stood him up, why would he now? My heart pressed against my chest. It was coming out, whether I liked it or not. There were only two ways this would end: it would escape through my throat or seize violently in cardiac arrest.

Hotel Frank was a new boutique hotel downtown. The closest parking spot was two blocks away, and I ran the rest of the way. But it felt like I was in a cartoon where the destination moved farther and farther away. Or maybe I was creating my own resistance. I had to get there. I had to go back to my car, drive away, and never know. A group of teenagers ahead of me were laughing and goofing around, trying to impress each other the way teenagers do. These efforts would not be stopped for anything. Neither rain nor sleet nor a thirty-year-old woman trying to get by them. I don't know how I got past them, how I made it to the hotel, but I did.

There were maybe five or six fans gathered outside. I could tell because two of them were wearing Separate Bedrooms shirts. "They're not letting anyone in," one of them said. It was only once I was inside that I realized the voice had been addressing me.

"Miss?" a security guard, a middle-aged Black man, called out to me.

I continued to the front desk. It was daytime, but the lobby was dark. The heavy velvet curtains of the hotel windows were drawn, the only lighting was ambient. Marble flooring gleamed under chandelier light. To my left was the bar. Empty except for a woman with balayage waves, leaning against an olive-green leather bar stool, talking on her cell phone. "It's so LA, right? Like, I guess I picked the right hotel." She laughed.

The man at the desk was small and trim. His suit the color of eggplant. He was scrolling on his phone. "Excuse me?" I asked softly.

He looked up. "Sorry about that," he said. "They're waiting to find out—it's nothing, ma'am. How can I help you?" I had gone from miss to ma'am in crossing the lobby.

"I need to speak to a manager. I need to speak to someone."

"Maybe I can help with something? Or connect you to guest services?"

"No, I'm not a guest."

"Then what is this in reference to?"

I should have said I was a guest.

"I read," I said. "I'm checking to see if it's accurate. Separate Bedrooms."

His face closed. He spoke as if reading something from memory. "We do not have a statement at this time."

"I just want to know if it's true."

"Ma'am, the hotel is not speaking to anyone."

Someone from outside yelled. The same voice that had been at my shoulder. "Why does she get to come in?" It was a man from the group of fans I'd passed. Now he was in the lobby too.

"She doesn't," the concierge said. He waved, trying to get the security guard's attention. The guard escorted the man outside.

"It's fine," I said. "I'm not a fan."

"We're not speaking to anyone," he repeated.

"I just need to know if it's true."

"Ma'am. We are not speaking to anyone."

My hands slammed against his desk. *"I know him."*

The concierge looked at me and seemed to believe this, but then some kind of training kicked in and he became rigid.

"Do you have any proof of that?"

"Proof?"

"Proof that you knew him."

I felt a pulling sensation in my chest. My hands were tense. I realized I was still gripping the desk. I could not talk to this man anymore. That was clear. I walked out, past the gathered fans. They were sobbing. While I was inside, it had been confirmed. I found out later Kathy had to reach Leora first, before the news broke. There was no time to tell the rest of us.

I LEFT PARC GÜELL. I WALKED BACK THE WAY I'D COME, BUT DIDN'T return to Roberta's. I sat in front of a café, under an umbrella, in one of those flimsy metal sidewalk chairs. Conversation and traffic blended together. A waiter came over and asked what I would like. I ordered an Aperol Spritz because that's what the women at the table next to me were drinking. I didn't drink it, I just wanted a place to sit.

I pictured in my mind what it would have been like if I could have chosen the last time I saw Gabe. A crisp white shirt, condensation forming around something like an Aperol Spritz, red lipstick, green flannel, whiskey, a really good song on the speakers, him mouthing along to the music, tapping his foot on the lower rung of my chair.

A memory flitted by like a hummingbird. The actual last time I saw Gabe. Gabe in the sun, leaning against his rental car, arms raised up over his head, the curve of his biceps. A ripple of desire replacing affection. He brought his arms down and held them out to me. I went to him. I wanted to go back to that last moment and change something. But what? Every time I puzzled over the picture trying to figure out where I went wrong, time was up, it was gone.

The ice in my drink melted. My phone buzzed.

Where are you? I didn't mean literally jump in the ocean

Now I feel like if the police find this and you are in the ocean it will look suspicious that I texted you something about jumping in the ocean right before you were found

She really could not help herself.

Elizabeth texted a third time. *Are you okay?*

I didn't know what to say, but if I'd learned anything recently it was that when someone was trying to get ahold of you, you should always text back. I wrote *no*.

I had been bracing myself for a massive upheaval. I had been waiting it out. But it wasn't something that would pounce on you, like a wolf, hidden by night, leaping from the bushes. At least, that's not how it was for me. Nothing took me over. I stepped forward. I met it. And then it was like a Frankenthaler painting, I became the heavily woven canvas, and it didn't undo me; it sank through, it stained.

People passed by. They talked to each other, some were alone. Then as the hours went by, there were more and more people, like buses were dropping them off. The sun set. The sky turned pink and gold. Then blue again, darker blue, that point in the evening when the sky takes on the hue of a blueberry, before subtly sinking into black night. Everyone in the world walked by. Except one.

WHEN I RETURNED TO THE APARTMENT, LEORA LET ME IN. SHE went into the kitchen. I figured Elizabeth was in Tamara's room and

I wasn't ready for that yet, so I followed Leora. She took a water pitcher out of the fridge. "Do you want some?" she asked.

"Sure," I said. She poured water into a glass, Gabe's bracelet slid down her wrist. She put the pitcher down, the bracelet slid back up toward her elbow. "What are you going to do with it?" I asked. "Will you keep wearing it?"

"I don't think so. I wanted to keep it close, but it's a little too big for my wrist"—she shook her arm back and forth to demonstrate how easily it moved—"and I don't want to do anything to change it from how he wore it." She took it off and placed it on the table, as if reminding herself that she should not be wearing it. "I think I'll find a nice box for it, maybe?"

"A box?"

"With the rest of Gabe's things."

So a large, tucked-away box.

I leaned over the table and reached for the bracelet. Probably too aggressively, like I was starving and someone had offered up this morsel of bread. I don't think Leora was expecting this desperation. She didn't try to stop me, she moved it closer to me. I put my hand over it. The warmth from the heat it had accumulated from Leora's body sank into my palm. It was lighter than I remembered.

"Are you angry with me?" That was it, wasn't it? That was why she didn't want to give me the bracelet.

"No." She shook her head. "I'm angry."

Angry. Full stop.

"It's not an excuse," she said. "And I should have said thank you."

"Can I have it?" I asked.

"Julia, I would, but—" She placed her glass on the table and sat down. She ran her hands over her hair, from her temple to the ends. The motion, the way she did it, it was so Gabe. Or he was so her. "He wore it every day. For his entire adult life. The entire time after he'd left home." Her voice snagged on this statement and I knew if she continued talking, it would rip her apart.

"I understand," I said. I did. When she wasn't there, the bracelet was. They were both meant to protect him, neither had saved him; they had this in common. It was a relief, after the many lies I'd recently told. Here was something I swore was true, and I was holding firm: Leora could have whatever she wanted. She could have the bracelet.

It might provide her comfort. Maybe she would decide to wear it, and it would feel like he was there with her, holding her hand in his. The chain knocking against a car door or countertop edge might remind her of his movements around her house. And maybe sometimes it would feel like a cold piece of metal. Kind of like it did in my hand now. I put it back on the table.

I sat in the chair next to her. This is all you will ever be able to do, a voice in my head said. We sat together in silence. I stayed there with her for as long as I could. Longer than I thought I could bear.

THIRTY

I went into Tamara's room. Elizabeth was lying on the bed, her laptop out. She said, "You're back."

Her tone was ice. I didn't blame her, but I did think about what Gabe had said. *She's a fundamentally cold person.* He was wrong. Yes, there was a chill in her voice, but in it there was also heat; a pleading, growing frustration that threatened to boil over. She was trying to cool *herself* down. But she could not self-extinguish on command. She was incapable of pretending things were fine when they weren't. And I could see how this would irritate him. Because Gabe, like me, was more than capable of pretending things were fine when they weren't.

I sat down on the bed. "I'm sorry," I said. I'd already apologized but I needed to do it again. "I wasn't trying to lie." The rest was hard to admit because it felt like an excuse but it was the real reason. "I just didn't know how to be honest."

She was quiet, thinking, then said, "Yes, it's harder than it looks, isn't it?"

I scooted back until I was against the headboard next to her. I saw that she was looking up flights back to London. I took out my phone and looked for the same, to America. Neither one of us was going to spend another day in Barcelona. For some time, the only sound was the clicks and whooshes of internet travel confirmation. Then Elizabeth said, "Did he ever do this thing when kissing? Like kind of tapping with his—"

"His foot, yeah."

She snapped her fingers at me, like yes, bang on, that's it.

"It was weird."

"Like a dog!" She cackled. Adding, "I quite liked it."

THIRTY-ONE

It comes in waves.

Sometimes a cliché is true. And sometimes it requires an addendum. I didn't dive into any bodies of water, but I did return to my life. Without Gabe.

Casey picked me up at LAX. I apologized for not telling him the truth sooner. He said he would have gone to Will first too. Outside my bungalow, I watched him drive off, then I opened the white gate, walked past the sun-streaked jasmine vines, and crawled into bed. The next morning I took a shower. I went back to work. That weekend, I photographed the jacket and skirt I'd worn to Gabe's funeral, then sold and packed them up. For the last month before the election, I phone banked with Casey and Will. In November, I thought, At least Gabe's not around to see *this*. I spent Christmas with my parents, I visited my cousin Ines. I finished Casey's and Will's rings. At their wedding, Jeanette said, "We need love more than ever." I pointed out to her that Casey and Will had fallen in love in LA, so it could be done. Elizabeth and I stayed in touch, texting throughout the year, plus a video call to introduce me to the baby. I went to New Mexico to see some of Georgia O'Keeffe's work in person. I stood alone on a mesa looking at the rock formations she'd painted. I'd gone there for peace and calm, but I ended up weeping. Which wasn't a surprise at that point. Weeping, wailing, laughing, throwing things, not getting off the floor for hours, going to bed too early, waking up too late. Sobbing! Oh yes, there are many ways to cry. I learned them all. "It's going to take some time," Elizabeth had told me at the Barcelona airport. "It just takes time." And then it was September, the anniversary of Gabe's death, his yahrzeit. I picked up Elizabeth and her daughter, Cosme, from the airport. Cosme Wolfe-Thompson.

"I know," Elizabeth groaned on the way to my place. She glanced back at Cosme, asleep in her car seat, then turned to me. "Every time I say her name, I think, You did not think long enough about what other people would think when they heard it. No one's going to know it was her father's favorite flower, they're just going to think I'm some twee idiot desperate to be unique. I should have named her Marjorie. You can rely on Marjorie. Marjorie's a stable girl."

"It's a good name," I assured her.

She gasped. I stopped short, nearly hitting the Audi in front of me. She yelled, "The Hollywood sign!" pointing to the white letters O-L-L visible in the mountains. Then, realizing we'd nearly had a road collision, she turned to me and said, "Sorry, is that so English-tourist-in-LA?"

When we walked into my house, Elizabeth had to use the bathroom and left the baby, in her car seat, with me in the hallway. I sat cross-legged across from Cosme, she was awake now. I'd seen her plenty when Elizabeth and I video chatted, but this visit was the first time I'd seen her in person. I already knew she looked like him, but to have his eyes, the same golden-brown color, looking back at me from that tiny, chubby face, I couldn't help laughing.

Elizabeth poked her head out of the bathroom, still toweling off her hands. "What?"

"I'm just marveling at your kid."

She smiled. "I know. She's perfect. Fuck Marjorie."

THERE WERE MORE PEOPLE AT THE MEMORIAL THAN THERE HAD been at the funeral. It was Elizabeth's idea to invite everyone. We never knew who might have been important in Gabe's life and we cast a wide net. Fans were invited too. We gathered in an art deco concert venue and theater in Hollywood and made it more of a tribute night. Not your traditional yahrzeit.

It was my idea to have a password at the door. His last secret show.

This time I volunteered to speak. After Jabari played a song, with Jeremy on keyboard, I stood up. I'd had a year to think about Elizabeth's question: If I had shown up at Hotel Frank that night, what would I have wanted him to say?

I could see Gabe telling me he loved Elizabeth and they were going to have a family together. *I mean, I thought we were over,* he'd say. *But with the baby, we're trying again, and it feels right. Julia, I'm sorry, that weekend was a mistake. If anything, I think it made me realize how madly in love I am with Elizabeth.*

Well, he probably wouldn't have said "madly in love," but something like that.

Or he might have pulled me close, whispering in my ear, *I mean, yes, I am an idiot. But no, I loved what happened between us. I just didn't know if you'd still want me.* We might have, I thought, stayed in that room for days. Just room service and sex. The worst thing to happen to us would have been me getting a few parking tickets because I'd thought I was only coming in for a drink and stayed for a week.

We could have been together.

Or, having explained everything he could possibly explain, we might have shared a hug and then an awkward kiss that didn't feel right. Gabe would have said, it dawning on him in the moment, *I think we might be better as friends.* And I might have laughed and said, *Thank God. How can we go back?*

We could have been together.

I'll never be able to choose one scenario over another. And how could I without Gabe? It would have taken us both. When I imagined these possibilities, it was like running a simulation, Gabe's avatar controlled by me. Every time, I played both roles.

I don't know what Gabe would have said. But these days when I think about stepping into that moment and walking into the hotel, I'd be the one to speak first.

I looked out into the crowd of people. And it was a crowd. Leora and Ramiro in the center, up front. Casey and Will in the third row, right behind my empty seat. Somewhere, I couldn't see, were David and Alice. The fans, the people I didn't know, the people I would know as soon as we shared our stories of Gabe.

I was looking for Elizabeth. I found her in the aisle, bumping Cosme on her hip. Our eyes met as I said, "I loved Gabe."

This is the only thing I can picture that I'm sure is true: I would go to Hotel Frank and tell him that. And he would say he loved me. There was no ambiguity in my mind. In that love, I felt certain. The question would have been what to do with it, how to express it, what to call it. I would have stayed with him in that hotel as long as it took to figure out whatever we were going to do next. And maybe, with an electric crackling underneath my skin, in the back of my mind, accessing some other life, I would have caught the wisp of another possibility, the one I'd lived through last year, and I'd have known that this was our chance.

"I loved Gabe," I said. My throat felt tight. I searched for the breath in my chest. There it was, and there we were. A glint, a flare, an aurora between our palms, a secret show and we always know the password.

Loved. Wrong tense. I corrected myself.

"I love Gabe."

And I opened, tender and free.

THIRTY-TWO

A few months after Gabe's yahrzeit, I was invited to a dinner party at Caroline's house. "There'll be single guys," she said, in the sing-songy tone of a mother convincing her child to attend a classmate's birthday party with *There'll be a cotton-candy machine.*

At the dinner party, as a not-at-all-spectacular playlist by Tim played, one of these single guys started talking to me about music, and then another, overhearing us, asked, "You knew Separate Bedrooms, right?" I was used to the question and could effectively field it, but for some reason that night I felt particularly drained and excused myself, retreating to Caroline's very large, very chrome kitchen.

Caroline walked in, holding an empty tray. She took a dish of meatballs out of the refrigerator and started loading them onto the tray. "Sorry about that," she said.

"No, it's okay. It happens."

"You're doing so much better. Such a difference from when I saw you in Europe to now." She squeezed my hand. "You'll find, over time, you'll think about him less and less. Meatball?"

"What?"

She held up the tray. I declined.

After I left the party, I thought about what Caroline said. It was true, I no longer looked stricken; I was better, and that was a victory, but better in this context was something else entirely. Grief was a large spectrum on a microscopic scale, and from where Caroline was standing, she could not see the gulf between better and—I don't know—done? Healed?

Sometimes I find myself thinking the thought that no self-respecting adult is supposed to think, the whine of a child.

It's not fair.

It's not fair he died at twenty-nine. It's not fair he died when we were in this complicated state. There was a throbbing meaninglessness that could at any moment spread into an ache and pull me apart. Over time, I did think about it less, but when I did, this wide gulf would open again, and even if I didn't fall in, just walking the perimeter of it was miserable.

Sometimes I try to escape it. There's always work. And wine, and sex, and books, and art. Escape it, not erase it. I keep one foot on the ground, which means it's never really a total escape, but it gets me out of my head and into my life. Sometimes I'll talk to Elizabeth or my other friends. Other times I stand still. I breathe, expanding like a drum, then letting go. I know that grief takes practice. And I'm patient with myself. Even though death happens all the time, no one could ever be a natural at this.

I took a rideshare from Caroline's, then once I was past the freeways, safely in my neighborhood, I walked the rest of the way home. I still walk all the time. I couldn't give it up after my London perambulating. I'm a regular *flâneuse*, I've kept it up for years. After work, I walk from my store to my house, about a mile and a half. The LA path is not as scenic or varied as Shoreditch, but it just means my focus must be sharper; I observe new flowers in bloom, the unique details of the other pedestrians I encounter. Sometimes I pass something that catches my eye, or ear, and I think, Gabe would love this; or remember when, together, we loved that?

I pause, grateful to run into him again.

ACKNOWLEDGMENTS

Thank you:

Marya Spence. Working with you is the single best decision I made for this book's launch into the world. A consistent confidant and champion, your dedication has exceeded all expectations.

Emma Leong for being my London advocate. Mackenzie Williams for your insight and assistance. Lena Little for your enthusiasm and care.

Andrea Schulz, Seema Mahanian, Sonia Gadre, Allie Merola, Logan Hill, Sara DeLozier, Molly Fessenden, Rebecca Marsh, Chandra Wohleber, Anna Dobbin, Kate Stark, Brian Tart, and everyone at Viking. Thank you, Lindsey Schwoeri, for leading the team and believing in the book from the start.

Elizabeth Yaffe for the gorgeous hand-drawn cover.

My UK editor, Katie Bowden, Lola Downes, Hope Butler, and everyone at 4th Estate.

Marissa Devins, Allan Haldeman, and Julien Thuan at UTA.

Lauren, Connie, Randy, and Ann Patchett: Each of you said the exact right thing when I needed to hear it.

Allison and David: I would not have been able to write this trio without our trio.

Mike Schur. I've learned so much from you about writing and solving creative problems. Thank you for being funny and kind. And for introducing me to JJ.

Jen Statsky, Paul W. Downs, and Lucia Aniello. For welcoming me into the *Hacks* writers' room and allowing space for me to continue working on this novel.

Maggie Shipstead for reading an early draft and your advice on publishing in general.

Leigh and Alexis for expanding my knowledge of Barcelona, Claudia for doing the same with Colombian music, Blair and Melissa for art history context, Josh H. for only-child inspiration, and Josh G. for answering my music business questions.

And for the rest of my research, thank you, Los Angeles Public Library.

My friends Harris and Ned. I miss you.

Dad and Heru, for everything.

Mom, when I was nine, you gave me *Alice's Adventures in Wonderland & Through the Looking Glass* and *The Elements of Style.* That is so you, and I'm so lucky you're my mother.

Ben, I dedicated this book to you because, like I said on our wedding day, our hearts are made from the same pattern. I love you. Thank you for running our household when I had to write, being the first and last reader of every draft, and being such a good listener that multiple people have assumed you are a professional therapist.

Ione, my darling, my love. The next one is for you.

100 YEARS of PUBLISHING

———◇———

Harold K. Guinzburg and George S. Oppenheimer founded Viking in 1925 with the intention of publishing books "with some claim to permanent importance rather than ephemeral popular interest." After merging with B. W. Huebsch, a small publisher with a distinguished catalog, Viking enjoyed almost fifty years of literary and commercial success before merging with Penguin Books in 1975.

Now an imprint of Penguin Random House, Viking specializes in bringing extraordinary works of fiction and nonfiction to a vast readership. In 2025, we celebrate one hundred years of excellence in publishing. Our centennial colophon features the original logo for Viking, created by the renowned American illustrator Rockwell Kent: a Viking ship that evokes enterprise, adventure, and exploration, ideas that inspired the imprint's name at its founding and continue to inspire us.

———◇———

For more information on Viking's history, authors, and books, please visit penguin.com/viking.